CHEERIO

CHEERIO

First published in Great Britain in 2025 by
CHEERIO Publishing
www.cheeriopublishing.com
info@cheeriopublishing.com

Printed and bound in Great Britain by Short Press

The moral right of the authors has been asserted.

A CIP catalogue record for this book is available from the British Library.

ISBN: 978-1-917283-06-9

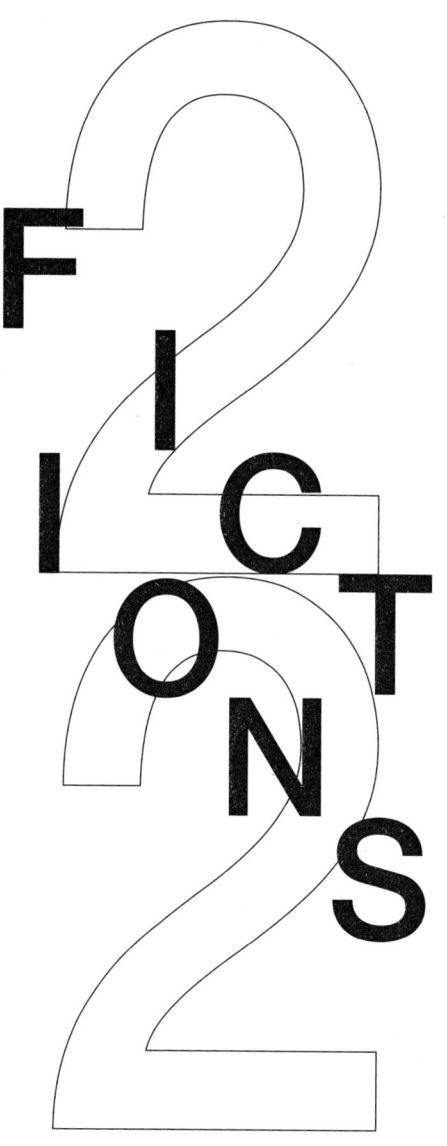

FICTIONS

2

**New Writing from
Desperate Literature &
Brick Lane Bookshop**

Contents

22 FICTIONS

Editors' Note

KATE ELLIS &
ROBERT LOYKO-GREER

The book in your hands is a celebration of the power and brilliance of the short story form, new writers, independent bookselling and small-press publishing.

In 2017 and 2019 respectively, the Desperate Literature and Brick Lane Bookshop short fiction prizes were founded. Established, plotted and driven by booksellers at these two independent bookshops, both projects have since created amazing platforms for new and boundary-pushing writing.

Along with cash prizes, events, writing residencies, and developmental opportunities, both projects produce annual anthologies of their short- and longlists. Between them, they have now published almost 150 writers, with many going on to win other prizes, publish elsewhere, and gain critical acclaim.

This is a collaborative anthology that showcases 22 fictions – eleven stories from the archives of each prize, drawn from their first five years. The book begins with an introduction by Wendy Erskine and foreword by Joanna Walsh (both former prize judges) who exalt the unique dynamism, force and playfulness of the short form.

We hope that you enjoy.

Brick Lane Bookshop was founded in London in 1978,
and Desperate Literature in Madrid in 2014.

Introduction

WENDY ERSKINE

I never set out to be a short story writer. I found the conceptualisation of the form off-putting: these literary Fabergé eggs, with every word driving the story forward, these miracles of construction, described using silversmithing analogies: burnished, filigree, finely honed. And didn't it seem that people could spend the rest of their lives going to 'art of the short story' events or looking at geometrical drawings which pinpointed where characters needed to have epiphanies? So many diktats: don't introduce a new character in the last quarter of the story; make sure you have a killer, bravura opening. It all sounded technically demanding and very exhausting, like Olympic pistol shooting or being incredible in bed. Plus, people who excelled at short stories were not just writers but 'masters.'

Then, in 2015, I was given Monday afternoon off work each week. Rather than spend it mooching around, I wanted to do something defined, and so had thought about spending the time at a gym or studying economics at a basic level. I happened to see that *Stinging Fly*, the Dublin-based literary magazine and publisher, was running a six-month fiction workshop on a Monday. To be considered for the course, it was necessary to submit a 2,500-word story or part of a novel. I'd long thought I could perhaps be a good writer if I gave it a go. My weighty empirical evidence for this was a primary school exercise book I still possessed, of stories I had written in 1978. To appropriate an Austen character, I felt I could have been a great proficient, had I ever tried. But now was the moment and, because I was re-grouting a bathroom floor, reading a Toni Morrison novel with a scene where one woman waited for another outside a prison and thinking just generally about the limits of filial obligation, a concatenation of those particular ideas resulted in a story about prison, mothers and daughters, and symbolic DIY called 'Locksmiths'.

It got me onto the course. Although I had some initial thoughts of trying to write a novel over the six months, what struck me was how democratic and accessible the short story form is. If, say, you are a carer, if you have a full-time job, if you have kids, if you have obligations that occupy your time and attention it may be difficult for you to commit to the long-term project of writing a novel. (That's not to say writing a novel is more challenging. In some ways it isn't. You have the luxury of residing in the same fictive world for the duration. You can have 'down time', sections of writing that aren't at the same pitch as the short story usually necessitates. You can stay with the same handful of characters for years.) However, what you are committing to, with the short story, is a form you can conceivably finish within a month. By no means is that a prescriptive approach to writing because people work in entirely different ways; I use it here solely for illustration of the short story's do-ability. Weeks 1 and 2, spend one hour a day on a long first draft, aiming to write about 500 words a day. That's 7,000 words. Spend the next two weeks, one hour a day, rewriting and revising. By the end of the month you have the satisfaction, the temporary euphoria, of a completed short story. You've created something from nothing. And if the story doesn't particularly sing, what have you lost? Nothing. That hour a day you dedicated to your work could have been spent sitting having a coffee or looking at nonsense on your phone. And so I realised that, while I had a full-time job, another job on top of that, and two kids, writing short stories was the pragmatic choice.

What I also understood, fairly quickly, was that much of the short story arcana was irrelevant. It's an enormously flexible form, capable of accommodating all kinds of ideas. Each story and how it operates just needs to be considered on its own terms. You can be experimental: narrative techniques that might pall over the course of a longer text can work wonderfully in a shorter form. You can deal, if you want, with an entire life – or a century – in the course of a story or you can expand a single minute within the same word count. No one needs to have an epiphany. You can run multiple temporal lines or move in a linear fashion. You can have stories where everything is freighted with meaning and implication, or others that feel looser and more spacious. And while it is lovely to come across a story where every sentence is a miracle of construction, there are also stories where each sentence, utterly unremarkable in and of itself, accumulates to produce an overall effect of great power. So, yes, it's wide open. You can write a compelling fabula, like Aisha Phoenix, or a story spanning a year that presents a community, as Aoife Inman does so skilfully. You can produce a brilliant account of a chicken-eating livestream, like Danielle Giles.

I suppose I also realised what I knew all along – that short stories are our natural mode. When we meet friends for a drink, to some degree we trade short stories and we all, consciously or unconsciously, employ our own little narrative strategies to make them engaging. They are perhaps the first literary form we encounter, in that children's reading books are short stories. So there's nothing intimidating about the short story. We have been reading and telling them our whole lives. It could be said that our sense of ourselves is a self-crafted set of short stories, experience made understandable by being tidied into narrative.

When I started writing short stories in earnest, my mum said she wished I didn't. They made her feel so stupid. I knew what she meant. She was referring to the different relationship with a reader that this form often demands. Sometimes, an ending's inconclusiveness or supposed opacity leads people to think they have misunderstood or missed something along the way. But short stories often offer something else. You as the reader might be co-opted into creating meaning in future time that extends beyond the final full stop of the story. And just generally there are gaps, lacunae, that the reader can fill. Although the enjoyment of fiction needn't necessarily reside in the idea of character, for me that is often a key dimension of reading. Sometimes I feel that I know characters as well after reading a short story as I have an entire novel. Quite often that's to do with the way in which I have supplied my own notions to fill those spaces. It's a creative project involving the story and the reader.

Since completing that course in 2015 and writing two collections of short stories, some other things have become apparent to me, one of which being that people's responses to collections can be a little peculiar in the tendency to want to determine which story is the 'best'. It is the rare review that does not proclaim one or other story in a collection the 'best'. Probably it's the one the reviewer most enjoyed, personal preference therefore masquerading as objective fact. This impetus to rank in order (and I do it too!) comes, possibly, from the short story's association with competitions. But it is always worth remembering that in any literary competition, what we have are the preferences of a particular person or group at a particular time. That's it.

Allowing that caveat, let's not underestimate the huge

significance of competitions. They illuminate and celebrate. There's such valuable feeling of affirmation in being shortlisted or even placed. As a sometime judge, I think it is a tremendous privilege to read work that perhaps has been shared with very few – or any – other readers. It's a responsibility too and needs serious engagement. Each story carries, I feel, some degree of hope, that its existence will be acknowledged, that it will make a connection. It was my great good fortune in 2021 to be asked to judge the Brick Lane Bookshop Short Story Prize, along with Kishani Widyaratna and Elise Dillsworth. At the time, I said that I didn't need convincing of the special power of the form, but these entries confirmed it once more, emphatically. This wasn't obligatory effusiveness. It was true. I think when you read the stories in this anthology you will see what I mean.

Why Writing Short Stories?

JOANNA WALSH

I was on a book tour in Mexico when I was emailed a dossier of press questions in advance of a reading. One journalist wrote asking, *why writing short stories.*

'Why writing short stories' is a bit like when Samuel Beckett wrote, 'what matter who's speaking?' a question that splits into import and export. Import is *what's it matter?* and export is material. The material that a short story exports is short. There are no other criteria. But still it's a question. The short story is always in question. It might be the question that matters.

The question I've always been asked about the short story is not about the short story at all. It's *when are you going to write a novel?* Despite the novelty that the word suggests, this question is never new, though a new novel still hovers eternally in my future, and though I've already written two books published as novels, which I didn't write thinking of them as novels at all.

I don't think I could have.

For one thing, I don't think I have novel experience. It doesn't arc, or follow a narrative: it loops, fragments, seems all beginning or all end, as so much of my experience doesn't move through time and space but through hope and memory.

Which means it moves through language, and language is a way of speaking matter that isn't there, or what matters that isn't there, like when Jonathan Swift's Gulliver wandered into a country that decreed 'that since words are only names for things, it would be more convenient for all men to carry about them such things as were necessary to express a particular business they are to discourse on'.

A novel requires a lot of material, 'but for short conversations', Gulliver discovered, 'a man may carry implements in his pockets, and under his arms, enough to supply him; and in his house, he cannot be at a loss. Therefore the room where company meet who practise this art, is full of all things, ready at hand, requisite to furnish matter for this kind of artificial converse'.

Because less matter is required to furnish a short story, less matters more. The short story is not Walter Benjamin's 'monumentally furnished ten-room apartment', which is how he described the nineteenth-century novel (Benjamin names Gaston Leroux's 368-page *The Phantom of the Opera* as its 'apotheosis') whose 'gigantic sideboards distended with carvings, the sunless corners where palms stand, the balcony embattled behind its balustrade, and the long corridors with their singing gas flames, fittingly house[s] only the corpse. 'On this sofa the aunt cannot but be murdered'.

Now we furnish with IKEA: flatpack, convenient, able to be set up anywhere, able to furnish a room in the way of Swift's short conversations. When everything is flatpack, everything is surface, surfaces that can be put together to create an illusion of volume. In a small space, the short story writer needs to be able to use surfaces. These are the surfaces of language. Inverting the object-oriented society that Swift describes, short story writers trade in illusion.

Writers of short stories furnish small spaces – not ten-room apartments – with immateriality that, fragmented, creates the illusion of volume. The fragment has been a thing ever since around the time Swift was writing, when rich Northern Europeans started touring the Mediterranean in search of encounters with leftover fragments of the classical world, the 'Grand Tour', an experience that *Gulliver's Travels* pastiches.

Swift's description of language as matter is a matter of international politics: 'thus ambassadors would be qualified to treat with foreign princes, or ministers of state, to whose tongues they were utter strangers'. No surprise. In 1726 the British Empire was already expanding in the name of trade, trading the immaterial language Swift wrote in for material goods. Language is not a material good. Jacques Derrida wrote that it's a poison. Gaston Leroux turned to short story writing in the pursuit of material goods after spending his large inheritance.

Leroux is listed on Wikipedia as a 'short story writer' although his best-remembered work is a novel. He might have been a short story writer because of the culture of the short story, the contemporary monthly and weekly publications that made writing short stories, in his era, a viable trade. But writing short stories is no longer a viable trade, as writers who choose to write short stories find: *When are you writing a novel?*

Who are the short story writers, these traders in fragments: the grand tourists, or the inhabitants of fragmented landscapes building pillars into single-room apartments to be furnished with flatpack furniture? Or either, likely either. Or both, which is either's opposite. In any case their fragmented material conveys hope and memory. Because the memory of these fragments is always created, as a matter of reconstruction. And creation is always hope.

Any writing is created from excavation: columns out of the dead ground. When I'm writing, I never think about making things up. The matter I write is waiting to be discovered/

exhumed/whatever. If I'm extractive, I'm self-extractive. Is that a good thing? I don't know. I don't have a choice. That's how I teach writing too: I tell students, you know it already. No need to learn, only to 'pick out', as Georges Perec wrote, 'what you've long ago picked out'. He wasn't writing about the short story but, when you get your material everywhere, why not apply it?

It's like when Chris Kraus told me that all novels are about real estate. Well that's novels, with their ten-room apartments. Perec wrote about apartments too, in *Species of Spaces*. Though a room is 'a fairly malleable space', despite any architect's intentions, and 'it is no good their trying to impress us with stuff about modules, and other nonsense'.

Short stories are for tenants, those who are aware that they are in a holding space. The short story writer doesn't have to build and doesn't have to respect the architect's intentions. That's because language isn't really an exchange of objects, only their surfaces.

But these are just some short stories. There are a thousand definitions, more, many of which lay down rules on how to build short stories, brick by brick. And a novel doesn't have to be a grand apartment. It can be a painting on a 'little bit of ivory'. Whatever, I'm not one for rules or craft, more for bricolage, for rearranging the furniture, or taking it apart and making it into something else, an IKEA hack, something you can do in a small space, Lautrémont's 'chance encounter of a sewing machine and an umbrella on an operating table', which is a very post-what-gets-called-the 'industrial revolution' range of objects and processes.

Which novels and short stories are too. *Gulliver's Travels* doesn't really count as a novel. It's sometimes called a 'proto-novel' and it was part of the emergence of the form during the eighteenth century, which also led to the emergence of the short story or, rather, the division of narratives into long and short, and both are something to do with the industrial revolution, with printing presses and newspapers, and railway stations, and education, and remoteness, and time spent between places, long or short. The Grand Tour stopped being a thing when the railways arrived.

A short story is an economic fact, and so is a novel. That's even before you've got to either's material. Each is defined by the systems that allow them to exist – like the prizes from which this collection is drawn, like independent bookshops and journals, and like this book – that encourage, that publish, that finance them. Short stories are often praised for their 'economy', which suggests a certain perspective. I'd like to see a short story praised for its expansiveness because the more something is fragmented, the more surface it has.

As writing becomes more portable, we have become less so. Now we work from home on our flatpack furniture. Wherever we are, we work 'remotely,' always ready to move but never moving. The short story used to be fable, then anecdote. Now it's something else. The short story is a reconfigurable, expansive surface of the immaterial material, of hope and memory, that is always bigger than the small room that only appears to contain it. It is a way of questioning spaces and the things in it, which is a way of questioning the distribution of space and those things, which is a way of questioning the distribution of language: what matter who's speaking? It is a question.

When the journalist asked me, why writing short stories, unlike Beckett they didn't use a question mark. It was – like the contribution dreaded at readings – not so much a question as a comment: for why. In which case, I could have answered, yes.

The Arcadian

SHOLA VON REINHOLD

Note on Text

It feels, perhaps appropriately given the 'themes' that appear in this text, that I wrote it in another era. The airs to which it was exposed were different. I remember when I started writing some of it, probably in about 2016/17, being concerned with Blackness on the page, in a British literary context (whatever that is). There were simply certain things I had not read rendered, nor anything close to them, and the sheer rendering of them felt like a kind of magic. Now, though things are still wanting (I meet Black writers of experimental or wayward or deliciously baroque and florid prose everywhere but how many of them are getting published?), there is a little difference and one might not feel the effects of 2017 or even 2019 when this came out by way of Desperate Literature. I'm curious how that might change again over ten years or more. Five years is a curious amount of history. The nearness and farness of it is always a little awkward. That said, reading back, glancingly, over this, I'm glad it was published and can see some merits against all those temporal odds.
— Shola von Reinhold, 2025

Bim will get to the hotel bar first. And it will be an old hotel; painted wall panels and a tinted glass dome, apparently once the house of a society hostess who was conveyed around Edinburgh in a coach pulled by zebras towards the end of the nineteenth century. Today, like whenever he comes, he will sit in the baroque alcove and fantasise about visiting the house in the 1890s, until he gets violently ejected from his own vision, recalling, with a shock, that he would probably not be invited to such a house in such a period.

Even his fantasies will not contain his Blackness, which will sometimes seem to keep him out of Arcadia however many loopholes he finds. He'll learn, for example about Black students in Edinburgh since the 1850s, at least. Surely any one of them might have been invited by the hostess? The child of a Yoruba noble, perhaps? This will get him a little further, but then he meets the hostess and her husband and they scream slurs at him, inform him that the reason he was invited was as an exotic specimen, like the zebras, and his vision ends. This Arcadian impulse will have always been doing this to him, sometimes seemingly against his own volition. Leading him down half-lit glittering corridors before slamming him against concrete walls.

To be born an Arcadian is to crave a paradise knit out of visions of the past just as a Utopian does with the future. Arcadian Personality Types therefore tend to have a general fondness for old things and buildings, such as this hotel; things which shall forever push Bim down mental avenues of history not conducive to constituting the grand ahistorical mythical paradise which is the ultimate Arcadian project (a collaboration with the Utopian Personality Types). Bim will know again sitting there that to be an Arcadian, hung up on fantasised pasts, but born in a historically impermissible body, is a kind of punishment.

That is why he will have been trying, for the past few weeks, to be Utopian. To be forward-looking. A futurist. It will be difficult. He will have just failed again by choosing this hotel and then fantasising about it, but these will only be lapses, he will tell himself. He is going to be meeting Henrik, a semi-muscular, semi-handsome Utopian, who will come in soon with a shopping bag and say, 'What are you having, mate?'

The 'mate' will make Bim feel sick. Conscious and deliberate. Bim will see that although Henrik's first language is not English it is not just a word he's innocently picked up. It will give Bim all the more encouragement to order the most elaborate cocktail on the menu, which Henrik will register blankly. Beer is of course what he will want Bim to order (and not because of the money). Wine will be barely tolerated. But this florid thing.

Maybe not, maybe Bim will just be in the midst of a self-fulfilling prophecy. After all, he first met Henrik whilst wearing a rustling shell-pink gown, every braid hanging entombed above his shoulders in small opal bars and each under-eye daubed to resemble violet petals blanched to the point of translucency and his cheeks glazed orchid. Bim will look much the same today minus the gown. Bim will think, 'If Henrik doesn't like it, he would not have come.' His displeasure in the choice of drink was not a matter of gender. It was a matter of 'political presentation'.

As if to confirm this Henrik will return from the bar and rant about the hotel. About 'such places'. Henrik, typical Utopian, will always be drawn to newer things. Old things will always be redolent of aristocracy and the bourgeoisie to Utopians like Henrik, and Bim, though he will understand this, will hate how this will, by default, make him look like a downright imperialist. The equation of utopianism with progressiveness, arcadianism with conservatism, will seem like a false one, a dangerous one. Still, he will wish he chose somewhere else more typically Utopian.

But Bim will be shocked and delighted when Henrik will say he has booked a room as a surprise. Bim will have tried many times to scam a room in this hotel, emailing the PR companies amongst other things.

Oh but darling the lord giveth and the lord taketh, for when in the room, he will barely have any time to look around before Henrik will say,

'Put on this, yeah?' and hand him the plastic bag and Bim will find inside a sort of football kit. He will start to get changed and Henrik will say,

'You're too skinny: a frond.' And Bim will immediately love the idea of being a frond but then Henrik will say, 'Come to the gym later.'

Bim will say no, barely concealing his disgust. Though why it will have made him so repulsed he shall not be able to say. Something in the atmosphere of *that* gym. He'll remember having been to the juice café there to meet Henrik last week. Afterwards, Henrik made him look around, and yes, whilst those bodies moving about like liquid; like oil; with a grace and strength that terrified and dizzied him; each torso different as if repeatedly impressed with another type of shell; razor clams over there; that one pink-white scallops; the endless ridges, furrows and hollows, were attractive, the bodies startled him, all together like that. Like any queer of his variety he should have rejoiced at the thick-cut ecstasy of that neck over there. But just like Henrik's body, they'd made him terrified in a different way, on top of the lustful terror. Made him sick with shock. It was shocking: Men.

He will feel dizzy as if some of his soul might easily spill over and out of him like iridescence, staining the hotel carpet forever, unless he contains his thoughts. He will go into the bathroom with the kit to finish getting changed and start to dry retch, so he will then lock the door and have a bath which will be delightful. There will even be gold swan taps.

He will shiver with joy in the foam.

In the bath he will know part of his being drawn to such *obvious* types, though morally anathema to him, not to mention basic, is, for now, vital. That it will have always been important to throw into relief his own femininity by physical and behavioural contrast, something which could be particularly hard if the men were white: somehow, they were capable of eliding such gorgeous signifiers as the shell-pink ballgowns. Or the brocade doublet he had met another man in.

'I reckon you'd look hot in a tracksuit, wear one next time.'

'Do I look like I would . . .'

'What?'

The mental gymnastics of these men was spectacular to witness. The image of Bim's Blackness overrode that of his femininity, blocked it out. For them, one could not even inhabit the same body as the other, never mind being atomically, monadically, the same, as they were to Bim. The gowns were taken to be an exception. As if they imagined it was fancy dress just for the night, to be blocked out, passed over, for a presumed otherwise regular masculinity.

'Why don't you shave your head?'

'But I've been growing it for ages,' he would tell them, fingering the crystal pendant at the end of a braid, wondering if he'd shaved under his lip properly.

Bim will think: And now this football kit, this really was *de trop*, it really was his worst nightmare and he will retch some more after the bath whilst putting it on – the feel of it! But perhaps this will be the Arcadian in him rebelling against getting fucked by a Utopian and all that went with it.

He will escape from his arcadianism.

***

The glass dome has turned silver, blue, indigo-black, black. It is midnight and Bim sits in the upper gallery looking down into the main bar. He has never sat upstairs before because it is only for hotel guests. When his drink is brought up he turns his attention to the painted wall panels. They are similar in style to the ones below. Eventually he finds himself standing up with his drink and wandering along from panel to panel until he stops and stands and stares at two of them for a very long time.

They both depict a courtyard garden. In the first it is early morning and the sky is copper green.

There are ghostly pear trees in white pots and stags supping from a large ornate central fountain.

The second panel depicts the same cloistered courtyard, there are many delicate Black and brown people gathered around the fountain. The sun has risen. They wear brocade robes with green velvet breeches and silk stockings in oyster and long trains of sheer fabric draped across the marble floor like swathes of coloured syrup on ice; crowns of metallic black stone and bronze project into the air like cathedrals. Outrageously embroidered slippers, high-heeled, in the manner of rococo court shoes.

The panels all date to before the residency of the hostess. He spends a great deal of time staring at these figures.

The two panels are beautiful.

It recalls when he was younger and the sky became powdered with green or flooded with rose and he would lie on the black-barred balcony of his tower, towels thrown over the railing to conceal him from anyone below who might look up. The sky looked not of that place but reflected from elsewhere. A charming lake where there were orchidaceous people. He would attribute the

31

sky to some time and place long forgotten. An arcadia. He would writhe around the balcony with loneliness which, once introduced to the system, to the soul of the Arcadian, never leaves.

He has come to know that such a sky *could* be of such a place and its not feeling so then was both his own lack of imagination and a sly aesthetic fascism that belonged to society at large. (And besides, that sky does not belong in the parties he now attends either.)

As an Arcadian he feels sure standing there that his sky is the one in the painting.

It makes the water in the fountain gleam. Silver and dun birds peck at bowls of fruit, perched on the lips of red glass vessels.

'Very funny,' Henrik said.

'Funny?'

Breakfast was also served in the upper gallery and Bim had woken up Henrik early just to show him the panels. Henrik looked at them again.

Bim's immediate worry was that Henrik would see it as a work of Orientalism. In his experience such people had learned to immediately dismiss as orientalist anything which is old and features bodies of colour near the ornamental. An improvement of kinds, probably, but now anything which reminded them of their own bodies' uncomfortable relation to power made them daily re-enact what they shunned by writing off work actually from 'the East'. And things like this: diasporic visions. A young Utopian like Henrik might not pick up that he was gazing on this Arcadia *with* the painter who was not separate from the bodies – something Bim detected but couldn't put a finger on.

That many of the figures did not fall along the gender line was something Henrik would probably also interpret as orientalist fantasy: the sexualised, demonised, feminised Other. Though to

Bim nothing could have been further from the truth.

This was not about something foreign.

'It's new. Modern,' said Henrik at last.

'No, it's not.'

'. . .'

'There were Black students living in the city at the time who might have modelled for the artist.'

'I didn't say there weren't,' says Henrik, quick off the mark, but Bim knew he didn't quite believe it. He needed him to believe it and spent some time arguing about the painting's age, but Henrik didn't want to argue any more and changed the subject. And, to Bim's delight, smiled and asked if he wanted one of those pink cocktails with his breakfast.

He also told Bim he liked his earrings.

But before Henrik stood up to order the cocktail his eyes flickered to the second panel. As they looked away from it, Bim caught them and was able to turn and see it as Henrik saw it.

Bim had been wrong. Henrik did not see orientalism at work. Not even. Instead, Bim saw how especially unconvincing Henrik thought the figures. Those predominantly androgynous Black and brown bodies. Unlikely in their setting: this building, a Victorian painting, a depiction of antiquity. They looked, to Henrik, like a kind of anachronistic, comical drag. Harder to believe than zebras in the streets of nineteenth-century Edinburgh.

Bim will visit the panel again. Will notice a figure leaning over the fountain. The figure Bim was most drawn to. A delicate youth (of twenty-five or so). Like many, though not all, of the figures, this one will once have been described as androgynous.

Bim will not be able to stop looking at the figure, at the light glancing off the mosaic in the fountain into Their face, hypnotising Them. Bim will not be ejected from this vision. They will be taken up, incorporated into the scheme of the hotel, the painted panels.

The blue marble niche.

                The giant fountain

The stags

                        The ghostly pear trees

          The figure in the corner, who will once have
                been referred to as a man

The figure on the fountain ledge who will once have been
   referred to as an androgyne

The figure by the pillar who will once have been referred to
   as a woman

The figure by the fruit who will once have been referred to
   by the word hermaphrodite

The red glass vessels

'he' but not He. To be said lightly without meaning. To be skimmed over surely rather than drawn attention to (They will once think).

        The dome.

Lots

LEEOR OHAYON

Her bluey-green eyes reflect in the bakery window, her surgical mask really brings them out, eyes like a cat's-eye marble, floating amid the display of tray upon tray of hamantashen: poppy seed and prune and something with sprinkles... the interior is decorated with crowns and clowns and bunting made to look like ra'ashanim... what do the Hasids call it? A grager? A groger? Those little Victorian things that rattle around to make noise to blot out his name – Haman's, who cast lots to kill Jews... and now instead, once a year, Hasidic Jews put on fez hats, get hammered on an open-top double-decker bus, cruising down Stamford Hill high street, klezmer music blaring out the back, and it's a shame there aren't more Purims in the average year, it's a shame people don't celebrate Second Purims any more... all those locally averted catastrophes turned into mini-parties like in Cairo and Rhodes and Ksar el-Kebir – the Purim of the Three Kings – or family-specific deliverances from tragedy, like the Plum Jam Purim or the one with the curtains... we could have had a scroll and sweets and dressed up in costume to celebrate the day Dad drove his car into the lamppost by the barber shop – Purim of the Hair's Breadth – or the day Mum got on the 253 with a suitcase because she said she was leaving for good... but she was back by dinner with puffy eyes and the table set, couscous soup on the hob... Dad slurping his bowl as if nothing had happened – Purim of Bus Stop H – but better than her couscous were the berkuks she made on Purim, boiled in milk and butter and dusted with cinnamon... and oh my God, her fijuelas – how could I forget? She'd wrap the thin dough around the fork while it sizzled in the oil, around and around until it came out a fried rose, syrup and sesame seeds on top... takes me way back... to being a kid, to the thrill around Purim, sifting through the mishloach manot – all that cellophane wrap and gift-basket filler,

looking for the good stuff: a packet of Klik, Bisli, Bamba, a
Chocolate Log, a small bottle of grape juice for blessing... we'd
receive them and Dad would open them up, dish the good stuff
out into separate baskets to send on, if he caught me rummaging
about he'd shout Don't you dare mix things up! He knew who
was getting what, who was deserving of the Klik or the Bisli or the
Bamba – who got the grape juice for blessing... Mum oversaw
quality control, she'd stand over the baskets, point to each one,
ask: Who for? then she'd open a fresh page in her notepad, scrawl
בס"ד in the top right-hand corner, invoke heaven's help onto the
page, so to speak, and jot down the things that they still needed to
buy... when the baskets were ready, Dad would wrap them up
with fresh cellophane, curl a gift ribbon with a pair of open
scissors, send them out to neighbours and friends, people from
synagogue and the community, saved money and trips to the
dentist, had everyone gushing how Moshe and A'liza went above
and beyond with their mishloah manot... he'd chuckle to
himself, proud... but the best thing about Purim, the absolute
best, was the costumes: Power Rangers and Pokémon and Dragon
Ball Z... until secondary school, after that it was all sexy cats and
slutty soldiers, girl gangs in joint costumes, boys too cool for it –
came into school wearing trackies – and always, always one prick
in a Bin Laden mask or a keffiyeh with a plastic gun... Hasidic
kids did it right: Queen Esther and Mordehai, and for twins:
the Ten Commandments... until they hit bar mitzvah, then
a fez hat forever after, and I'd come all the way here, to this
bakery, just to remember home... as if we'd eaten... as if we'd
made hamantashen at home... Mum wouldn't have made
hamantashen, she'd be annoyed hearing me call hamantashen
hamantashen, she'd have given me one of those looks and said:
Oznei haman, with a stress as if I'd misheard – an i-na'al abuk at

the end for comic effect . . . she hated it when me and Rach came back from school with their pronunciations: it's brit not bris, say, levaya not lavoya, and if we said I'm shvitzing or Don't be a shnorer – wohohwoh, she'd slap a hand to her cheek, look up to the ceiling and ask, Why are they trying to make my kids like theirs? Didn't want us like *them* . . . but also, didn't want us as we *are* – though she wouldn't say that bit out loud, God forbid, tfu tfu tfu . . . she watches in silence as her friends talk about their grandkids, seconds and thirds on the way, Pesach in a four-star hotel in Eilat . . . if pushed she might say: God is the neck – or was it the hand? Is it God's hand? . . . the girl with the bluey-green eyes is tapping for my attention . . . her hand on my shoulder, her bluey-green eyes in the bakery window . . . and I know those eyes . . . of course, I know those eyes . . . Natalie Yehoshua, Nat Yesh of Asher and Gina from Kyverdale Road, Margalit's granddaughter with the bluey-green eyes – eyes like a cat's-eye marble . . . because there's that anecdote, that joke, that someone way back, a great-great-something-or-other, must've hooked up with a British officer in Aden – on the hush – which was quite disturbing because you couldn't tell it without imagining Nat's grandma Margalit fucking a soldier in the back of a jeep, not Margalit herself with her pop socks and cardigan, just her face cut out, superimposed on a sepia-tinted ancestor . . . to be fair, I've heard it before, every Mizrahi, Sephardi community with a few blond kids in its ranks and a history of colonial rule will tell you a version of it . . . she comes in for a hug, pauses, leans forward then stops, sorta swaying in the air, decides to pat me on my arm instead, rubs her hand up and down . . . Dan-Dan, she says, Daniel! How are you? It's been so long . . . How's your mum? How's your dad? How's Rach – haven't seen her in years . . . I give her the protocol line: everyone is good and healthy and happy –

no dramas ever – but she's only half listening, she reaches into her big Fendi bag, pulls out a tickets book, flicks it into the palm of her hand ... What're your plans for Purim? she asks ... My plans? No plans ... Purim, haven't celebrated in years, I say ... instant regret, told her too much ... now, she's smiling, Amazing, she says, I'm organising a Purim party, La Maschera in Camden Town, complimentary drink on arrival with wristband, ten till three, come Dan, please? Will be an opportunity for us to catch up, rendezvous, remember the past! ... I parrot the words back at her: Purim party, wristband, rendezvous ... I don't know what else to say, don't know what could be worse, swaying awkwardly on a sticky, glittery floor to an electro-house mix of Rihanna's 'Umbrella', with all those people from school ... all those kids from the suburbs: Barnet and Harrow and Hertsmere ... except no longer kids, now fully grown, actual adults who sound like their parents ... Becky Green and Sophie Rose and that lanky one with the attitude ... Julie Oppenheim – Goolie Open Hymen, Rafi Silver used to call her until one day she clapped him straight in the face, red handprint on his cheek for all of fifth lesson ... then there were pricks like Josh Gold, Josh Cohen, lesser pricks like Danny Haddad, Michael Hajaj – tanned skin, Hermès belts ... who has the energy for that? Who has the strength to answer: What are you up to these days? and Where do you live? Is there a missus Elfassi? What about kids? Josh Gold grinning in silence because it was always Oi Fassy, never Elfassi ... and I'm thinking this, the setting, the guests, rubbing shoulders, mixing with that lot, and how did Nat Yesh from Kyverdale Road become a part of that world? ... and she looks up at me with those bluey-green eyes ... those cat's-eye marbles ... Come, please? she says, everyone will be there, Sophie Rose always asks me about you, and Julie Oppenheim as well... We'll be crowning an Esther and Mordehai, she says... Weren't they uncle and niece? I ask, but she just shrugs at me, says, Honestly, can't wait to tell Mum that I saw Dan Fas on Stamford Hill high street!... How is your mum? I ask... she sighs... Not doing well, she says, bed-bound, arthritis, Parkinson's, a salad of health issues, all downhill after Asher passed away, this time two years back... and I can't believe it, *Gina*, Nutter of Nat – that's what people called her behind her back... Nat overheard once, burst into tears, had all the girls on the school bus lining up to console her... what was it Mum used to say about Gina?... called her the thing that blows air into the fireplace... she could set the whole place ablaze with her words, big smoker as well, one after the other, wasn't shy of a slanging match at all the wrong times, usually with Rina and her sister Ilana... on the synagogue stairs on Kippur, on Simhat Torah during the hakafot – one araq too many in the synagogue kitchen, let it all rip about Rina's husband Shimo'n... knew how to open her mouth, and she was always washing that concrete patch she had for a front garden, you'd see her outside with a sponja stick and a bucket, in her house flip-flops, gold anklet studded with turquoise, soapy water running onto the pavement... if you walked past and called out Hiya Gina, she'd stop, rest her hand on the stick, head propped up on top, her attention all yours... Hello sweetie, Hello darrrrling – Rs rolling into next week... Gina... Nutter of Nat... the thing that blows air into the fireplace... she had enough on her plate: Asher with the gambling and the betting and the cheating, apparently... she caught him twice with Luna, Rina and Ilana's younger sister – the unmarried one – and if she ever came up in conversation, Gina would make a face like she was about to spit, Gina never forgave her... never forgave Asher, didn't forgive Shimo'n of Rina either, he provided the alibis, the ruses, pretended they were at his bakery playing cards in the room at the back . . . Mum always said Gina was miskeena because she'd had a hard life, she carried her mum and all her siblings on her shoulders after they'd kidnapped her brother from the maternity ward, then God gave her a husband like that, that's her lot in this life . . . Mum used to say there are two things in life we don't choose: you don't choose your family and you don't choose your luck, which was her way of saying in life you just sucked it up, God wrote it in the stars . . . maktub . . . we don't know the lots that have been cast up above . . . and now Nat's pleading with me, with those bluey-green eyes, disposable mask at her chin, and I've got no excuse, no business meeting at ten, no dinner reservation with a husband or boyfriend . . . as if I could tell her that anyway, on the high street outside the bakery, so that it can make its way back round to Mum, so she can stand there with her hands in her hair again: Why did you tell her? I told you not to tell her, don't you know Asher and Gina have a big mouth? . . . but Asher is dead and Gina's too ill to care – does it even matter? Does any of it matter? And what if I knocked on Mum's door and said: Listen, Mum, I'm not gay any more, would she put out some treats and put on a costume? Would she declare it a Second Purim?

Stuart Hall and Stuart Hall

TOM BENN

Stuart Hall is a BBC presenter of north-west regional news programmes and national gameshows.

Stuart Hall has fallen a long way, Krishnan Guru-Murthy says on *Channel 4 News*.

Stuart Hall is a Jamaican-born left-wing academic and occasional BBC presenter.

Stuart Hall is racially abused on the street in sixties Birmingham while out with his wife.

Stuart Hall says *we are all hybrid . . .*

Stuart Hall calls it *the beautiful game . . .*

Stuart Hall says *when I ask anybody where they're from I expect nowadays to be told an extremely long story; they're from really five different places . . . and in their heads, their sense of themselves, to be juggling a set of world identities . . . they're trying to find their place . . .*

I can't be doing with coloured men no more, my nana says to a friend, in '90s Hulme, Manchester, *the lot of them brung me nowt but pain.* While her lover, the docker from Trinidad, his hands calloused and patient, teach mine to play dominoes and show a child what colour town is of a dry night: across high-rises, low-rises, deck-access flats, like this one; above pubs, parks, courtyards, radial routes, side streets. All is amber. Lazy amber. Scurrying amber. Tassel-shaded-sitting-room-fishbowl, greased-bus-window, lamppost-blinking amber.

Stuart Hall says *the everyday and mundane elements of our lives can affect the person we become . . .*

Stuart Hall is a millionaire from the small market town of

Ashton-under-Lyne, Lancashire, in the east borough of Greater Manchester known since 1974 as Tameside, after the River Tame.

Tameside includes the towns of Hyde and Droylsden.

Stuart Hall pleads guilty to indecent assault, crimes committed between 1967 and 1986.

Stuart Hall is found guilty of two further charges and receives an additional sentence.

Stuart Hall loves Shakespeare, loves English literature. Stuart Hall's football commentary is highly allusive. Stuart Hall, in 1958, reports on his first match: it is at Hillsborough.

Stuart Hall, more than fifty years later, no longer living in not-yet-Tameside, breaks his garage door motor. He rings my father for a quote to fix it. My father sends two lads round to fettle Stuart Hall's garage door.

My father buys his first house, a two-up-two-down red-brick in Droylsden, Tameside. It is 1980. For eight months he cannot afford furniture beyond a bed.

Stuart Hall is brought up in Hyde, not-yet-Tameside. Hyde is home to the Moors Murderers and two of their victims, and to Harold Shipman's medical practice and hundreds of his victims.

Ian Brady is from Glasgow. He is born Ian Duncan Stewart; his father is unknown.

Myra Hindley grows up in Crumpsall, Manchester, brutalised by poverty, a family of four living in a single room. She dies of bronchial pneumonia, age sixty.

My father, age sixty, cannot bring himself to say her name. *She is too wicked*, he says.

Harold Shipman is from Nottingham, and until his arrest, he is my friend's family doctor in Hyde, Tameside. *He was very good,* my friend, age sixteen, says to me. *He used to listen. He helped my mam when she was pregnant with me. I was a nightmare.*

Later, a one-eyed man from Tameside shoots a man to death, possibly over an inherited slight. There is long-standing bad blood between two Tameside families and their allies. The one-eyed man then shoots and grenades the other man's father to death, then shoots and grenades to death two female police officers dispatched to a house in response to a hoax 999 call he makes about a broken kitchen window, kids' vandalism. I listen to the audio on YouTube. He sounds exactly like a chef I worked with in a pub kitchen one summer who believed in his own lies so completely he did not feel the need to remember them from breath to breath. After the ambush, the one-eyed man drives to Hyde Police Station to hand himself in. He is five months past his first murder, six weeks at the centre of a city-wide manhunt.

Stuart Hall and George Formby Snr are both born in Ashton, not-yet-Tameside, fifty-four years apart.

George Formby Snr pretends he is from Wigan; nicknamed the Wigan Nightingale because of his trademark terminal cough, on the music-hall stage he coins 'Wigan Pier', giving name to a place that does not exist; and, by inventing a place he invents being from, he gives a road a destination.

George Formby Snr spends his adolescence touring the north-west, sleeping on coal carts, inhaling the coal dust that will kill him aged forty-five.

George Formby Snr's mother has one hundred and forty-one convictions for soliciting and dies in the workhouse; his father is unknown. George Formby Snr is given his stepfather's name, James Lawler Booth, but sheds it for others.

In Manchester he watches coal waggons labelled and destined for Formby, a seaside town north of Liverpool. As Formby he develops his Lancastrian tramp persona, John Willie: white make-up, oversized trousers, cane and bowler hat; seen and stolen one night by Charlie Chaplin.

George Formby Snr, the Wigan Nightingale, dies nationally famous, a Professional Northerner, a wealthy bigamist from Ashton.

His children are born in Wigan.

Mary Ann Britland, the first woman to be executed at Manchester's Strangeways Prison, lives and marries in Ashton, not-yet-Tameside. In 1886, when Formby Snr is eleven and out singing for his meals, Mary murders her nineteen-year-old daughter with mouse powder from the corner chemist. Mary soon murders her husband Thomas and moves across the street to live with another Mary and another Thomas. Mary murders Mary, of course, to be with Other Thomas; but three deaths are too many; even here; even now. Mary confesses to killing her family and neighbour for the insurance, so she could afford to marry Other Thomas, and leave Ashton, not-yet-Tameside.

Mary hangs.

In Ashton, Mary works days in a factory and nights as a barmaid. George Formby Snr says *it's not the cough that carries you off – it's the coffin they carries you off in!*

Hulme, inner Manchester, is built and demolished twice before my mother is forty-five. When Embden Street is bulldozed for slum clearance my mother's father, my mother, her two brothers and sister are relocated to Droylsden, Tameside. Her schools are wrecking-balled. My mother cries.

My mother is ten when she sees Jimmy Savile get out of a Rolls-Royce and enter a butcher's shop by Embden Street. She touches the bonnet of his Rolls-Royce. *Blinkin' kids*, he shouts, *get out of it!* and chases her down her street.

A group of Moss Side Rastas see my mother entering a nightclub. She has gap-teeth, black lipstick, an afro. A box jacket and pencil skirt. She works through the week in a boutique, goes about with scooterboys and is courting a footballer.

Hey, Sista, a Rasta says.

I'm not your sister.

Handsworth Revolution, an album of Birmingham reggae, is my father's favourite LP and, on some days, mine.

Stuart Hall, lecturing in Birmingham, prefers Miles Davis.

Stuart Hall is the son of middle-class Jamaicans of mixed descent.

Send them home, my mother's father, Liberian Kru, says of the Jamaicans. *They refuse to speak English.*

Stuart Hall is the son of an Ashton baker.

Stuart Hall collects antique clocks; each tells the right time for some bugger, somewhere, somewhen.

George Formby fettles watches in his dressing room at Ealing Studios to pass the time.

My father is the son of a D-Day veteran, an amateur boxer, a second-generation Irish Catholic.

My father is the son of a seamstress, a Protestant girl whose family leave Wales and settle in Ancoats.

My father's grandfather is a kitchen porter at Manchester's Midland Hotel. His wife-to-be is a tea waitress there. He has come from Limerick to work nights, to throw chopping knives at the rats.

My mother's father arrives in England from Liberia in 1950 and marries a white Mancunian girl who chucks a brick through her headmaster's window on her last day of school.

The Kru tribe make poor slaves. They gain a reputation for chucking themselves in the Atlantic at any opportunity. It is reported that the ones who make it across continually try to escape. For this they fetch a low price at auction.

Stuart Hall says *we are all hybrid . . .*

Liberian Kru and Mancunian welder, my mother's father dies of pneumonia, not yet sixty.

George Formby Snr says *it's the coffin they carries you off in!*

A nana walks out on a mother's father, a mother's brothers, a mother's sister, a mother. This is before Hulme can be razed once, let alone twice.

I remember my cousin's hands, child's hands, cleverer than mine. Pinching coins from a pool table in a Moss Side pub after my nana's funeral. Coins spread on his palms like domino pips.

Stuart Hall says *the everyday and mundane elements of our lives can affect the person we become . . .*

Stuart Hall is the son of middle-class Jamaicans of mixed descent.

Stuart Hall is the son of an Ashton baker.

The Closed Door

ALICE HAWORTH-BOOTH

The baby was going through a phase of only saying Hello, though it knew a lot of other words. Hello! it said to Rona when she came home. Then Hello! when Rona gave it a yoghurt, and Hello! when Rona put it to bed. It was nice to be greeted but Rona wondered where Cat and Dog and No had gone. She wasn't even Rona's baby but of course Rona had a certain investment in her. The baby wasn't sleeping well; the nights were too hot. Her face with its glaze of distraught boredom, paralysed on the verge of tears in the cot, was too much sometimes. Rona had gone back to bed to listen to waves crashing through her earphones.

The baby, if it belonged to anyone, was her boyfriend Joe's. He'd had her by accident with a short-lived sweetheart named Dawn. In the delivery room they had named the baby Brenda, making her seem, Rona had always thought, more like a colleague or an aunt than a baby. For Rona, having this kind of baby solved a lot of problems. She could see how she liked it and leave at any time. She could choose to cancel plans with the baby if something else came up. Joe was grateful if she helped even half-heartedly.

They had met when Rona was handing out flyers for a protest. In a way, Joe had been her only real political success. There was something about flyering that emboldened Rona: instead of hating her, people on the street hated something much bigger. They hate life itself! she told herself. 'Piss off,' a man with a wheelie suitcase had volleyed at her as she smiled and shouted, 'Save the world! Next Saturday!' A woman had taken a flyer and started reading it before asking if Rona had any facts, and Rona, caught off guard, had replied that she didn't have a mind for facts. The woman was shaking her head.

'If I were you I'd *get* a mind for facts,' the woman said, 'if you're going to go around asking people to sign up for this drivel.'

She'd walked away, looking back at Rona at intervals shouting, 'Educate yourself!'

Rona did know a few facts, but she was philosophically resistant to repeating them. Either you could imagine the apocalypse or you couldn't. She didn't want to convince anyone else the world was going to end. It felt cruel. Rona preferred to smile at people without saying anything.

Other passers-by had been nice. A dental student who had been at Tahrir Square complimented Rona on her government: 'You have a wonderful country – don't try to change it too much. Just a couple of tweaks, OK?' Rona nodded and wished him luck in his orthodontic exams. She felt good again; this was good, people were real, they were all fighting their own battles.

A man in a blue shirt had come over to her and asked for a leaflet, though she was already holding one out to him.

'Hello,' she said, when he didn't walk away.

He said he didn't agree with their methods, though it was true something needed to be done. Rona's group were known for irritating people. She wasn't sure if she agreed with their methods either, but their methods were really the main thing about them.

'I don't like conflict,' she'd said. 'Actually, I don't really like doing anything.'

'We're alike, then,' he said. 'I work there,' he added, gesturing to a government building Rona couldn't name.

'Right, I hear they hate doing things in there,' she said. Though most people wouldn't call it a dictatorship, the government was still no good, as far as she knew.

'I shouldn't even really be talking to you like this,' he said. 'I'll get in trouble.'

'Can they see us from up there?' Rona said. 'We could pretend to be having an argument.'

The man started to jab his finger at her, knitting his eyebrows together, looking as if he might say something like, 'Now listen here.'

'But anyway. It's good that you've thought so carefully about the inconvenience that you're causing. That's reassuring.'

'I frequently think about it,' Rona said.

The man pointed to the flyer. Whose Future? **OUR FUTURE!** it said, answering itself in bold, in capitals. 'It's a little possessive, isn't it? Who are "we"?'

'I didn't write the flyer,' Rona said. 'It's got nothing to do with me.'

When he left he said, 'Well, keep up the good work, but, you know, not really.'

Joe's baby must have already existed then, in a controversially embryonic, cellular, sloppy way. Rona was oddly stirred by thinking of Brenda's conception, her formation by the meeting of what she imagined were two steaming-hot substances – Rona had always had a loose grip on the science. She thought of it as cosmology: things happening in strange dimensions, at unfamiliar scales. Brenda was so small then, but Rona imagined planetary gases melding and churning.

Having a baby by accident was wildly out of Rona's character, which is probably why it hadn't happened to her. Her womb was resolutely closed. She knew you shouldn't think this way, but she felt familiar by now with the kind of person her reproductive system was. A strait-laced jobsworth, a woman in a pleated skirt, named . . . something like Brenda. It worked against desire; it put its calling on hold. Joe was obviously, somehow, pro-life, not in the political sense but optimistically, lustily in favour of it all.

***

She had next seen Joe at the protest she'd given him the flyer for.

'I'm not staying,' he'd said, when he found her with a bucket, shouting, 'Donations!' into the wind.

'No one's staying,' said Rona, feeling light-headed and hungry. 'The world is literally ending.' She laughed. 'Imagine if it was ending right now,' she said, striking a runner's pose, making as if to dash for it. Would it be like that?

'Aargh,' Joe cried, shielding his face against his destiny. 'Help!'

Rona shrugged. They stood for a moment, looking at placards.

'Anyway, thanks,' he said, and disappeared again without telling her his name or anything else about himself. He was wearing Nikes. Time felt short to Rona. She didn't have any to waste, but it also felt like a silky nothingness, whipping around above her head mockingly. It wasn't the tick-tock, sun-up-sun-down, winter-spring-summer-autumn, birth-middle-age-death time she'd grown up knowing. It was new, urgent and meaningless.

Joe started coming to meetings in community centres and in the tea-stained attics of obscure trade union buildings.

'Hey! You! Government mole! State-funded spy!' Rona yelled when she saw him, and people spun round to look, but he stayed while they discussed recycled sticker suppliers.

'I'm Joe,' he said.

Their fingers touched while putting the mugs away – the mugs all featured the faces and slogans of unsuccessful candidates and forgotten campaigns. Rona was comforted by them. She wanted to produce things that would become dusty, redundant and inexplicable. What did Choose Queues mean? To work away patiently at the margins of things, neatening them like a pastry crust. To contribute to life without being at its centre. Revolution is not a piece of embroidery, said Mao, who was wrong about so many things.

'Don't you find these mugs depressing?' Joe asked.

Rona shook her head. She wasn't sure she should say out loud that she was reassured by years of political failure. Joe was into progress, the irresistible thrum of it. Rona wouldn't mind if time stopped and pooled in on itself, making a large grey puddle.

'I'm just saying I would never want to end up on a mug,' he said.

Rona went to the toilet, locked the door and couldn't unlock it again. She pawed at the silver bolt for minutes, growing hot with embarrassment. Finally she saw Joe's shoes under the door, pacing for a moment before stopping, squishing under his weight as he crouched. His voice was saying, 'Rona? Rona, is that you?'

Rona had tears in her eyelashes by then. How can we go into the future with our noses pressed against a closed door? Is that what Virginia Woolf had said?

'Are you upset?'

'What?' Rona said.

'This is going to work,' he said. 'It won't be a mug.'

'A what?'

'A mug.'

Rona was thinking about Joe's face, imagining its concreteness. Was he talking about the revolution, or something more important?

'I'm not upset,' Rona said, weeping. 'I'm trapped.'

'Take a deep breath,' Joe said. 'Count to ... six. After that, try the lock again?'

Rona didn't like to take a deep breath, but she wiped her

eyes and looked up. There was a sign on the door that read: To unlock, pull towards you. Rona pulled the door and the bolt sprung back. Belief! It could be administered like WD40.

At the next meeting Joe was wirier, more glistening than usual, smelling of mineral water. Rona was kind of high, psychologically speaking. One of the leaders (there were no leaders) had asked her to be part of a secret cell. She couldn't tell Rona the details but it was high profile, very risky, very exciting. Rona had quickly said OK, though now she was thinking about it it seemed like a wild thing to do, whatever 'it' was going to be. She clutched Joe's shoulder, said 'Hi!' too charismatically.

'Guess what,' Joe said uncertainly when they'd sat down and people were still talking around them and making their tea. 'I'm having a baby.'

'Haha,' he added.

Rona nodded, thinking about all the things it could be, how they would get away, *whether* they'd get away. Would they have to get a taxi? They would have to lie about getting the taxi afterwards and say they rode their bikes.

'I'm sorry,' Joe was saying. 'I don't know if it's weird for you. I mean, it's obviously weirder for me. Maybe.'

'Sorry,' Rona said, 'what?'

In Any Other Business a drama teacher in orange leggings was suggesting they all lie down on their backs for fifteen minutes in town centres up and down the country, flailing their arms and legs. It's called the Dying Fly, she explained. There was some disagreement.

'I think it might be considered offensive,' said a soft-looking man.

'We'll look silly. Vulnerable. Like dying flies,' said another.

The drama teacher nodded.

Rona looked at Joe, who was contemplating the Dying Fly placidly.

'We would, of course, imbue it with pathos,' the woman said, finally.

Rona put her hand up, voting in favour of the Dying Fly. She wanted to lie down. She wanted to flail miserably. She wanted to die.

The end of the world sometimes seemed like a frivolous thing to get upset about, an existential crisis of last resort. There was going to be a sombre procession – mothers and children would dance sadly through the streets. 'Throwing another funeral for yourselves?' said a different man with a wheelie suitcase as Rona handed him the flyer.

Joe's baby was the size of an aubergine by now. *Your baby is the size of an eggplant, and can blink and dream*, Rona read online, googling '28 weeks'. It was depressing looking at the cut-out photo of the aubergine, so large and real. *Your baby has a strong chance of survival if born now!* the website congratulated. Joe went on the march for mothers and children. Rona had gone too, though when she got there she looked out for the papier mâché skeletons and skulked along behind them. Skin in the game, the mothers were saying. 'What I'd really like,' said a small child into a microphone, 'is to live to the end of my natural life.'

She was sad, but what about? What was the end of the world anyway? Was it a substance like a gas that they were all walking through at all times, getting on their skins, making them feel grubby and itchy?

'Stupid time to have a baby,' Joe said when he found her.

'Ah, someone didn't do their research,' Rona said. Still, it wasn't imaginative to assume the worst. Got to enjoy it while it lasts. 'How about a drink?' she asked. It started raining hard.

They both ordered tap water at the pub, which was full of mothers and placards and prams. Rona kept bumping into children eating tin-foiled sandwiches on the way up the stairs.

They drank their water quickly and Joe went to get more. While he was gone Rona listened to two friends talking about open borders. Joe came back with two glasses of water each.

'What's happening with your baby?' Rona ventured. 'Is it quite big by now?'

'I don't know,' said Joe. 'I don't get to see it much. You know, the bump. *In embryo*. I'm not with . . . It was very . . . ' He trailed off and smiled downwards.

When they left the pub it had turned into a scorching evening. She could feel the heat pumping off the brick walls all the way back to Joe's house. 'Climate change in a day,' Rona said, to say something.

'Kind of a relief,' Joe replied. 'It would be better if we could just get it over with.'

He lived in a nice place with two other well-paid men. The walls were all subtle greys, the carpets were seagrass; the kitchen had a wooden counter smudged gently with olive-oil stains.

'I love you,' Joe said as they ate spaghetti in the dining area of the eat-in kitchen. His housemate was cooking behind them with his headphones on.

'Did you mean to say that?' asked Rona.

'I think so. What did I say?'

'"I love you."'

'Really?' Joe said.

Joe was trying to save the world; everyone was now. Joe's job title actually was Environmental, and Rona forgot the end. Officer. Liaison. Lead. Joe truly did do things every day. He made a difference. There were statistics that he was directly responsible for. Rona googled it. Eighty-nine per cent decrease in this, 154 per cent increase in that. Joe didn't tell her about it.

Then Joe's department put out a report Rona couldn't even look at the title of, and she didn't know how he could copy and paste it into spreadsheets and emails without shivering, but he always seemed pleased about something, and sent her texts that said things like 'Are you happy with linguine?'

Two months later Brenda was born. Brenda means Queen of the Land, Dawn told her when she went to the hospital. When Rona looked it up on her phone she found out Brenda meant sword. Brenda was a person, it was true, detached from Dawn and Joe, more Rona's, she felt, as she sat in the visitor's chair holding her. With Brenda in her arms Rona felt a dizzying love for the future, but when she handed her back to Dawn, it was gone again.

In the hospital Joe looked at Brenda like someone he truly loved. His eyes became browner, his eyebrows wriggled with a high-frequency pleasure that seemed both transmitted and received. Rona had never seen anything like it.

Now they were here in Joe's flat, the three of them and Brenda's chosen family of stuffed animals. This kind of motherhood required nothing. It was shockingly easy to make a life. Rona bought large pots of geraniums and put them on the windowsill.

She ate two hours before yoga; she finally owned a camisole. Joe was here too, of course, though his life seemed mysterious and separate. Watering plants by a special method Rona didn't know the details of, over the sink. Sterilising things. Cutting slices of bread precisely, to Brenda's exact requirements. He put up shelves and laid a blue fluffy carpet in Brenda's bedroom. He's handy! said Rona's friends winkingly.

Rona had a small worry that she and Joe would break up at a bad time developmentally. Would Brenda carry with her the vague, disturbing memory of a non-committal woman? Or remember nothing of Rona at all?

'Just when I've made a life, life on earth ends,' Rona said to Brenda as she chopped up a banana.

'What do you mean by "life"?' Joe asked.

'What do I mean by "ends"?' Rona replied.

Rona wondered if Brenda already knew about the end of the world in her wise, large-eyed way. Children were smarter than anyone, and more brave, though it was an irony that they did lack certain capabilities, that their access to power was indirect. The youngest of all of them, she was the closest in a way to not existing. It was very recently that she had not existed, within living memory you might say.

'Is existing better?' Rona asked Brenda, putting the banana down in front of her.

Joe was printing a report and the words 'doomsday clock' were coming out of the printer.

'Do you think Brenda will print things out?' Joe turned to Rona and asked. 'Do you think Brenda will know that jagged sound of cartridge on A4? Do you think Brenda will queue in shops and not know where to look as she taps her card to the card reader?'

'Brenda will place her items in the bagging area,' said Rona.

'Do you think Brenda will put elasticated blue plastic bags around her shoes when she goes swimming?'

'Do you think Brenda will have a terrible moth problem, will spend thousands of pounds trying to kill moths?'

'Do you think Brenda will desire nothing more than a pink pencil sharpener from the Natural History Museum?' Joe tapped Brenda on the head.

'OK,' said Rona.

In the bed which they have made an ocean, with the sea sounds on a speaker now, Rona wonders what constitutes a raft, whether two human bodies are enough.

'What will happen to Brenda?' Rona asks.

'Let's hope Brenda's life is strange,' says Joe.

A column of light appears at the sea's furthest shore, then broadens into a lighthouse beam. Brenda in her striped pyjamas climbs aboard. 'Hello,' she says.

'She's here,' Rona says.

'The future,' Joe says.

Damsons

N.G.F. CLARK

There are times when the fading of the season permits the embers of the old gods to glow through the cracks.

When September comes, and the trees deepen their greenery, when the damsons grow soft and heavy, and the morning light spills aged and oaken – this is one of those times.

On the awakening of the old god Pendyn a sign is put up on our street to let others know of his return. The sign is a stiff white board on a wooden post that appears in the garden of a house owned by a man named Marlon. The god's name is handwritten in thick black marker pen in evenly spaced capitals.

I walk past this house on my way to work almost every day, all the year round. And when the sign for the old god Pendyn appears, it is as if an old friend has returned. The sign appears only briefly – a couple of weeks at most – but each time I pass, and I glimpse the sign ahead, I feel a quiet joy, and all is well.

Our street is a long, red-brick avenue, leafy with tall, full-grown limes. Looking down it on a summer's day you could be forgiven for thinking the road disappears into dense forest only a few yards in. It takes a full fifteen minutes to walk from one end to the other, longer if it is wet, as the York stone becomes slippery underfoot. Once, this street would have been an affluent part of the city, but the wealth has long since departed. Now, the pavement is as wild and untended as the gardens. Now, it is ours.

At one end of the avenue is a mosque, and cars are parked nose to tail every Friday afternoon. At the other end is a Polish church with an attached bakery selling fresh bread and *kołackzi*. No shrine exists for the old god Pendyn aside from the end-terrace house. The stone rows that once guided his priests have long been interred beneath the turning of plough, pick and JCB. And yet the old god's genius still clings to this place like the stiff clench of a mummified claw.

Marlon, who owns the house where Pendyn occasionally resides, didn't know what he was taking on when he bought the property. The world is so different now – how should one honour the old gods, especially when one becomes your lodger?

We bring our gifts anyway. The Sikh family next door always provide a tray of homemade samosas and flowers from the minimarket. I like to bake something sweet. Sometimes it feels like a harvest festival, other times a bring-and-buy sale, or a wake.

This year there is a bottle of vodka, *pączki* from the bakery, some old CDs, poster-paint drawings of Amelia – aged five and a half – and her cats, a birthday card with the price tag still on, and a fat roll-up. Even if the old god Pendyn isn't keen on the gift, Marlon can usually find a use for it. No one really knows what the old gods like any more and we have forgotten the language they once spoke, so there is no use in asking.

Marlon gathers the gifts in his living room and sets them out on a trestle table. This year there are fewer gifts than usual. There are no samosas from next door.

I have brought with me a fruit crumble, made with blackberries I picked myself and apples from a tin, and a pack of tobacco as an afterthought (Marlon smokes like a bonfire). I asked my son what he thought Pendyn looks like, and he made a Lego figure of the old god, which I thought was a clever thing to do, and so my son has brought that too.

Marlon has a smile for everyone who enters his home with gifts. He'll always return in kind, usually with a mug of Jamaican rum, or a bag of damsons from the tree in his garden, or a chat. He has time for everyone, has Marlon. He wants to know who you are, why you're here, why you care. Or sometimes he'll just talk football.

Today, when we visit, Marlon tells me about the time a high

druid of the British Druid Order paid a visit, but he was out. This is what he left, says Marlon, and he shows me a card with a Celtic knot trim and a sickle stamp. We both laugh that such a thing could happen. The high druid has not called since.

My son places his Lego figure of the old god Pendyn on the table next to the other gifts. He asks if we can see him. Marlon says he is resting.

The next day the sign has gone.

It has only been up a few days and I ask Marlon why he has taken it down so soon. Marlon tells me some kids in the neighbourhood stole the sign and haven't brought it back.

The days of the old god's awakening slowly pass. No more gifts arrive at the table for Pendyn. It is only a few more days before he will slip back between the cracks once more. Who will know to visit without the sign? Who will care to bring their gifts? It feels like the year has gone wrong.

Marlon could make another sign, I think, but a dimness at the back of his wrinkled old eyes tells me he will not. One year, perhaps soon, a different sign will appear in his garden, and the developers who buy the property will not care to accept visitors or gifts for those two short weeks in September.

I take different routes on my walk to work, searching across streets and down alleys for the lost sign. I get to work late, and home later, but I don't mind. I ask the Sikh family next door to Marlon, but they don't know who I am. I ask the kids hanging out in the park whether they have seen it – they shrug and laugh and one spits on the floor. I ask at the Polish bakery, and at the mosque, but no one has seen it. They do not seem to understand why it is important.

I begin to wonder if it is. No one else seems to realise something is wrong. The world moves on without pausing to think of Pendyn.

Five nights after the sign was stolen I stop in the park in the cold and the damp. Why am I doing this? I could make a new sign myself, if I had the materials. But somehow that seems wrong. It is not my sign to put up, not my god to announce. It has nothing to do with me. Yet it was only me searching these past few days.

The shadows are thick in the park, and the streetlamps from outside can't puncture the darkness. There is a man sitting alone on a swing, smoking. He wears an enormous rastacap that perches awkwardly on his head, as if caught on something. The end of his cigarette glows softly.

There is no one else around, so I ask the man if he has seen the sign.

He asks me why I am searching for it, and I feel foolish.

'I thought people would miss it, but I think it's only me. It's a stupid thing to be doing.'

The man's eyes glint with the light of his cigarette end, then fade just as quickly.

'Do you know why I am here?' he asks.

I shake my head.

'I am here because it is the only place where the stars are visible on a clear night – look . . .'

I look up, and realise he is right. Without the streetlamps the stars can be seen clearer than I could have thought.

The man points out constellations to me: 'There is Cocidius with his spear and shield, there is long and flowing Verbeia. And between them is Belatucadrus, shining bright most of all . . .'

The man's joy is tangible as he speaks the names of the stars, even though I don't recognise any of them. As he talks, I feel very calm and peaceful.

'Do you see anyone else with me, looking at the stars?' asks the man.

'No.'

'And yet here I am all the same, because it is important to me to be here. A task is always worthwhile, no matter how small, if it means something to you.'

My eyesight has adjusted to the gloom by the time I leave the park, and on my way out I see the sign lodged, upended, between the park fence and a bus stop. Aside from being slightly ragged around the edges it is in good shape, and the marker pen has not run. I take no small amount of pride carrying it over one shoulder, a lone pilgrim to a sleepy god, and my heart is light as I return it to Marlon's garden.

Afterwards, I feel more sober. Am I really such a creature of habit to feel the loss of a sign so keenly? But the next day, gifts start reappearing on the table for Pendyn. There is fresh bread from the bakery, silk from the mosque, and there are flowers and home-baked samosas from next door. I see the smiles on the neighbours' faces, the gratitude in Marlon's grin, and I know I'm not the only one who draws comfort from this small ritual of the year.

Marlon's granddaughter is playing on an old videogame console. It is a game I used to play, when I was younger, so whilst Marlon is outside having a smoke and my son sits on the couch looking at my phone, I pick up a controller and join in. Marlon's granddaughter is impressed; she doesn't usually have someone else to play with. I once knew this game very well and, as I play, the same feelings I once associated with it resurface. I wonder how it is that some memories stay submerged for months or years or decades until something tugs them back up, and how nice it is to share them with someone new.

There is a clatter as my son drops my phone on the floor. I turn around – he is staring open-mouthed at a shadow moving in the hallway. The room feels suddenly damp and cool, as if we are sitting inside the trunk of a hollow tree. We hear the soft creak of the stairs, the gentle scrape of antlers against the ceiling. On the trestle table, one of the samosas is missing.

The following week, Marlon takes down the sign. The year has moved on already and all along the avenue the leaves of the limes slowly turn to lemon. The only damsons left are those half-hidden in the grass. For another year, we forget the old god Pendyn.

WATCH AND SUBSCRIBE!!

Artemisia eats entire Chicken Shop Menu – Mukbang LIVE!

DANIELLE GILES

takes me an hour to prep (wifi, angles, make-up, lighting)

I get the bags of food ready and visible on the desk, waiting like bombs, and I open the first one and take out onion rings, hold them up to the camera, and then begin

I'm chewing before I even start to stream

got the jump on all the viewers as they log on, loyal as Praetorians, to watch me eat

wings, thighs, breast, got chips delivered too and even the flaccid salad and I say this last one aloud and get

              17:00 [no profile pic]: >:(

              17:00 [no profile pic]: porn gif, the

                      woman's eyes sometimes shown

but my eyes twinkle as I eat, I have special contact lenses that make them brighter and bluer – anime beauties, Superman X-ray, Merlin who could see into the future

today I'm eating the entire chicken shop menu – Kent Fried Chicken, the copyright-avoiding colonel with a brown beard instead of a white one

I went there once after a night out and a man said to me cheesy chips were a girly order when all around us was lovely meat, cut and portioned right to fit in greasy little boxes

              17:05 [no profile pic]: Flat 7, Naples

                    Road, Islington, N1–

17:05: deleted

17:05: sorry babes that's private, wink gif, haha

              17:06 [profile pic him in graduate gown]:

                    that her address?

it's wrong anyway, idiots think I'm still at my old place but now if anybody went there they'd find only a baffled bougie couple and an underexercised greyhound

              17:07 [the graduate gown accented by

fur]: she's not interested in you losers

salad is too warm, chicken is too cold, its skin pimpled, my skin pimpled too from wearing only a strappy top, the kind that mothers in films would look at and say you're not going out in that but I wasn't going out

I wasn't going anywhere because my hour of streaming today would keep me for the week

wool scratches below my waist from the blanket that none of my viewers can see

17:13 [profile pic a cartoon girl]: feet pics?

I send him my business email address, those cost more and only when I am in the mood – £100 per foot, my little toes expensive as saffron, more reliable than gold

my face, back at me, deliberately pretty

my room, behind me, discarded PhD drafts, sheaves of paper stuffed into bookshelves, laundry whirring through a cycle downstairs, shuddering my feet, maybe I put a red in with that white wash, I can't remember and can't check now

they like a messy room, makes me human, though they don't know how I watch them back

they aren't aware of the hours I spend on my academic research combing through chatrooms:

skinny boys with painted-on abs

women pointing to the bags under their eyes and asking whether they are hideous

flesh edited out of existence by filters, girls becoming hourglasses, men turning triangular

oh, they are all a little lovely, my audience, all have beauty in them

17:22 [profile pic a little girl]: fatty

17:25 [profile pic a ninja]: I want to
turn you inside out

17:25: blocked

17:25 [profile pic a fitness model]: he
was complimenting you

conference days I speak about all this online chatter in rooms that smell of coffee and sweat and all these scholars look at me and wait for what insights will come out of my mouth next

I once overheard this professor say she was working class because she sold her ideas and wasn't that comparable to retail/ factory/delivery drivers/cleaners?

now into the burger and chips, classic as a nuclear family grease drops and hits my blanket

it'll smell of burgers for the rest of the week, even after I've aired out the room and lit some incense, vanilla? cinnamon? no it's a lavender sort of week after this, for rest and forgetting and sweetness

there were lavender sprigs under my pillow every night when that deepfake video first came out and I couldn't sleep without thinking of all the angles from which I could be seen (couldn't be seen – that version wasn't me and yet it had my eyes, sometimes, because they'd sourced my face from my hundreds of streams, accurately, carefully)

I wonder sometimes about the body they stitched me onto, who she was, whether she knew that they'd taken her head, whether she cared

sometimes I dream I meet her

we hug, finally complete

we turn into something incredible, a robot, a unicorn, something more than the sum of our parts, but I still never see her face no time to dream, I keep going with the chips, sprinkling vinegar onto them, so strong it pouts my mouth

    17:31 [profile pic a fitness model]:
      rub it on your tits, £10

17:32: not that kind of channel babe x

    17:32 [profile pic a fitness model]:
      fucking right it's not

they sign off, another viewer lost but one in 10,000, as statistically significant as the odds of being injured by a toilet or winning an Oscar and I don't worry about those

the Academy is still yet to contact me of course

I smile, and my viewers think it's for them

    17:37 [no profile pic]: it's all fake

    17:39 [no profile pic]: making me feel
      less lonely this evening, thank
      you xxxxxoxox £50

17:40: thanxxx love u guys

    17:41 [profile pic a bear]: too skinny

    17:41 [the bear is fighting]: vomiting
      gif 1

    17:41 [profile pic an actual bear-baiting
      screenshot]: bet she throws it
      up afterwards

wrong

there's a wilderness survival programme I watch where the women always do better than the men, and this woman kills a squirrel and as its flayed skin is steaming heat into her eyes she looks up to heaven and then to the ground and says thanks, like that squirrel was put in that forest just for her

so I have never thrown up any of the food I eat for these videos because there was a potato once in the dark warmth of the soil that was destined for this: for picking and chopping and freezing and frying, and that unsuspecting potato is now covered in ketchup and glory as I stream it to thousands of followers

there's a reason for everything, I've heard many times, said to me like an apology

the vibration on my feet changes from heavy bass to whining melody and on to a final spin, can't leave the clothes in there too long or my housemate will leave a passive-aggressive note full of :) and ! and ?

it's not me in the deepfake but technology can do some marvellous things and stitch a girl's face onto another girl's body so neatly that nobody can tell the difference, and that was three years ago so imagine what they could do now, have probably already done

I still don't know who made it, no way of finding out the police said, and not a crime anyway so why bother them, don't I know there are proper villains out there not some little weirdo I should pity, maybe even forgive?

> 17:49 [profile pic a Kardashian]: she's
> got a filter on

no filter right now, and I'm on to the ice cream which is so sweet I taste only pink not strawberries (strawberry flavour says the packet defensively)

I frown when I bite into it and feel the cold bloom up my teeth and you can't fake that and this is mine, all the tips I get, an honest living

> 17:51 [profile pic a white man in a suit,
> it's his real picture and he should
> be careful talking to strangers on
> the internet, a man like that
> could be taken advantage of]: £176

apart from the 15% platform fee
there have to be ways to diversify
17:55: I'm thinking of moving into ASMR x

       17:55 [no profile pic]: so cool!
       17:55 [profile pic a famous blonde
            singer]: yesss
       17:55 [profile pic maybe not that
            blonde singer, maybe a famous
            female fascist]: porn gif, no eyes
            shown

an email is sent to my work from a burner account every year or so, titled: *re inappropriate video*

the department are kinder than they need to be about the deepfake, and offer counselling each time (as if I don't already do it), though they think thank God not my daughter/wife/ girlfriend but I bet some of them don't even know, haven't checked how somebody can turn an image sour

I sometimes think about finding out who did it, stitching their head into some awful video but that would be lowering myself to revenge and that never works out in the films though it looks such fun

my outfit for misguided, hollow, entertaining revenge: trousers (leather), blouse (red), gloves (many pairs for different crimes)

the ice cream is done now on to the showstopper the finale

       17:57 [profile pic definitely a famous
            blonde fascist]: she's not going
            to manage that whole chicken
            now

I'm going to more than manage it, I'm going to develop it like an underperforming employee, I'm going to give it a performance review and team-building days

it's the size of my head but I've always liked a challenge
and I eat it methodically from the bottom up like bears do to
unfortunate hikers and I pause when I can and tell the viewers
to follow, to like and subscribe and pay and they do and I see my
heating bill, a good night out, a new laptop and still the money
keeps rising and still I keep eating

my stomach doesn't hurt at all though it should, my insides
are resilient

fingers have wrinkled from the grease and my palms smell
of fat

mascara has run a little

               18:01 [no profile pic]: hot

               18:01 [profile pic a selfie of a boy not
                          even old enough for the platform
                          and he's got a little dog in
                          his arms]: £4.50

a jingle from below and my wash is done and the chicken is
done too and what a well-planned day

I log off and I collect my laundry – the housemate has put
her next load on top of the machine to mark her spot in the queue
but she's out now at her nine-to-five

I put my blanket in next for a whole three-hour cycle and
look at cottage getaways for next weekend while I wait

So Long Sarajevo/
They Miss You
So Badly

FRANCESCA REECE

A pair of actors talking to an Englishman in a basement all hung with blue and lilac smoke. Candles. *Aleksander is Vedrana's boyfriend*, the Englishman with his RP voice tells us. It's still winter and she's wearing a boxy coat and fingerless gloves. Gold hoops glint in her dark, reddish-black hair. They were putting on *Richard III* and it was the end of the Siege of Sarajevo. *Now is the winter of our discontent*, says the Englishman, who's not much older than them really. They're teenagers, prematurely aged. Grungy, '90s feedback sounds fuzz and blur with the needles of smoke, and then are eviscerated by the thud of shells and mortar. A bakery queue. Old women in headscarves with hands all pressed with the rhizomes of age. Soviet buses in barbershop colours with jagged hollows where windows used to be. BBC voices saying words like *you enne, ethnic, intervention*. Great, gauzy gusts of fire clawing apart gaping tower blocks and a man in Wranglers and a sweatshirt dragging himself along the pavement on his elbows. The Siege of Sarajevo is my first memory. It's framed in a polished teak TV set with a dial, and it feels like woodchip walls and the tight, pubic curls of our living room carpet.

'We should put Sontag's Sarajevo-*Godot* in the box,' says the Student, self-importantly. 'It was the epilogue to the century.'

I don't know what Sontag or *Godot* have to do with Sarajevo or even each other but the Student thinks they should go in the box with Oil, International English, Auschwitz and Binary Code. It's just the kind of thing he would say.

The Siege of Sarajevo is my first real memory.

The radio says: But if your childhood memories are really so unreliable, are you sure that you are who you think you are?

Red, spectral light is the colour of the bar. Campari light, filtering out to green around the pass, and a sinister, jaundiced yellow fug at the Gents. Sometimes, the colours make me think of stained-glass windows and sunsets, and then sometimes they make me think of those grotesque videos they used to show you at school where someone took too much ecstasy and ended up foaming at the mouth in a dirty toilet stall. Light that is holy and sleazy all at once. 'This bar is full of fucking weirdos,' said the Student when he first started coming in. 'That's why I like it,' he said, 'It's full of the kind of people who've washed up here at the end of the world.'

Now he rolls two cigarettes – one for him, one for me. Everybody smokes at the bar after close. He's allowed to stay on the basis of the fact that we sleep together sometimes I guess, and my boss is fond of him because he once expressed a passing appreciation for the song, 'Roxanne'.

I didn't think that there would be so much blood.

I want to decorate the box with newspaper cuttings about the solar eclipse. I looked it up on the internet; it was on the 11th August 1999. It was the summer that we buried the time capsule in Nain's garden, where the light was clean and direct and bored down into the lurid green of the lawn and tinted our skin. Skin that smelt like sunlight, tree sap and soil. All summer, I scraped the sap off the leprous bark of the larch trees. *I'm harvesting amber for the time capsule.* Mum is lying in the grass pretending to sleep so she doesn't have to speak to me. We watched the eclipse through film negatives and now, when I try and really think about what it looked like, my mind bulges with tiny silhouettes of Nain on the beach at Aberdyfi. When it's over, Mum drops the negatives on the patio tiles and goes back to lie on her bath towel in the grass. Her face is calm when she closes her eyes. The same features are replicated and aged on Nain's face, and now, when I look in the liver-spotted mirror behind the bar, they're traced right across my reflection. I wonder if they would have come out on yours. If hours and days and weeks would have ended up biting into your soft, July-peach-features with the same kind of tide. Mine are split now; spliced by the brassy shadow and the plume of the Student's cigarette.

Am I washed up here at the end of the world? I suppose so. The Student likes the game with the box and that in turn gives me a swell of pleasure. I invented something *cerebral*. I am limbs and breasts and a pair of ankles and fingertips that press hard on his mouth when he moves inside me. Sometimes I wonder how my body has the right to experience, express such isolated pleasure. I didn't think that there would be so much blood.

On Saturday mornings sometimes there's a jumble sale on our street. Trails of trestle tables are un-stacked before dawn and by the time I get out they swarm and *Andrić* multiply from the church steps right down towards the Old Port. A racket of saline, southern light this morning. There is a man with sickly, light-bulb skin and a brown leather jacket who sells memories – heaps of old photographs, postcards and letters. Twenty cents for a shard of someone's past-tense life. I leave with a clutch of family photographs.

Paul, Café de la Poste, Hendaye, 1955

Brunnen, Septembre '64

Papi et Jeanne, Chez B. 1953

The pencil strokes tail off like contrails, so they're almost in motion I guess. They're so empty now, though, that they may as well be Viking runes.

The radio says: It is thought that we don't have memories that early in life because we don't have the language skills that it is thought are necessary to produce the narrative structure that characterises later recall.

Silvio is drinking *I'd save Andrić till the last* coffee on the balcony. Silvio is one of my two flatmates and the one I find the most offensive. He's sitting outside where I wanted to sit, in hibiscus-print board shorts and the kind of straw hat that irrefutably indicates that the wearer is a twat. Silvio is a DJ – and by that I mean, he works in a bar like me but is generically aspirational. I sort through the post, picking out the flyers of the neighbourhood mediums for my collage. M. Samou promises *prodigious natural gifts* and claims that his inherited, supernatural powers can cure heartbreak, bereavement, legal woes and back pain. M. Sosostris insists that your loved ones are waiting for you. *They miss you so badly.* Silvio gives me a withering look and carries on eating his cereal (it's half past four, incidentally). Silvio thinks flyers should be abolished because they're bad for the environment. Silvio once saw the beginnings of a collage I was accumulating and described it as *mignon.* When I said that it was like his music – sampling, layering, fragmentation – he said: *I made a really good collage in primary school when France won the World Cup. My step-mum still has it up in the kitchen*, and then he asked me if I had a good number for coke, because it turned out his dealer had voted for the National Front.

I'm not trying to be obtuse. All these scraps concertina out and proliferate, and I'm trying to collect them and make them something coherent. I'm trying to synthesise them and make my memory make sense. This is how my body felt.

The gynaecologist asks me why *the eighteenth floor* I have so many bruises, but not in a gentle kind of way. Her mouth is burred with disapproval. I say that *and of course because they cut the electricity* I bruise easily. She sneers. What about this one? she demands. Or this one? She thrusts a condemning finger towards a little blue angel on the softest part of my thigh. The press of a thumb. How on earth does a person get a bruise here? She talks to me like *I can't use the lift* I'm a silly little girl and when she tells me the result, part of her wilts and dies as if she's staring down the compact incarnation of everything that's wrong with humanity. I feel light. I was one. How will you react when I tell you? Will I even bother to tell you at all?

I'd save Andrić till the end. Till the last coffee!

I'm building something. This is how my body felt.

The pain was quite spectacular really, and after it I felt fragmented in turn. I was one. We were two we were three and yet we were one and then I let go of you both. They miss you so badly.

Tall thin windows like arrow slits. *You can't even remember what you ate yesterday.* It was a very difficult moment – a very painful one for me. *You remind me of a friend of mine who said she can't even remember the names of her favourite film stars.* It was very late at night and we couldn't see anything. We managed to enter the building through *I'd save Andrić till the end* the front door.

They used white phosphor bombs. It was impossible to extinguish the flames with water. One thing I still remember *till the last coffee* was that a woman who lived opposite the library was crying. She told me, 'a part of Sarajevo is burning. A part of me is burning.'

Blodeuwedd made of flowers. *Eithin. Erwain. Dderwen.*

Do you know why they stopped shelling the Television Tower? About 100 grenades in, they realised it wasn't a mosque!

When I leave the bar after close, the old port is rinsed with the indigo tones of dawn. Night here in the summer is never really complete – it's picked apart with snatches of light, and by the time my boss pulls down the grille with a Victorian factory *clank*, the seam where the grey, speckled sea meets the horizon is smudged with it. I didn't think there would be so much blood.

The pub in town. *Dyf Bryn Glas has belted his trousers with bailer's twine I swear to God.* I cackle. Somehow I'm lying across the pool table, licking the back of my hand anticipating tequila. Sting sings, and you sing, that you won't share Roxanne with another boy. You were loud, brash and incandescent. It was the total silence in the end that really threw me. I never thought you'd get rid of me by withdrawing any kind of language. I thought we'd go out with a real bang.

The radio says: But if your childhood memories are really so unreliable, are you sure that you are who you think you are?

Nain once told me that her mum's first memory was the end of the First World War. She was sitting on the cold tiles of the kitchen floor and her father – who was a wheelwright – came in from work.

'Well, it's over,' he apparently said.'

'What's over?' her mother asked, 'Something in one of those Balkan countries?'

'No,' her father, the wheelwright said. 'Everything's over. The war is over. It's done.'

My first memory is the Siege of Sarajevo. It's framed in a polished teak TV set with a dial – but I'm not even sure if that's real all things considered, because it was the nineties, and in the nineties I'm pretty sure TVs were made out of plastic. I'd save Andrić till the last coffee.

The Four Kind Women

MELODY RAZAK

The women are very kind. Their gentleness bewilders me. They smell of almond oil and stewed mutton. They hop on flat feet like crows, whispering from inside their black chadors. They think that because they speak a village dialect I can't understand them, but I can. They're talking about me. Little moosh they say, so far away from home, her bones so brittle we could chew them, pick our teeth with them. Her marrow would taste so tender in a stew. They lick their lips. Look at her eyes! Have you ever seen such a colour?

They want to eat my eyes.

I think they want to eat my eyes.

I close them at once. I don't want to be seen.

I'm not here and I am here. Consciousness evades me. When I am awake, I feign stupidity. I will not talk. I can't remember my name.

It hurts to move, so I stay still. One of the kind women sits beside me and with great care, as though I am a child, begins to spoon thin soup into my mouth. I purse my lips, refuse. Another kind woman pinches my nose. My mouth opens, the thin soup trickles in and is good. Some of it sticks to my stomach. Some of it they clean with a damp cloth from around my chin. The soup is different here, spicier, darker.

It hurts to eat.

'She's not used to it.'

'She's not had it before.'

'She must eat it. It will nourish her. Fatten her in time for the wedding.'

'Little moosh, so far away from home.'

Wedding?

I don't stink of my own piss and shit any more. Someone has cleaned me, bathed and scented me. There is a whiff of talcum powder on my skin. Rose.

At night I wet the bed. In the morning I leak hot blood on the mattress. The four kind women lift me and change the sheets. They use damp towels to clean in between my legs and when they do this, they do so with sorrow and the fourth woman, the youngest, always cries. They comfort her, bring hot tea and stroke her head.

It's almost as if my wounds are not my wounds alone, but hers too. It annoys me. This sharing of the wound.

We live in one bare room in a big house. The four kind women sleep on rolled-out mattresses on the floor and I have the bed.

The four kind women pray five times a day. I watch them perform their ablutions with half an eye. They wash their hands, their feet, faces and necks, even inside their ears. They mutter and lie prostrate on pink prayer mats, marked by the soles of their feet, and they face the same way.

In the evenings, the four kind women read from the holy book. They take it in turns to sit by my side.

I am not stupid. I know it's not company on offer. It is a keeping-an-eye.

I begin to heal. One day, I can move my arm. The next day I move my leg. On the third day, I sit up in bed. The four kind women are so pleased they coo like warm-throated pigeons and bring me a dish of sweetened cream.

I listen to them talk and learn that I am over the border.

'A pity she is mute.'

'It is appropriate. Anything else would be difficult.'

'It's a blessing.'

Oh. I had not wanted to make it easy for them. I have landed myself in a catch. I will need to find another way of inflicting harm. Do I really want to harm them? Yes. I do.

'It will suit baby brother perfectly, him being so simple himself.'

'She has been sent to us from Allah.'

'She is a gift.'

'A miracle.'

'You will be married soon, dear child,' says the eldest kind woman. 'A modest wedding. Just us and your husband-to-be. He saw you when you were sleeping. He loves you already.'

'Mashallah, little moosh.'

I will do what I am told, and when I am strong enough, when I remember, I will work out how to get home. This, this is not home.

'Today is your wedding day,' says the eldest of the four kind women.

Of course, I know their names by now but I will not acknowledge them.

They help me off the bed, put me in a tub of warm water and bathe me. They rub me with jasmine-scented soap, wash and oil my hair, dress me in silken undergarments and whilst they dress me they sing in rounds and harmonies that are beautiful to hear. Beauty hurts me. I sob, inconsolable, until I am sick and dry. Ever patient, the four kind women bundle me in towels and wipe my mouth. They talc me as though talcing is the cure for all grief.

They place gold earrings in my lobes.

'Pretty one.'

'Jewel-of-our-hearts.'

'Allah in his greatness has blessed us.'

'You are one of us now.'

No. No, I am not.

They guide me. Help me walk. I have not left the bed in days, weeks, perhaps months? They lead me through a garden and the air is cool on my face. It must be nearly winter. If it's nearly winter here, it will be nearly winter over there.

Imagine a room with two red-bowed high-backed chairs and I must sit on one, and I don't want to sit on one, knowing what it would mean to sit on one, but gentle hands push me gently down and keep me gently in place.

The carpet is all shades of dark blue. It has a gold border of dusky roses and there are peacocks in the centre. I have never seen so many peacocks before, their plumes in fanned coquettish display.

Marzipan-stuffed dates are pushed between my lips.

'A wedding is not a wedding without delectable morsels to sweeten the heart.'

The four kind women take it in turns to kiss my face, and they are so kind and so full of love when they kiss my face that I almost begin to cry with something like hate, though I don't know yet that this is hate, having never known such revulsion to be possible before.

Two men enter the chamber. The first man is shy. Awkward. His mouth is twisted out of shape. He looks at his feet.

The second man looks straight ahead and when I look at him, prodded as I have been to look at him by the fourth kind woman because one must respect one's elders, I smell him, like a bottle of vinegar pushed to the nose, before I catch his eye.

I remember.

The shock of the flood is caught in my throat. My knees shudder. My stomach heaves like dry rot pickling and all along my spine ice-cold sweat stinks. I vomit. I am like a struck thing. My skin blanched and peeled off, my ligaments, bones and muscles exposed. Marzipan-stuffed dates are all over my dress and the fourth kind woman is quick to clean me up.

The man with the vinegar smell catches my eye for a second and then he looks away. He will never look at me again.

I stare at the dark-blue carpet for ages. I am married to the man with the twisted mouth and simple brain. He sits next to me, blushes crimson. My husband.

After the wedding feast, I am led into a new room.

'This is your marital chamber.'

'Where you will lie with your husband.'

'He blushed when he saw you!'

'You will still sleep with us in the zenana.'

'We are always separate from the menfolk. Allah requires it.'

'But for an hour each day, you will lie here and do your duty by your husband.'

'Sisters, does she know?' asks the fourth kind woman.

The other three are silent. The eldest gives the youngest a look and there is something in that look that fills them all with shame.

'Allah. Forgive me. I am stupid to ask such questions.'

They guide me to the bed and lay me on it. They remove my garments and massage my feet. They dab droplets of blood from my thighs and dust them with talc. Rose. They place a brand-new cotton sheet across my naked trembling body.

They look at me in adoration, in envy.

The eldest kind woman uncorks a small vial and feeds me drops of bitter liquid. She has been holding the vial in her hand all this time, hiding it in the clench of her fingers as though it were a secret.

'This will help.'

'It will be over before you know it.'

'It is never enjoyable.'

'But it is a duty.'

'And then there will be a child.'

'A child will bring you joy.'

What is joy? I am growing sleepy. What is joy? I sleep.

I come to with a thick head. The man with the twisted

mouth is next to me. My husband. I try not to look at him, but there is an unfamiliar movement and my eyes are drawn involuntarily across. His hand is in his pyjamas and he is frantically touching himself. He heaves a heavy release, leaks a tiny patch of moisture on the cotton crotch, grunts like a baby pig snuffling and then he falls asleep.

Oh!

This, the daily act of my husband frantically touching himself, touching his cock, too simple, too timid to actually look at me, becomes the pattern of our marital bed.

This is joy. It is small joy but I will take what I can get.

I continue to heal. I learn to walk. I go to the toilet by myself. I feed myself.

I learn that the four kind women are the wives, mother and sister of the man with the vinegar smell. There are other women too, servants and cooks who flit around like vagrant spirits and never once catch my eye. They are always cleaning. Sometimes there are guests, women in black chadors, but I don't see them. I hear them. I smell the saffron tea. I am kept in the bedroom and then I know for certain that I am not free. I am a secret and the door is always locked.

My nipples and belly swell. The four kind women examine me with shrewd sideways glances.

One day, I am allowed into the garden. The garden is full and rich with shrubs and flowers in bud, desperate to bloom. I dig my hands into the earth and like a starved seedling turn my face to the winter sun.

The four kind women watch me with pleasure.

'We should let her sit outside for an hour a day.'

'I have not seen her so happy.'

'She has lost so much.'

'Sun spots will stipple her complexion,' says the fourth kind woman with an almost-there-but-not-quite sly upturn of the mouth.

There is a boy who tends the trees. He lives in a small hut at the bottom of the garden. I see him from the corner of my eye, looking at me, trying not to look at me, trying not to be seen looking at me as I sit on the ground beneath the guava tree.

The four kind women instruct the boy to stay in his hut between 3 and 5 p.m. so that I can sit outside and put my fingers in the soil. He is not to approach me. It would be a sin. Punishable by flogging. They are stern about this and of course he agrees. He has no wish to be flogged.

They dress me head to toe in a billowing chador several sizes too big. My shroud. They watch me carefully at first, as I sit beneath the guava tree, but it is boring watching me. They grow sleepy and yawn, go inside for an afternoon nap. I sit there for two hours and talk to the tree.

I tell the tree my plan. The leaves rustle and try to dissuade me.

The four kind women have not always lived in this room. They all agree that the rose water here is not as rose-scented as the rose water over there. There is no kebab seller here on Friday nights, behind the Jumma Masjid, grilling and chilli-pepper adding, rolling the meat of the newborn lamb into the pliable naan and twisting it up in newspaper. A roll that to bite into, they all agree, juices on the hem of the hijab, was the closest thing to paradise, as they knew it.

They had not necessarily wanted to cross the border. They were just told that that was what was going to happen. Here, they're not allowed out at all. Not yet. The streets are awash with fresh unrest.

'Do you think we will ever be allowed to go to market?'
'Inshallah.'
'Do you think we will ever make friends?'
'Allah will provide.'
'Did you hear the gunshots last night?'
'They say it is worse across the border.'
'What kind of border is it?'
'A line on paper and men with guns.'
'I'm not sure I like it here.'
'It was better over there.'
'Our house was nicer. We had furniture.'
'For shame. This is God's chosen land. When matters settle, we will send for our things. Our home will be ours again.'

'Do you really think she has been sent as a gift?' asks the fourth kind woman, eyeing me up and down.

'Yes. A gift from Allah to reward our faith.'

The fourth kind woman, the second wife of the man with the vinegar smell, likes it best when they cover my face with the veil. A bud of envy unfurls at the back of her eyelids, like a bright-green fern in the monsoon rain. She tries to pretend it's not there, but I smell it. It smells like sour milk.

One day when the air is crisper, the eldest of the four kind women wraps a wool shawl around my neck and whilst doing so feels each of my breasts. My breasts are swollen. I flinch. I don't want her to touch me.

'Daughter! Daughters-in-law! It has happened,' she calls out.

'What?'

'What?'

The fourth kind woman puts a hand on her stomach. 'A baby,' she says, softly.

In the garden, my legs buckle. I sit on the ground. A new kind of nausea rises to my throat. I put a hand over my mouth and swallow my vomit until I can't swallow any more. I spit into the nearest bush. The bush is dark green. It will flower red hibiscus in the spring.

The boy is in his hut, as instructed to be. Nevertheless, like all people who are told to do one thing but are then, on account of being told, compelled to do the other, the forbidden thing, he stands half in and half out of the door. He watches me vomit.

When I finish and turn around, the footsteps recede. There is a handkerchief on the ground behind me, and a steel cup of water. The handkerchief smells of cheap brown soap, of the buy-by-weight variety. I almost don't want to use it and really how dare he approach me with such stealth when he has so specifically been warned against approaching me at all?

Loneliness wins in the end. I rinse my mouth and wipe the faded cloth across it. The handkerchief is soft on my skin. It might have belonged to his mother, or his sister. I don't suppose he has a wife. I tuck the handkerchief into my sleeve and leave the empty metal cup on the ground.

If I sit beneath the guava tree several days in a row, the boy will know that that is where I'll be. He will watch me and I will like being admired so long as he doesn't come too close. I am not sure by what logic or sense I have worked this out, but somehow I just know.

Every day at three in the afternoon, I sit beneath the tree and wait for the boy to come and ask for his handkerchief. He doesn't.

Fizzy restlessness gets the better of me. One day, I pep myself up with encouraging words, one eye on the big house to make sure I am not being watched, and walk to his hut. My cheeks burn. The palm-frond door is slightly ajar.

'The guavas are pickling on the tree,' I say. The absurdity

almost makes me laugh. This is the first sentence I have spoken in months. 'No one has thought to pick them. They will ferment up there. They will spoil.'

The boy laughs, a warm inviting sound.

I push the palm-frond door open and go in. It is a dark, not unpleasant hut with a narrow bamboo bed nudged to the corner.

'Can you pick some guavas from the tree, and put them beneath it, so I can find them and eat them tomorrow? I'm craving sour fruit.' And then because I am already in the hut so I might as well, I sit on the edge of the bed. He is surprised and then he is not surprised. There is safety in my black shroud.

'This is yours,' I say and give him the handkerchief. 'I washed it. What's your name?'

'Bhaumika,' he says. 'It means from the earth.'

'I can't remember mine,' I say. 'Where are you from?'

'From the south.'

'Why are you here?'

'I came for work.'

'Your skin is very dark. You look a bit dirty.'

He averts his eyes, unnerved. 'I'm outside all day.'

'They will wake up soon. I should go. Don't tell them I can talk, OK? They think I'm mute.'

'Even your husband? Does he think you're mute? I'm not going to tell them. They'll blame me that you're here.'

I flush beneath my shroud. 'My husband is a stunted idiot,' I say. 'I didn't choose him.'

The boy nods sympathetically.

The next day, there are three guavas beneath the tree. I lift them to my nose and inhale the heady perfume.

I go to his hut. The palm-frond door is open. 'I have the

guavas,' I call. 'Do you have a knife? I'm not allowed sharp things.'

He comes out. Puts an old jute sack on the ground for me to sit on and on a scratched tin plate he slices the fruit into quarters with a paring knife. He places the tin plate between us.

'Shall we eat from the same plate? At the same time?'

'I only have one plate,' he says.

'How old are you?'

'I'm not sure. I've never known my birthday,' he replies. 'How old are you?'

'I can't remember.'

'Have you forgotten everything?'

'Not everything.'

He brings me water to wash my hands. I dry them on the hem of my shroud.

'You should go. They will wake up soon.'

'Each day I hope they will die in their sleep, but each day I go back and they are still alive.'

He laughs. 'You don't really wish that do you?'

'I do actually. If I could poison their food I would.'

'You don't seem that type of person.'

'Don't you know that everyone is that type of person now? War will do that.'

'For someone who has forgotten so much, you seem to know a lot about a lot.'

'When I was across the border, I liked to read. My brain is full of useless information. For example, did you know that rats will eat their own tails before they die of starvation?'

'No,' he says. 'I didn't.'

That evening at the allocated hour, in the marital bed, my husband one hand on his cock as is his way, the four kind women with an ear pressed to the door as is theirs, I look at the wall and think of the boy and whether his skin smells as dirty as it looks. I imagine pressing my nose into his skin, so that my breath leaves a moist patch in the crook of his arm, the crook of his arm being specifically that hidden bit inside the elbow.

I sleep. I dream. The boy's dark arms from fingertip to elbow covered in grime that is not the soil of the earth, but the mucus, the blood and guts of a human. Of me. I wake up. I am cold all over.

It is midwinter. The four kind women watch me and whisper amongst themselves.

'Is it normal to sit outside in the cold?'

'Should we stop her?'

'How can we deny her? She has suffered so much.'

'I'll ask the servant girl to keep an eye,' says the fourth kind woman.

A few days later, when a servant girl is sent to keep me company, I am so furious I hit her. I slap her and push her to the ground. Go! She curls into herself and I pummel her small body until she cries out in pain.

I march back up to the house, stand in rigid fury above the four kind women who are dozing. I clench my fists. I scream.

The noise of my scream comes from some deep unknown place inside me. Deeper than my longing for the boy in his hut, deeper than the food forced through my lips, deeper than my husband with the twisted mouth and back to the night, to the exact time and place when I was dragged off a train and punched in the face by the man with the vinegar smell. I had screamed like this then, too.

I was on a train. I had tomato sandwiches in wax paper, a red ribbon in my hair. I was going to see my grandmother. I was raped. I was left for dead. A curious contrition must have got him in the end, because he came back and fetched me. A girl-bride for his simple brother.

The four kind women flap in agitation.

'What has happened?'

'What shall we do?'

'Be careful. The baby.'

'The servants will hear. They will tell the neighbours.'

'The neighbours will tell their friends and relatives.'

'They can't!'

'Shhh. Little moosh. You shall have your heart's desire.'

'We are indulging her,' says the fourth kind woman, the bright-green fern behind her eyelids unfurling into existence.

We are complicit, whispers the eldest and most knowing of the four, but she whispers this only to herself, too ashamed to say it out loud.

I stop screaming. I listen with interest as they panic. I sit on my raised bed and refuse food or water. When they bring the servant girl and question her, she exaggerates so much they don't know who to believe, only that no matter what, there can't be screaming of this sort again.

They whisper, worried. The baby.

They try to push food through my mouth as they did when I was weak, but I give them a look so fierce, they stop. They are afraid of me.

I go to the boy's hut every day now. I sit on the edge of his bed.

In an old saucepan balanced on a metal grille, over a small wood fire, he puts tea and crushed cardamom in boiling milk and, because sugar is rationed, he uses local honey, purchased on the black market. He cleans and polishes two condensed-milk cans for us to drink from.

'I heard you scream.'

'I shocked myself.'

'I saw you hit the servant girl.'

'I was angry. They had sent her to spy on me. They don't trust me.'

I drink my tea and smile. The tea in the boy's hut tastes like the tea at home.

The winter air is cold. The boy gives me a hand-stitched blanket and builds a newspaper fire in the middle of the hut. I tell him stories about tigers and djinns and fairy kingdoms.

He tells me about the sea.

'When you are in a boat on the water, the wind whistles in your ears and you can taste the salt on your lips.'

'I've never seen the sea.'

The next day he brings me a small fish from the market. I poke it with the tip of my finger and stroke the scales so that they prickle sharply before falling back into place. The fish is iridescent.

'I've never seen a real fish before,' I say.

He sharpens a knife against a stone, feels for the vertebrae, slides the blade along the thin frame and deftly cuts the fillet away from the bone. The long thin skeleton is delicate and the cut so clean that there is no gut wound, no bleeding of the organs. I had not thought death could be so clean.

He spears a flake of flesh on his knife and holds it out.

'I can't,' I say, squeamish. 'It's not cooked.'

'Go on. It will taste of the sea.'

I try it. I close my eyes and pretend I am on the seashore.

'You are fearless to come here every day,' he says.

'You would be fearless too. If what happened to me

happened to you.'

I tell him about the baby growing in my belly.

'I know,' he says.

'How?'

'Servants talk.'

'What do they say?'

'That you are with child.'

I look at the floor. 'If I tell you a secret, will you still be my friend?'

'Yes.'

'No matter the secret?'

'Yes.'

He spits on his palm and holds it out. I spit on my own and we shake. His hand in my hand.

I tell him my secret and wait to be banished. I don't look up from the floor.

'It happened to each of my five sisters,' he finally says. 'In my village, our landlord took his property as he deemed fit. It was considered an honour that our womenfolk were beautiful enough. It is a strange thing to witness your father beg and plead with another man, when you are just a child. It makes you think that you too will spend your life begging and pleading for things that you should not need to beg and plead to protect. If I had stayed I would have killed the landlord and then I would've been shot. Ma forced me to leave. She was not ready to see me die.'

'Oh,' I say and look up. 'Oh. So you know?'

'I know.'

The boy's eyes are black-coffee-coloured. His skin is like dark wood, like walnuts in their shell. Of course he is beautiful.

He gives me a pencil and a blue airmail envelope with red go-faster stripes along the edge. The envelope unfolds into a sheet of paper.

'You could write a letter,' he says. 'If you remember your address. I'll post it. There is a new post office in town.'

'Write a letter home?'

'Yes. They say at the post office that letters are travelling easily across the border now. Girls who were taken are being rescued. There is a new law. An Abducted Girls Recovery Law.'

'Oh. A saving-face law you mean? By the very men in the white houses who caused the war in the first place?'

I write a letter to my father, but of course I can't remember the address.

The fourth kind woman has started to bathe in orange-blossom water. She arranges choice morsels on a plate and takes them to the chamber of the man with the vinegar smell. In sleep she is restless. She wants a baby. Her own baby. She can't take her eyes off my stomach.

The cashew-sized baby in my belly grows, and I start crying over nothing.

'It was the same with my sisters. First you're sick, then you cry, and then you are full of joy. The more you swell, the happier you feel.'

I shake my head. No. 'There is no joy in this.'

I get bigger. 'Look how big I am,' I say to the boy, crying. Even in despair, I am vain.

'Did you know,' I say one day, 'that he has never once touched me? Not in the way that a husband should touch his wife. I don't think he knows what to do.'

'I did know that.'

'How?'

'Gossiping servants.'

'So, you know then that the baby can't be his?'

'I guessed it.'

One day the baby kicks. I am so startled, I yelp.

'Feel this,' I say and take off my shroud, lower my pyjama bottoms. 'Put your hand on here,' and because he is hesitant, I take his wrist and put his palm on my belly.

He breathes in the wonder of it. The wonder not of the baby's lively foot demanding attention, but the wonder of his own hand, etched with daily graft, placed on the smooth milk of my belly.

'Can I kiss you?' I say and kiss him quickly on the mouth. He tastes iridescent.

He kisses back. Slowly. Gently probes the inside of my mouth with the tip of his swollen tongue. I want his hand inside me. I want him to reach up and feel the wet warmth of me so I take his fingers and guide them inside.

He gasps. He was not expecting that at all.

The old wounds unravel and unroll to reach my tender heart. I am full of tiny aches. I bleed on his fingers.

His breath is short. I can feel him burning so I move against him. Put my hand on his cock. I whisper in his ear.

'People kill babies all the time,' I say. 'Especially if the baby is a girl.'

He doesn't answer. Doesn't look at me, but I know that he knows it was always going to be this way.

No Visible Wound

MARIANA ROA OLIVA

I just want to say two things about Pachuca. First: Pachuca es una ciudad darks. And second: Rebo, my source, had a centipede named Scully and a dog that took itself out for walks.

About the first, I need to clarify one thing. Pachuca es una ciudad darks roughly translates as Pachuca is a haunted city, but that doesn't capture the humour contained in the word *darks*, which came from a meme about Mexico City goths.

Pachuca is a haunted city for two reasons. First, because the municipal government turned most historic buildings – including a beautiful twentieth-century cinema – into parking lots. And second, because of how much time Rebo has spent playing ouija board here.

I was not a fan of the ouija board when I arrived at Rebo's. In fact I had never played it and had no intention of doing so, and so I did two things to prevent him from playing while I was around. First, I asked him to tell me about Pachuca.

He started by telling me the story of one of the leaders of the affordable housing movement, whose name was also Rebo. Rebo was well-loved in Pachuca because he had helped many people keep their homes when the municipal government tried to turn them into parking lots. One day, he went to Mexico City to watch the soccer match between El América and Los Tuzos and, after the match, while drinking at a bar, accidentally got into a fight. He ended up so badly hurt that his opponent thought he was dead and took him to the train tracks outside the city to make it seem like he had been run over by a train. Hours later, a train passed over him, but didn't kill him. When he came back to Pachuca, the municipal government had turned his house into a parking lot. Rebo then painted his whole body grey so nobody would recognise him, and moved to the train station's awning, where he has lived ever since.

Then he said it was my turn to tell a haunted story. First, I told him about the time I worked as an undercover journalist at Barnacle Farm, writing about the living conditions of seasonal workers. I shared a trailer with Rulo, a self-described nomad who put the electric tea-kettle on the stove, and asked me every night why I didn't want to sleep with him until I decided to just sleep with him so he would stop asking. That strategy didn't work – Rulo simply tweaked the question: why don't you want to sleep with me *tonight*?

The second thing I did to prevent Rebo from playing ouija board while I was around was ask him to play a different game.

— Ouija board is not a board game.

— If it's a board, and you play it, it's a board game.

— But you don't *play* ouija board, you *use* the ouija board.

— I see. What if we play a game that has no board, instead of using a board that has no game?

— What game?

— It's called Twenty Questions.

— Is it about asking questions?

— Yes.

— We could just ask the ouija board.

— The whole point of the game is not to ask the ouija board.

— Why not?

— Just ask me a question to figure out what I'm thinking.

— Okay, is it a game?

— Yes.

— Is it a game in which I have to ask questions?

— Yes.

— Is it the ouija board?

— You just said that's not a game!

But every time there was still the rest of the day, and Rebo knew that I knew that I had to either play ouija board with him or just tell him what I had come to him for, why I had been in Pachuca, staying at his home, for more than a few weeks now. Instead, I did two things.

First I told him about Cándido, who had been to twelve different cities in the US, or rather to twelve different prisons in twelve different cities in the US. The part of the country Cándido knew best was the section of the desert he walked for days at a time for more than fifteen years, first to try to make a living in El Norte, then to help people from his town get there. *Yo he caminado harto. Días en el monte, jamás dejé a nadie tirado – por eso me aprecian aquí.* He had crossed the border more times than he could count, but the last time La Migra caught him, he decided not to ever do it again. *La mera neta yo soy paisa, le dije a la ley.* The first thing he did when he went back to his town was go see the sequoia trees, which are all connected underground.

Then I told him about Omar, the van driver from Oaxaca City down to the coast, whose first words to me were *Si se marea, me dice.* I vomited three times in the same plastic bag.

— Do you not get carsick any more?

— ¿Cómo cree? Esta es la tercera vez en el día que hago esta ruta.

Omar had been on the road for over sixteen hours by then, and still had that trip and one back to complete before he could go home and get some rest.

— Yo crecí en el campo, tengo siete hermanos, pero el campo no da para vivir.

Omar learned to drive in the US. He arrived there when he was eighteen, got a job driving people through the Mexico–US border and up into New York City. His boss would send him money to get a new van for every trip because that way La Migra was less suspicious. Omar would take the seats out of the vans in order to fit more people, and would set a support over the wheels to prevent them from getting pushed down by the weight. Then he would drive for days, arrive back in New York, and keep the van and a good amount of money – a lot more than he made now.

But eventually he got caught.

— Me preguntaron quién era mi jefe, que quién conectaba a la raza. Me dijeron que si hablaba me soltaban luego luego. Pero no les dije nada. Les dije que venía yo solo con ellos. Me dijeron que me iban a dar diez años. Para asustarme. El abogado que me estaba ayudando me había dicho que me declarara culpable. Ni madres. Claro, el abogado me lo puso el Estado. Me declaré inocente y salí en seis meses.

That winter, he got a job plowing snow.

— Mi jefe me estuvo llamando para que regresara. Yo le caía bien porque nunca lo eché de cabeza, ni me rajé.

When I finished telling Rebo about Omar, he told me to wait at the kitchen table, and went to get the ouija board. I had one last resource to avoid playing: I asked Rebo to teach me how to sing. First, he told me that teaching was all about choosing the right metaphors. Then he demonstrated –

— Do you know what part of the body the sound comes out of when you sing?

— The mouth?

— The bones.

And made me touch different parts of my own skeleton so I could feel them vibrate with the notes produced by my lungs and my brain.

But to my surprise, he said he preferred it if we just shared more haunted stories. So first I told him about the time I reported on ladderberries, a forest fruit that makes you feel afraid of heights after you eat it.

— Why would they do that?

— The berries? It's an evolutionary trait. To get people not to pick them off the trees.

— That makes no sense, fruit wants to get eaten.

— Fruit doesn't want anything. Fruit is just fruit.

Then he told me the story of when the municipal government was tearing down the walls of an old woman's house to build a parking lot and the security guard at the site saw a goblin run away from the property and into the street. The morning after, when the guard woke up, he found his alarm clock completely disassembled. At night, when he came back home after work, the clock was fully put together again. This same event repeated every day for the rest of the guards' life – his bedside clock disassembled every morning and reassembled again every night.

***

The next morning when I got up, Rebo was waiting for me in the kitchen with the ouija board all ready on the table. I finally had no option but to play.

He made me close my eyes and then held my hands. I realised this was a more serious engagement for Rebo than I had given him credit for. The morning light was touching the edge of the kitchen door, and I could feel a slow ray of sun climbing up my back. He put my hands on the planchette and let go. I felt my weight shifting slightly, back and forth, isolated in time from the past and the future, floating in space. Around me I started seeing the train station by my place back in Mexico City. A woman and a child were crouching on the platform, painting each other's faces to go work in the trains. My vision switched to the inside of the car and I saw them come on. The child told a joke not meant to make people laugh, and then the woman walked down the aisle – *una moneda que no afecte su economía. Esta moneda no me va a hacer rica, ni a usted la va hacer pobre.*

I opened my eyes and Rebo was calm, his hand on a pen with which he had written down the words I spelled with the planchette.

***

I started getting used to the ouija board, just like Rebo started getting used to my presence in the house. He would ask, sometimes me and sometimes the ouija board, what I had come to him for, why I was in Pachuca. In response, I would sometimes tell him a haunted story, and sometimes ask him to play a game.

Last night, the ouija board told us that the municipal government was going to turn the city's music hall into a parking lot, and there would be one last concert before they demolished everything but the façade. On the walk there, Rebo asked me if I believed in reverse bad memory.

— You mean good memory?

— No, I mean remembering more things than have happened to you.

— I don't know. I don't know how to know.

We were late to the concert but still caught a hand moving like a pained tarantula over an upright bass.

Today I asked Rebo to play ouija board with me one last time. Painted all grey, invisible, sitting at the ex-train station's awning, now a parking lot, we both closed our eyes and put our hands together over the planchette, our fingertips – the oldest, most democratic printing press – touching.

Tipping

GIO IOZZI

In late July the heat dome you've been following on the news lumbers over from Canada, squats over London and refuses to move for days. Temperatures creep up past 37 degrees into the 40s. The humidity sweats your eyelids and you stop wearing bras. He has taken the kids camping on the Welsh coast, leaving you to finish a proposal for work and to *try to relax*, but the heat makes it impossible. You wander from room to room trying to find cool spaces in the house. In the last year, just like the earth, your body has begun a slow-boil, to magic up tepid moisture on your chest, between your breasts, in the gossamer-soft creases of your groin, below the lip of your C-section scar. Recently, your flesh has developed weird hot spots as if someone is holding a match to some of its parts – calves, cheeks, lips, base of neck. Each of these spots seems to burn hotter when you are angry. Before they left, you had been arguing more than usual.

'You love conflict,' he said.

'Oh yeah,' you said. 'Can't get enough.' You licked your lips, made a canine sound. You both laughed, but it could have been crying.

'Are you OK?' he said.

'I may be losing it,' you said and when he tried to hug you, you pushed him away.

Perhaps you do feel more alive in the operatics of a row? When you surveyed yourself in the mirror afterwards, your cheeks were flushed with tiny broken capillaries, your eyes flashing, your lips murmuring excited curses. Your chest was moving fast, like you were drunk or turned on. The final issue was about sun hats. The kids – your boy, ten, your girl, eight – had lost theirs. How was it that all the ones you had bought had vanished? He had to buy some on the way, you growled, or they would all get heatstroke at the campsite. You think of their hair partings tenderising. As you do, you bite a nail down so much it bleeds a little. You bite down on other images before they start. Your children lying in a room with no food, no running water, dying of thirst. You wonder why you decided to have kids, a totally selfish act, if you think about it now.

Have you settled in? you text on the second morning.
Are they OK? Did you find hats? Sorry about all the shit.
He texts back, *We have hats. Now relax!*
Over the next few days, as it gets hotter, you start to shower three times a day, and take to wearing a white linen sack dress of your mum's, and although you feel sloppily middle-aged in it, it's the only thing your flesh can endure. At night you turn the pillow over again and again to experience moments of coolness; in the morning you sit on the edge of the bed and then get up slowly, your armpits already damp. The cats play dead in the front room, their jaws open, showing the jellied corrugation of their mouths. The male spreads his legs wide, his claws blanched chicken feet. You start to talk to them, and then in small moments to yourself. 'Hey fellas, hot isn't it?' They look out of their fur at you and say yes with their lemony eyes. You place bowls of water for them in different rooms which grow warm quickly, rejected.

They say brain fog is a real thing.
Brain fog is a real thing, they say.
It's a fog, they say, in your brain.
He says you repeat yourself more than you used to. One thing you read about was menopause and vaginal atrophy. A friend told you that once when she sat down, she felt herself split. But you are heating and flooding, all liquid; every few months blood drops out of you like your uterus is raining. Then the fire, which seems to shudder from your core and shatter inside the

upper casement of your chest, driving its way up further into your head and popping into your cheeks as if a child has drawn bad red crayon all over your face. There are times when you are so hot, you imagine steam or even flames rising from the top of your skull as if you are a flambéed saint or she-devil, depending.

The leaves of the new fruit trees outside are bronzing when they should be gleaming green. One late afternoon you go out and fork up the earth around them, feeding water slowly from the can into the soil. The earth is like sawdust and some of the water pisses away its grey fingers into the gutter. You wear wellies and feel like a farm girl in the tropics. The street is quiet, palpating in the heat. At first there appear to be no bird sounds at all, but then a scatter of lime parakeets screech over the trees. *Kawa, kawa.* They came in a few years ago – smaller bird species fled. In fact, you haven't seen a sparrow in a long time. Or a thrush. Or a robin. Or a blackbird. Ten years ago there were dozens. The pavement still radiates heat. You stand, your hand on the small of your back, looking up and down the street but there is no one about. You are waiting to see someone, a friend passing by, a neighbour, to be reassured of some normality. But it's still high noon, deserted spaghetti-western silence. It's 35 degrees and you know it will be another tough night.

Later, when the earth balloons its fever, you touch yourself. You want release, the release you sometimes still get when time, the room, the bed seem to fold in on themselves like spatial origami. But now you can't seem to come at all, your body is hot and slippery and there's no traction. Perhaps the earth will not allow you this release. She is heating, you are heating, there's no real break any more. Maybe no one deserves to feel pleasure in the Anthropocene.

***

It's Earth-sized, the crisis. Too big. Your brain tries to wrestle with it. The planet is over 24,000 miles around. Almost 8 billion people. But you are not like Superman, who flew around the world thousands of times, trailing strings of light, to reverse time. You are not a deity, not a goddess. Still, you imagine yourself as a giant woman, striding through the seas and cooling the earth by using your arms and skirts for shade, erecting high fences around the Amazon and the Congo Basin, throwing vast cooling nets over the oceans, pushing deep-sea trawler ships away with the force of your hands, snuffing out new gas and oil plants with your fingers. You feel angry that there isn't some magic you can do. You feel rage at the men who got the earth into this fucking mess and the fact that you probably won't be able to save your kids.

You are obsessed with weather forecasts, watching heat graphics lick over the UK on the weather app on your phone. Which is the most accurate? AccuWeather, XCWeather, the Met Office, the BBC? What's it like in Liverpool, Manchester, Glasgow, Skye? Milan, Paris? It's cooler in Spain than England, but the orange crops are decimated this year.

The weather men and women are smiling and joking as if this is a one-off event, promising it will break in a few days. They all seem to be getting it wrong while the heat doubles down. The women gleam and say *phew* a lot with mock gestures, stroking sweat from their foreheads.

They must know the science.
They've got to know.
Everyone in power knows.
By the end of the week, they say.
They say by the end of the week.

***

'This doesn't feel right,' you tell him on the phone. He doesn't respond. You have caught him at the end of the day with a warm beer in his hand. You can hear your kids' voices in the background, squealing about something they want, then their voices fade. They have made some friends, he tells you, they run in a ragged group around the field every evening. It's sweet and gives him a break, he talks to the other parents, he is getting lots of brownie points for doing it alone, he says, especially from the mums. He has to round the kids up each evening and almost strap them into the tent, sleeping bags half unzipped as even at night it's too warm.

'Is it bad there too then?' you ask.

'Not too bad,' he says. 'Bit overcast today, thundery, but still tons of people on the beaches. The BBQs fucking stink.'

This is geniality, this is getting on. You have shoved rolled-up facecloths under your breasts to absorb the sweat. Unusually you have tried on an old pair of vintage cowboy boots you wore in the 1990s, and as you lie on the bed speaking to him, you lift your right leg up and down, admiring the look of the toe and heel. You feel sexy. Maybe this is the moment to touch yourself again. His voice is low and you match it.

'I'm wearing the boots.'

'What?'

'Do you remember, my cowboys? The white ones.'

'Ah . . .'

He doesn't want to say no, he can't remember.

'Don't worry.' You have over ten pairs of boots at the last count, coated with dust in a cupboard.

'I've never known it like this,' you say, returning to your subject. 'I can't hear birdsong. There are no normal birds left.'

'They must be in the shade,' he says, his tone changing. 'Under the trees and bushes. Taking refuge – like us.'

He says the sea is like the Med, like a warm soup. Everyone's in the water. There were jellyfish yesterday, thousands of them, and people were screaming, falling over each other.

'It was like *Jaws* but in Porthmadog,' he says.

You laugh long and hard, a tincture too much.

The kids are tiring him out though. Your son likes to bury his little sister up to her neck in sand.

'Don't let her suffocate,' you say. 'Children can die in sand holes. The walls collapse.'

'Don't worry, I'm on it,' he says.

You think about the moment when everyone's back, all the needs crashing in at the same time, pots and pans, clanging in your eardrums.

My babies, I don't want them to die.

'I don't want the kids to die,' you say.

'What? Why would they die?'

'Starve.'

'We've got plenty of food.'

'Not now, but when—'

'Please,' he says. 'Not the bread-basket stuff . . . I can't . . .'

'Handle it?'

He can't handle it. Neither can you.

'You forgot her teddy. Is she OK without it?'

Familiar ground.

He doesn't respond. See, the negativity put him off.

At the socials that are starting to happen, you experience the moment when people's eyes glaze over and they edge away. 'I've decided to stop flying, I feel so guilty,' you say. 'Don't you?' But you hear them speak later to someone else about their family trip to New York. They deserve it after the last three years, they want to see family and friends. Everyone needs fun and pleasure again. You feel like Fiver from *Watership Down*. Fiver with his nervous twitching, his wet eyes, his sweet neurotic mumblings. *But where is Hazel, listening, comforting?* In your head, Art Garfunkel's singing 'Bright Eyes' and your eyes brim with tears. You wonder if people see you as Marvin, the depressed robot from *The Hitchhiker's Guide to the Galaxy*. Or Debbie Downer from *SNL*.

No you are Fiver, you are Fiver, definitely Fiver but without Hazel. You are trembling and wet all over. You wonder who your Hazel is – and you realise it is not your husband any more.

It's a slow walk to the shops. The roads, the houses, seem to be holding their breath. You imagine paint melting, the grouting cracking and shifting. Heave, they call it. The air basks, bewildered. The plane trees, pollarded back like knuckles, have dry white dust on them, now useless and empty of birds.

In the supermarket the meat-locker light reveals humans in beachwear, topless men showing hairy nipples, wet curls of hair peeping out from armpits, women in complicated backless dresses showing small bulges of flesh under bras. Everyone seems to have earbuds in. No one is looking at you. But then, your face is red and for the first time in your life you're not wearing a bra in public and you have flannels tucked under your tits. The woman at the cash register flicks her eyes to your nipples and asks you if you want a free coffee.

'Is it iced?'

'No.'

'Then I'm OK thanks. This heat's intense, isn't it?'

'Yes,' she replies, her face stodgy under a severe fringe, 'lovely.'

Wish I was at the beach.'

 'It's the climate crisis you know.'

 The eyes glaze.

 'I like hot summers.'

 'Yes, but not like this.'

 'Well,' she says, 'lucky you, to be able to enjoy it. I'm stuck in here – although at least there's air conditioning.'

 'Yes.'

 'Enjoy it while it lasts, love.'

How long will it last? Outside, you zombie-walk back into the blast of the street. Luckily your thighs are separated by some long granny pants. Your hair parting sizzles. You remember the documentary you watched about Karachi in Pakistan, where a young man fixed air con for the people who could afford it, and those who couldn't, including his own mother, lay in the heat of their small rooms panting. They were feeling ill and needed to lie down a lot. Some officials were painting the roofs of the houses white. There was a woman who was planting small oases of green where she could, but Karachi is burning up.

 On your doorstep you find a dead swift. You crouch down, trying to detect a heartbeat in the fine geometry of its feathers, but there is nothing. You take it through to the garden and begin to dig a grave in one of the flowerbeds. Two summers ago, in the pale pink of dusk, you watched dozens of swifts wheel and flicker excitedly across the sky. They so delighted you, a man came to fix you a nesting box and you hoped, your whole body in a swell of hope, that some would start to nest high up on the wall.

It does not break,

 it does not break,

and this is one week, just one week.

When will it break? you ask.

By the end of the week, the forecasters promise.

But they are tired now, even the weather people. They've stopped smiling so much and are making smaller, floppier signs with their arms, as if the studio itself is warping. The weather forecaster has his shirt sleeves rolled up and tie loosened, his teeth are white and keep moving in a grimace, a terrible smile, like the Cheshire Cat.

'Liars,' you shout at the screen and your own cats jolt.

At night the windows are open in all the houses on your street. You look out at the street lamp, trying to see insects. You recall a windscreen twenty years ago with insects piled up in crusted armies. You want to see swarms and swarms in the blue UV light but there are just one or two skidding around in the air. Opposite, in the first-floor flat, some people in their twenties are having a party. The music's loud. You are lying on your bed, the blind open at the bottom allowing you just enough of a view to watch as they drink late into the night. The women have long hair and bra tops. 'Fucking yes!' they shout when a tune comes on that they love. By the end they're swigging from the wine bottles and snorting lines off the table, a cheese plant casting tessellations of shadows on the walls. They kiss, thrash and embrace in the heat. You long to be in the room, to forget yourself for an hour or two. You remember clubs and dancing with him, grinding your hips together. He used to come up behind you and kiss your neck and jaw so much it would shiver your nipples into knots. At one point one of the men is hanging half his body out of the window, his torso sweat-bright, his voice seeming to join the clotted mess of the humid night.

Are all the other neighbours lying on their beds trying to sleep like you? The heat makes your body heavy, like a doll whose strings inside need rehooking. Your thigh sockets hang slightly, breasts loll like empty bagpipes. The temperature is somehow worse at night, as you expect release and it's like a planetary press bearing down on you. The orangey-brown dark is menacing, the earth's core ordering up a nightmarish entrée from the future. Are the other humans naked like you, their body hair saturated, their limbs sweating in the stillness, like yours? Worries and anxieties looming like stone monoliths of the mind. The fan stirs the hot air around the room. Your eyeballs are hot. Your brain is cooking. Can a body start to cook? You will not be googling that.

On the fourth day, before they are due to return, you are hunched over your phone, scrolling through heat graphs and online data. Twitter is a screaming corridor of people who are very afraid. You read that there's more than 416 parts per million of carbon dioxide in the atmosphere, a fifty per cent increase since the 1700s. This is very bad. Someone posts an image of five giraffes lying dead in a circle in Kenya, their beautiful necks almost touching, like a withered jigsaw dropped a few feet from the sky.

Hell is almost complete, you think. Now what to do?

A daddy-long-legs skitters across the ceiling. When you were a child, on a caravan holiday in the 1980s, you got one caught in your hair. You cried out and made your brother smash it against the wobbly plastic wall. Now you watch this one, absorbing each jangly puppet-dance of its body. It meets its shadow-twin on the wall, jazz-shaking its long legs, then drops down into a corner of the skirting board and you try not to feel horror. 'Don't come near me,' you whisper, but then, 'Don't die, don't die.'

There was the summer of 1976. Naked in the garden with

your mum, proudly pushing out your stout belly and chest. The heat was a miracle, an exotic one-off when London was hotter than Rome. Your mum and her friends wore their underwear as bikinis. You were all smiling, squinting into the camera. Mum brought out a basket full of beads and you wound them round and round your neck. 'It's like being somewhere else,' she said. There was your own birth, when you emerged from your mother's womb with teeth and your head full of black hair. You think of your own daughter, the way she burned you as she came out.

The next morning there is a shift, not sudden, just like an electric hot-plate is slowly turning off. You remember the drama of downpours after heatwaves when you first met him, when the sky was refreshed and the earth smelt of petrichor. You remember making love with the windows open and rain lashing in. This is just a loosening of the belt, a slow outbreath; a sluggish rain dropping a scatter of wet. The walls at the front of the house are still baking when you put your hand to them.

He phones from a motorway service station to tell you they're an hour away.

'I thought you said it was unbearable?'

'It was,' you say.

'It feels OK now.'

'Yes, but it scared me.'

'The kids want to see you.'

You hear the agitated squawks of your children in the background. Your heart quickens.

You have not worked at all, but you will say that you have and that you managed to relax. You have bought a range of bamboo toothbrushes and a small pot of charcoal toothpaste. After holding the pot under your chin you dip the brush into the powder and feed its salty grit into your mouth. Halfway through, you see that your teeth are black, as if an ink cartridge has exploded in your mouth. You laugh into the pot which sends a fine layer of powder onto your white dress and the sink. You return the kids' plastic toothpaste tube back between the taps.

In the remaining moments of silence before they return, you allow one last fantasy to play out in your mind. Every microbead on sand, soil, sea and ocean, every rat king of plastic in every whale belly, every particle in every city, every molecule in every placenta, begins unsticking, extricating itself, finding an exit, rising into the air, gradually levitating upwards through space into the blue ozone, joining a queue that begins its slumberous journey into another galaxy. Once there, it disappears into the mouth of a sluggish goliath who enjoys chowing down on plastic and farting it out into something alchemic. The world in an epic self-clean, a plastic resurrection.

You think about the plastic threading through the planet, you think about him and the kids coming through the door, their faces which now fill you with pain when you look at them. You feel sick for a moment, as though the room is tipping – the earth, even. All the spots on your body flicker on. The pools on your flesh liquify. You feel your belly fire up and you lean over the sink as the flames begin burning upwards.

Mapping Chillies

SUEY KWEON

My mother used to lay out her chillies to dry from around August time each year on the pavements that lined the tower blocks of apartments. The best real estate was naturally the concrete road which was dark and absorbed the hard sun most robustly, but it was hard to find enough of this space where cars rubbed shoulders, and were given preference over chillies. She used to lay out the blue tarpaulin and scatter the chillies in an even layer across, allowing them to surrender to the dusty sun. Unmelting blue plastic; the brown, nasal drone of cicadas – this was the palette of summer. There were always those women who would hedge their bets and action their chilli-drying earlier, when the rains had only just seemed to have cleared up, and it broke my heart to see their chillies slumping on sodden newspapers after a surprise renegade shower. Dried chillies, if successfully pulled off, were a wealth beyond themselves. I would have guessed that the drying itself took up the best part of a month, but I'd count myself lucky if I got to witness even the early chillies' debuts; would imagine, instead, redness overrunning the pavements; love the view of darkening fruits spilling onto car bonnets and boots. Chillies bringing a city to stillness.

After the drying, I know that they are ground into fine powder, gochugaru, with instruments of kinds noseying in on the process. Powder goes to all sorts: reconstituted into familiar food things more solid that come out of long hours' pounding, massaging, waiting. There is something so proud about the word 'homemade' and it gives me capital in this land of peas and carrots. My carrots should be crunchy, fresh and seasoned; made by a woman older than me who was raised firmly in the understanding that she would grow up into a wife. I like the sizzle of food against hot oil, sounding like the last pitter-patter of the season on the mosquito nets that provide the first barrier to a home. Thin metal mesh that you dragged along outside your window, sieving creatures out of the kneaded breeze. When the weather is this hot, though, the elderly would be sitting in the sheltered benches that litter the apartment complexes, some minding or guarding their chillies. There is a cooler breath on these kerb-side benches than where the air conditioning units pump out heat into the stale height above the streets. Catch the right angle, a good bearing, and the wind will whip the sweat right off your back.

'I come from a land where chillies are a gift or a curse from the exotic, and when I first saw schoolmates eating the skins of pears I was astonished,' I would say dreamily. I remembered thinking it was dirty and unpleasant. This is how I could explain to my mother something about England that she didn't ask to be explained and I knew that she heard the gratitude in my voice. That I knew of grapes you could swallow the skins of. Shiny exteriors on apples for gripping onto and biting into. Even as an adult, seeing a friend crunch through a fruit until its emaciated core dangled on a saliva-thread from its stem – this brought me fresh wonder. At home, my mother would cut these things into bite-sized pieces; I think, to encourage slow consumption, easy digestion. Grapes would be highly prized in the summer, when I might be there, with their skins tough and sour, as were the beetle-like seeds inside when chewed upon. My aunty and cousins would rupture the ashy skins with their teeth and let the smooth ball inside roll out through the slit – a sweet hidden gem. So many skins spat out in Korean kitchens.

***

My laptop screen shows me a blister in time when Google's camera-on-wheels skulked through, capturing a man who's just dropped his phone, a silver Hyundai struggling to park, a uniformed boy sweating to fulfil his restaurant's thirty-minute delivery promise. I know that it's pretty recent because of the fresh colour on the complex. I remember when suddenly the taupes and beiges were more than just blemished; when in the next impression they were licked up and blinged out by soft lavender. Maps these days speak much more than their ornamental forefathers: they are triangulation, satellite, traffic, a way to find home and to leave it through a voice in your ear. You can skim-read a city like this.

There is a shop I see in my aunty's apartment complex called Bling Bling, in English (as in medallions that could be dumb-bells, or grills that make your jaw ache), that sells I <3 NY T-shirts, children's Disney costumes, and everything in between. It looks sort of like a charity shop here from the tiny shape of it visible on the street, but it's called Bling Bling and wants to make a quid. Squidged between signs for a laundry service and a lettings shop, Bling Bling is crisp white Tipp-Ex swept through veteran smudges and frayed edges; plastic on watercolour that makes you wonder how it's stayed so lifelike. This corner of commerce: shops holding up cram schools for kids in English, maths, piano upstairs. Next time, Bling Bling will be gone after maybe a year of blundering exchanges, replaced by something called something like Blossom selling the same T-shirts and costumes recycled.

That was close to where I was sitting waiting for my cousin's daughter to get off the school bus to nursery and back. The bus was television, American-anorak-yellow and she was being taught in the English language whilst she was young enough for it to stick. I didn't really need to wait for the child because the bus was only ten paces from her apartment block's entrance, but it wasn't a disturbance to me and I liked sitting in that peace within a city with roads that used to put me on edge with their wide, many lanes. I was stressing about the time that comes when this baby reads her books more fluently than my sing-song cadence. Rhythm afforded me secret time; afforded her a performance. Stutters became staccatos and my adoring audience liked the tension before a plot. That patience is the product of good child-rearing, my cousin probably thought. Then, her babble with the grasshoppers and ants, splintering their spindly legs by stepping on them. She was so cute I wanted to eat her.

***

A split-second failure between street view to satellite shows a parallel universe marked by gridlines on a digital screen. We compose ourselves: recover to see the same same green rooftops of these cloned buildings; remember my grandmother's old house, peculiar because it was a house with its own private walls and roof – a lovely arcadian past now from the seventeenth storey. Her roof was still also coloured in this green paint. There are rumours slipping around online that this is a result of a monopoly of roof paint by a chaebol corporation, or that this paint helps to waterproof homes, or that the green reflects light to help cooling. We amuse ourselves by thinking of travellers flying overhead awed by cities verdant and lush, oxygen abundant. Most of the green tiles visible are the tops of towers edged by thick borders of their own shadows. We pinch and part my fingers like gods – the universe blunders, trips up; names of places become vaguer until 'SOUTH KOREA' (then, 'THE WORLD'). The icons of magnifying glass and arrow, serviceable euphemisms for a body, probing to the unsullied depths of this land until we can count the little squares that make up a factory. We hunger for blocks of stone, fabrics to finger, microscope on atom; to move more inwards into populated streets faster than you can walk, to be in an autumn-coloured day and stare up for a long time without neck-craning or eyes blinded by sky; for a city of right-angles and rectangles found at the bottom of a kaleidoscope; to see a tree that is tree-like and stays in its place; for a chilli to shrink in its skin at the snap of a button. See a screen scramble to keep up with the wind on a cool day and compute this jagged flow of pixels into gibberish. Make the earth a ball against blackness, and this little corner less than a smudge under cloud forms. My greenery made snotty.

Fix

K. LOCKWOOD JEFFORD

A teenager goes missing from a seaside town. By the time his disappearance is reported to police, he's not been seen for three days. At least not by anyone in his family.

Before the city across the estuary reached out with its award-winning suspension bridge and seized it as a suburb on its western edge, a dormitory for commuters, the seaside town was its own place. A pebbly beach, a pretty esplanade, a pier restored with EU money long before the referendum, an international sixth-form college perched on the cliff.

A Local Enterprise Partnership has been established, with a Local Industrial Strategy. There are plans for a new football stadium on an old landfill site and – the pet project of the deputy leader of the city council – a clifftop complex with commercial units and a creative hub of workshops and studios for letting at subsidised rents to artists with proven financial need. The fate of the old maternity hospital, a grey-stone Gothic Grade II listed building, is out to tender.

House prices have risen, rents increased, the retired population has swelled. Teenagers hang about on street corners or dodge the expensive fares on buses over the bridge to the city.

The teenager's sister is in her late twenties and lives near the city end of the bridge in a studio flat bought by her parents. She paints portraits of small children brought to model by doting mums and dads. She watches the traffic zipping both ways along the bridge's four-lane highway like electric beetles, the racket rasping at her ears like a cloud of raging hornets. Sometimes she blocks it out by listening to music through headphones. This is what she was doing the day she had six missed calls from her brother.

***

The area around the massive concrete slab anchoring the bridge to the seaside town becomes a destination for drug drops and dealing.

Some months previously, police stopped a van being driven over the bridge with a known drug dealer as a passenger. The driver, a thirty-one-year-old unemployed hospital porter, tried to flee but gave up on realising his only escape route was a fifty-metre drop into the estuary.

In court, the ex-porter admits to driving a man who supplied drugs. His counsel states he'd pleaded guilty at an early stage, that at the time he'd been addicted to heroin and his relationship had recently broken up. The judge says the drug dealer couldn't operate without his help and that an immediate sentence is justified.

A consultant psychiatrist in her early forties arrives for the clinic she runs from a Portakabin in the grounds of the city's hospital. The clinic where she sees the teenager for the mood swings he self-medicates with illicit drugs.

The consultant's secretary hands her an armful of case notes and points at a headline in the local paper: FORMER HOSPITAL PORTER JAILED 18 MONTHS. Beneath, a photograph of a man with small black eyes in a sickly-looking face set somewhere between tearful and telling you to fuck off. Her secretary is excited because the ex-porter used to work at the hospital's sterile-supplies department until he was sacked for stealing surgical gloves. The consultant doesn't recognise him. She feels the first stabs of a headache, takes two of the dihydrocodeine she keeps in her desk drawer and opens the teenager's file.

She has been seeing him for a few months since his parents' BUPA insurance ran out for the Priory. Typically, he skips along to his appointments late, neck swathed in silky scarves, long hair swept up in a ponytail, fingernails painted blue, fishnet tights peeping out from under skinny jeans. He talks about his life in an upbeat way, insists the six-inch scar on the inside of his left forearm is due to an accident with the bread knife.

His mother does something in the art world and the father's a senior civil servant. They are in their fifties, and have a huge house in the seaside town where the teenager attends the expensive sixth-form college. It was the school that raised concerns about his poor attendance and failing performance. A sister died in a traffic accident when he was only seven. He says his mother hasn't smiled since. Another sister lives in the city so it's just him with his parents at home. They're old, he says.

They don't know about the heroin he buys off the dark web.

The teenager's sister sees the report and the ex-porter's name rings alarm bells. She googles it and finds a newspaper report of her sister's death ten years ago: MOTORCYCLIST RESPONSIBLE FOR DEATH OF TALENTED TEEN. It's the same name but a different address in the seaside town. The dilapidated bit behind the old maternity hospital. She calls her mother who asks if her brother is there.

A trainee psychiatrist who works in the consultant's team sees the ex-porter's picture and recognises him as the man he was called to see a week ago on the medical ward. The man had come in by ambulance, whining and writhing about, complaining of pain all over his body. He was keeping patients with serious medical conditions awake, they said. It was murder to find a vein, but all the blood tests were normal. A heroin addict, they said, nothing medically wrong with him, but his girlfriend had thrown him out and there were no hostel places or crisis beds. We can't just let him go, they said.

The trainee remembers the man's papery skin all shades of grey and blue, etched with scars and track marks barely hidden by botched DIY tattoos. Waves of sobbing shook his flimsy body, which looked as if it limped from fix to fix, got itself kicked, punched and bashed about. His sunken belly gurgled like water pipes. He was trying to sort himself out, he said. He'd rowed with his girlfriend. His drugs counsellor was off sick, he had a court case coming up and couldn't get hold of his solicitor. He'd felt so bad he started punching the walls. His head. Then he got the pains all over.

The trainee knows they hate people like him clogging up beds. He arranged a transfer to the mental health unit and prescribed plenty of sedation. The nurses called in the morning to say he'd discharged himself.

The teenager doesn't turn up for his appointment or answer his phone when the consultant calls. Her headache intensifies, untouched by the painkillers. An email marked URGENT! drops into her inbox. *All consultants must attend a consultation on reorganisation of mental health services.* She knows 'reorganisation' means cuts forced by years of austerity and, in her view, 'consultation' is a box-ticking farce. We hear what you're saying. Thank you for attending.

She writes herself a prescription for tramadol and slips out to a different chemist to the one she used a few days ago.

Police officers ask for consent to search the teenager's home for any evidence or leads as to why he has gone. This is normal procedure. Police officers ask the teenager's parents for consent to make public the fact he is missing. The parents don't have a recent photograph, but the teenager's sister has a selfie the teenager sent her, taken when he was high on heroin. A smile lifts his face, the corners of his mouth, brightens his eyes.

The teenager's mother tells police it's not unusual to not see him for a few days. Both she and her husband have intensive careers that demand time and focus. Ultimately, their children benefit. Private schools. Travel. Her son often visits his sister, a talented artist, in the city. She had assumed he was there. They are a very close family, especially since another daughter died in a tragic road accident ten years ago. She was only sixteen.

It appears the teenager's father was the last person to have seen his son. He tells the police his wife was in bed and he was working on his laptop at the kitchen table. His son came in for a drink of water. He doesn't tell them his son saw he was masturbating. He tells the police they didn't speak. Which is true.

The missing teenager's disappearance is reported in the local paper and on radio and television news programmes. The police issue a statement to say they are concerned for his welfare and are urgently appealing for help from the public to trace him. There is a special phone number to call. A reference number to quote.

The missing teenager's picture is on page two. The front page carries a photograph of the deputy leader of the city council shaking hands with a local entrepreneur who has a major stake in the new football stadium.

The service director tells the consultant she must attend the consultation meeting even though it means she will have to cancel a clinic. He tells her there is a serious proposal to build a new mental health unit on the site of the old maternity hospital in the seaside town. He says this is fantastic news for her.

The old maternity hospital is where the consultant's son was born by emergency caesarean section. They did everything they could to save him, but it wasn't enough.

The baby would have been five years old next month.

She believes she wasn't cut out to be a mother. Her husband thinks she'll change her mind. He doesn't know she's taking the contraceptive pill. She places two tramadol on her tongue, swigs her bottled water to wash them down.

The ex-porter sees the missing teenager's picture. It triggers flashbacks of the girl. Looks just like her. That night. Ten years ago. Girlfriend was right pissed off with him because he forgot to pick up the chips for their tea. Sent him straight back out. He'd zapped down to the takeaway, didn't see the girl. It was January, foggy, frosty. Yamaha brakes were dodgy. He didn't see her.

Felt her though.

Did four months inside for death by careless driving. When he came out he had no job. He'd felt like shit. Couldn't sleep. Lost weight. His relationship was on its last legs and he didn't want to lose access to his kids. His doctor prescribed valium. But he felt pathetic taking a woman's pill, so he stopped. It was his uncle gave him his first hit. Have some of this. You'll feel warm and nice.

His relationship fell apart. The next one didn't last either. He lost contact with his kids. Couldn't stick any of the crappy jobs he got. Heroin stayed. At first it numbed over the bad stuff and let some good squeeze through. But it got harder to squeeze, to stay the right side of sick as a dog. His uncle said, Take more, no problem. Only a tenner a hit. Then it was, Inject, it works faster. Have one on me for free.

***

Too distracted to paint, the missing teenager's sister cancels all her portrait clients and googles 'missing teenagers' instead. She finds herself scrolling through screen after screen after screen:

A nine-year-old boy and a fourteen-year-old girl go missing after a trip to the library.

Police launch a search for a thirteen-year-old girl, last seen leaving her home at 6 p.m. on the 10th of November. Police are growing increasingly concerned for her welfare.

Police are appealing for information to help find a fifteen-year-old boy last seen at 4 p.m. on 6th February leaving a friend's house. He is described as white, five feet four inches tall, of slim build, with brown hair and wearing a grey hooded top and dark jeans. Officers are becoming increasingly concerned for his welfare and ask anyone who has seen him or knows where he is to call police quoting this reference number.

Two teenagers aged sixteen and seventeen are found safe and well. Police will not release the location of where they were found.

After an extensive police search and campaign by family friends, the girl's body was discovered at a quarry close to her home. Her family released a statement asking for privacy. Police say there are no suspicious circumstances.

A missing teen's body was found six days after he went missing from home.

A thirteen-year-old was found dead yesterday, nine days after disappearing.

The missing teenager's sister sets up a fresh canvas and starts to paint the images inside her.

A car is found abandoned by the concrete slab anchoring the bridge to the seaside town. It is identified as belonging to the missing teenager's father, who didn't know it was missing. DNA found inside doesn't match the missing teenager.

The trainee psychiatrist reads a report in the *British Journal of Psychiatry* that suggests suicide has overtaken road traffic accidents as the major cause of death in fifteen- to twenty-five-year-olds. He is determined to make a difference in his chosen profession.

When he attends supervision with the consultant, he sees a pile of the *British Journal of Psychiatry* as high as her desk, still wrapped in their cellophane sheaths.

The consultant was on the trainee's interview panel, where he'd described being 'passionate about mental health'. This had impressed the service director, but the consultant is concerned about people who say they are 'passionate about mental health'. It's a job, she thinks. Be passionate about other things.

A body is found in the estuary. It is not the missing teenager.

In prison, the ex-porter gets pains all over his body. No physical cause can be found. He is seen by the visiting forensic psychiatrist who takes a detailed history and says the pain is psychological and that his family had no language for emotion. The ex-porter disagrees. He tells the psychiatrist his family did have a language for emotion, only not in words. The last time he saw his mother she tipped him off a chair like he was a bag of rubbish.

The psychiatrist puts him on one-to-one suicide watch and refers him to the hospital wing. The referral gets stuck as there are no free officers to escort him.

The missing teenager's body is found in undergrowth near a clifftop path by police. Postmortem examination reveals the cause of death was hypothermia. The coroner is notified.

The service director calls the consultant in the middle of a clinic to tell her. There will be a routine Serious Incident Inquiry, of course, he says.

She excuses herself and rushes to the toilet where she sits in a cubicle and cries so hard her head hurts as if her skull will split. She should have seen it coming. He was only eighteen for Christ's sake. Somebody knocks on the door to ask if she's OK.

Afterwards her eyeballs feel like they've been rolled in grit.

At the Serious Incident Inquiry, the consultant describes how she tried to engage the teenager, how she believed he was depressed beneath his upbeat veneer. A false self, a defence, she says. She was concerned when he didn't attend his appointment and had tried to contact him. She had not been in contact with his parents in treatment as he'd asked her not to. He'd given his sister as next of kin. It's a fine balance, she says, managing the clinical risk and maintaining rapport. It's all detailed in his risk plan. He was eighteen. If I'd spoken to his parents about him without his consent, I could have ruptured the therapeutic relationship.

In her interview for the Inquiry, the teenager's sister says he'd had a row with their parents about running up thousands of pounds on his mother's credit card, buying stuff from Gucci.

Their parents didn't have a clue about the drugs, she says. He said they helped numb over the bad mood swings, calmed him. But it got harder and he needed more and more. He had to get a dealer. Then she'd found him on the toilet in her bathroom peeing like a girl. He had a syringe in his teeth, a scarf tied tight around his arm and he was slapping his vein, going, Come on. One more fix. She didn't know it'd got that bad and threatened to tell their parents. He pleaded with me not to, she says. Promised he was going to the clinic and the consultant was going to get him on a treatment programme as soon as a place came up.

The teenager's parents lodge a complaint about the service received by their son, citing 'lack of communication and confidentiality taken too far'. They say he should have been admitted.

The service director emails the consultant about the complaint. *Please review notes ASAP esp. concerning crisis and contingency plans so I can write a response.*

The consultant sees the email on her phone while she is attending a presentation about reorganising mental health services in line with evidence-based data. She takes an extra tramadol.

That evening her husband prepares a special dinner to mark their tenth wedding anniversary, which she has forgotten. Afterwards he tries to persuade her to come to bed and she tells him she won't be long. She tweets about the fetishisation of data which is idealised so managers making cuts to services feel justified. Feel better. Inured. *The reality is we need properly trained, experienced staff to see complex cases. Instead, services are put out to tender to the cheapest bidder.*

At 4 a.m. she wakes on the sofa with a cricked neck and throbbing head.

The teenager's sister reads the report from the Serious Incident Inquiry. It says, *When she was found she was blue.* She doesn't know why the report says 'she' in several places.

To her, her brother always looked like a boy who looked like a girl who looked like a boy.

The teenager's mother is interviewed by the local press. Services for soaring numbers of young people who have self-harmed or are having some sort of breakdown are grossly inadequate, she says. It prolongs suffering for children and their families.

She tells the reporter that she and her husband and daughter are closer than ever in grief.

The local entrepreneur's son gets a studio in the creative hub despite having an income well above the minimum wage from a job in the company run by his uncle.

The teenager's sister watches the traffic on the bridge at night. A glimmering necklace of ruby gemstones on the left, a string of shimmering diamonds on the right.

The mental health service relocates to a new unit at the old maternity hospital. It is cold and smells of plastic. Files are lost in transition. Two staff leave and their posts are frozen.

The teenager's parents announce they are setting up their own charity for young people with mental health and drug problems.

The trainee psychiatrist goes to see the teenager's sister's exhibition at the new clifftop complex. A series of abstract portraits called *Missing*.

He buys a painting. It is more than he can really afford. The teenager's sister smiles, thanks him, places a red dot on the canvas.

The consultant's application to sit on a panel advising the Local Enterprise Partnership on services for young people with mental health problems is blocked.

The head of procurement at the local NHS trust is under investigation for receiving VIP tickets and hospitality from a bidding company during a tender process for converting the old maternity hospital into a specialist mental health unit.

A twenty-one-year-old man with a long history of substance misuse while in prison dies after he sets himself on fire when smoking drugs in his cell. A thirty-one-year-old man who had previously self-harmed in jail, and had been assessed as having an increased risk of suicide, is found hanged in his cell.

Cracks are found on the road surface of the bridge. It is closed for investigation. The consultant's drive to work is increased by five miles and fifty minutes in the morning rush hour.

A teenager goes missing.

Raise

or

How to Break Free of the Ground

or

The Lakeland Dialect for 'Slippery' Is 'Slape' and to Form It in the Mouth Requires an Act of Falling

KATIE HALE

Begin at yon coffin stone: flat-topped boulder at the foot of the fell, positioned for resting the burden of the dead. Your hand is small but your brother's smaller. It twitches in yours, a caught insect, and when he grins at you, you roll your ten-year-old eyes, keep on climbing for the beck. You drag the plastic net behind you.

/

No. Stop. Let me begin again.

/

Up aback of yon coffin stone, your brother's hand in yours a caught insect, a metal bucket in his other. When you offer to take it, he tells you, 'No way, José,' even though really it's too big for him, even though the path is steep and difficult, even though the rocks are stern. Sometimes it clangs against the ground. Sometimes he kicks it accidentally and stumbles, but he always pulls himself back up, barrels out his chest like the bodybuilders on telly.

He's going to fill the bucket from the tarn at the top of the fell. He's gonna catch a flickering silver fish, he says: a tiddler he can scoop in his insect hand, let it wriggle in his palm, go still. Then, he says, he'll put it back. After all, he's not a monster, just a small kind of god.

The sky out over the lake is a centrefold, a glossy falling open after rain. You climb to where the path becomes trickle, becomes syke, becomes beck. This happens sometimes: boots and water pulled by the same gravity. The rocks are slick with moss.

Your brother has tramped the bottom of the dell till his trainers are clarty with mud. He stomps through the water, saying, 'Jeez, it's cold.' When you ignore him, he stamps harder and says, 'I said, *jeez, it's cold.*' His soles are worn from where he's scuffed them along the pavement, and his laces trail like unfinished sentences. It's the summer holidays before you turn eleven, before your last year at the little village school, and you're almost an adult in your fake suede jacket, your purple dungarees—

/

Again.

/

It's the summer holidays before you turn eleven, and you're almost an adult in your fake suede jacket, your purple dungarees. Your mam has said, 'Look after your brother,' and, 'Make sure you're back by lunch.'

So you begin out past Town End aback of the dead poet's cottage. Past the car park, the coaches, the disgorged tourists here for long-wilted daffodils and a clutch of gingerbread from the famous shop. Past yon coffin stone with its box-flat top, where two collies beg as a woman tucks into her bait, as she ignores you and your brother and the dogs.

Happen your grip is a gin trap, and your brother keeps twining on about the climb. 'Let us rest a mo – go on.'

Somewhere in the deciduous garden of Wishing Gate House, a squirrel taps hazelnuts against its teeth – a scrape, a patter, a tumble of shells between branches. A clutch of sparrows. Thrum of wings. From the opposite fell, a white flock of birds merges with the sky: inconsequential gods departing a dead religion. Out on the lake, an old man rows the disturbed creases of the water, and a skein of geese skitters in to land.

'Stop twining and move.' You pull your brother up to where the path becomes trickle, becomes syke, becomes beck, metal bucket a clang against the rock.

/

Metal bucket a clang against the rock, you walk out through Town End, past the sheep skull nailed to the lintel, up, aback of the dead poet's cottage. Yesterday's rain furrows the edges of the track, gathers leaf mulch in the gutters. The mizzle is a spider's web clinging to your face. Already your calves are heavy, your breath a helicopter whirring across the valley.

Look after your brother. Make sure you're back by lunch.

Up the curling border of the dell – fringe of kingcup, thunder flowers with rainstorms locked inside – happen your brother starts twining on about the climb. 'Let us rest a mo – go on.'

But it's the summer holidays before you turn eleven. You're almost an adult in your fake suede jacket, your purple dungarees, and your mam has said, 'Make sure you're back by lunch.'

So you tell him, 'We've not got time. Come on.'

Your hand is a gin trap. You drag him up to where the trail begins to tack, a zigzag of tumbled rock, which your brother calls, 'Tougher'n climbing to heaven.' He must have picked this up from school, because you've never heard it from your mam, and anyway it's childish, thinking heaven is somewhere like a mountain you can climb to.

/

Once, your teacher asked: 'If you build a ship and sail her across an ocean in the middle of a storm – then, when you arrive, swap out the oars for new ones – then, when the hull begins to rot, replace the boards – then, when the sails are blown to tatters, stitch up another set from different cloth – then, when the rigging can't hold you up, buy a bunch of rope and knot yourself some more – and so on, and so on, till you've substituted every part – is she still the same ship that crossed the ocean in the storm?'

'Yes, cos she's still got the same name.'

'No, cos there's nowt of her old self left.'

Your teacher told you, 'That's the point – *you* get to decide what you mean by *same*.'

/

Past yon coffin stone – flat-topped boulder at the bottom of the raise, aback of the dead poet's cottage – past the duck pond with its watchful heron, its fringe of thunder flowers and kingcup, happen you climb the curling border of the dell. Rain dashes you, the weight of a hefted flock. At the driveway for Wishing Gate House, your brother begs again to hear about the boggles and their hauntings. So you tell him he's ladgeful. 'Everyone knows they're only stories.'

His hand twitches in yours, a caught insect, and mizzle like a spider's web snags at your face. The gate is looped with binding twine, your fingers too cold, too wet to untie it. Happen in this telling, you struggle with the knot. Happen the sneck is rusted shut, the gate a sudden ending, so you run home in your fake suede jacket, your purple dungarees – your brother's trainers clarty, scuffed and slape. Your mam has said, 'Make sure you're back by lunch.' And so, happen in this telling, you are.

/

162

Out past Town End aback of the dead poet's cottage, you climb to where the path becomes syke, becomes beck, becomes force – becomes fierce white hurry that rushes the clart from your treads. The water tugs at your skin, unzips you like a boot.

Happen you remember that saying: how you can't step in the same river twice. Happen you tell it to your brother, who calls you ladgeful.

The water dodges and slips – happen it weaves between your bones, so from your toes, you can feel your flesh unknitting, becoming flood. Next, your soles. Your ankles. Legs. Happen your brother's hand twitches in yours, a caught insect, and when you fall – him first, pulling you after – both of you fall without breaking: liquid dance down the fellside; tumbling ghyll; water remaking itself as wish. Happen when you fall, you fall for something beautiful and calm, for the mirrored oblivion of the lake.

/

Again.

/

Past the duck pond with its watchful heron, loose change of kingcup at the fringe. Up the curling border of the dell.

Your mam has said the dell was dug out years ago, to unearth the bones for Wishing Gate House, which everyone knows is a rattled haunting, a cluster of boggles and ghouls. It hunkers between the trees, between the fleeting deer, the dead still playing out their stories on repeat.

/

Your mam has said, 'Look after your brother,' so happen when your brother stumbles, you're the one who falls. Your head against a rock. Your eke of blood. You spreading, leaking your own red tarn across the path.

/

Your brother clangs the metal bucket, you drag him after.

Your brother's trainers worn and clarty.

The rocks are treacherous and slape, boots and water pulled by the same gravity.

/

Your brother was a full pail of water, and you spill it: you've been telling this story your whole life.

/

Past the coffin stone, aback of the dead poet's cottage, up the curling border of the dell. As you climb the path to Alcock Tarn, your brother's hand is a caught insect, the mizzle a web on your face. Happen his hand grows stronger. Grip a gin trap. Dusting of dark hairs at the wrist.

Up through deciduous woods, squirrels flash the branches with red. Unloop the binder twine, unsneck the gate. Happen your brother is taller now, an Adam's apple riding his throat, his chin bearded with the wild. When he smiles at you, little sister, your small hand twitches in his.

You have been telling this story your whole life – how, when the trail begins to tack, you will say, 'Breather?' but your brother shakes his chiselled head, and the first silver flutters from his hair like a blown cobweb.

His breath will become a helicopter whirring across the valley.

By the time you reach the open summit, happen Alcock Tarn will lie still and gleaming as a promise, and your brother will stoop, his skin a tumbled crag. His feet are bare. He has lost the metal bucket. When he smiles (when he smiles at you, little sister), it's a god ray splitting the clouds after rain. When he walks, shuffles, out into the tarn, he is a full pail of water, emptying himself back into the flood.

/

They say yon coffin stone is flat for the resting of burdens, flat from the repeated weight of the dead.

At school, you learned how the universe is infinite, and also still expanding, and how somehow both these things can be true.

/

Happen you perch a moment on yon coffin stone, to decide what you mean by *true*. You have been telling this story your whole life, and now, when you gather your words, they flicker, fish circling a metal bucket, waiting for you to return them to the tarn.

Catch your breath, the way you would snatch a tiddler from the beck, the way you would catch a hand to stop it falling.

The path is always there, aback of the dead poet's cottage, curling up the border of the dell. When you stand, send the roe deer askitter between the trees, the heron panicking away towards the lake. Up at the house, the boggles will continue their relentless haunting.

The path is always there. And so now, begin.

Riding Lessons

MAX LURY

Kieran met Nina on the steps. They were flat and grey and climbed up the shallow slope towards the house, which was all glass and clean white stone, unblemished. The sky was an open blue and the clouds were the colour of spit. Nina was smoking and wearing new glasses.

New glasses, Kieran said.

She nodded. Then, after a pause, she said it too. New glasses.

Kieran laughed. She had made the word 'new' long and hollow, like a tunnel, or a tube of dry pasta.

Then she stood up and hugged Kieran and said it's so nice that you've come, really. He said have you been in yet, and she shook her head. Gestured to the butt between her fingers. He nodded and took a seat next to her, folding his hands and squeezing them between his thighs.

Nina studied the end of her cigarette for a moment or two. She spoke without looking up.

Nervous?

You know, Kieran said, I haven't seen Tim in a long time.

Nina looked at him like she didn't buy it. Her black hair was cut short and it framed her face in a way that Kieran thought made her look like a celebrity. Not anyone in particular, just someone famous. Features you would remember.

She said is it the eating thing?

He paused, toyed with extending his silence. Decided against it.

Yeah, he said, it's still the eating thing.

She said is it still just in front of people, and he lied and said yeah, just people.

He had told her once when they were drunk and then in the morning he had texted her saying please don't tell anyone and she had responded of course not :) with a little smiley face that at first seemed mocking and then he realised, was a way of communicating something else. He didn't know why he'd told her. He could only guess. Sometimes he thought maybe he had told her because he wasn't attracted to her, because maybe there was nothing to lose by exposing that part of himself.

But he knew that wasn't entirely true. Once, he had convinced himself he loved her and he had drafted a whole message asking if they could meet up because he had something very important to tell her and then, in the same movement, his thumbs never stopping on the screen, he had deleted it all. When he woke up the next day he pushed it down inside himself until it sank, and the memory of the feeling now would come to him only for a moment, barely there, whilst he was on the bus or doing the washing-up.

There was space between the houses here, outside of London, enough room for bright-green hedgerows and flowerbeds. A squirrel stopped and stared at them, its head moving in little spasms. A yellow car drove past and Nina punched Kieran's thigh and said yellow car. Then they were silent again and watched the squirrel move in stops and starts across the lawn.

They heard a voice from behind them, and they both turned to see Ellie coming down the steps in an apron, waving a hand in an oven mitt and saying hello my lovelies. She had slicked her dark hair back so it was tight against her scalp and her free hand had a ring on each finger. Ellie gave Nina two big kisses and said her tits looked great and then when she gave Kieran a hug she did it slowly, like she was handling a porcelain doll. She squeezed his hand and looked him in the eye and said oh it's so lovely you've come, really.

Kieran put his hands in his pockets and said it's been a while and Ellie said yes, Tim's so excited to see you. Kieran was not sure

Tim had ever been excited about anything. He thought it over as Nina and Ellie talked about something on the walk up to the house and then Ellie turned around and put her hand on Kieran's arm and said I'm excited to see you too, you know.

Nina said it'll be just like uni again and Ellie said oh God, I hope not. Kieran was not sure what Ellie meant and judging by the way Nina stopped for a moment he thought she wasn't either.

They hung their coats on a wooden rack by the front door, Kieran's a formless blue mass and Nina's sleek and black, almost liquid. As they moved towards the kitchen Kieran could smell something rich: meat, garlic, onions, pepper. Tim was stood behind the marble island with his hands in the sink and when he saw them he squinted like he was looking out to sea. He was shorter than Ellie by a head and when he stood next to her the effect was slightly comic. Tim placed the soap in a little china dish and wiped his hands, once, on a tiny cream towel.

Tim gave Nina a kiss on the cheek and then shook Kieran's hand. His were still damp and the hot water made them slightly too warm, like small sacks of blood.

Ellie said when was the last time you two saw each other and then Tim and Kieran looked at one another for a while. Something passed between them.

Kieran had not seen Tim for years, but they were still members of an old group chat that was pretty dead, apart from the occasional message. Kieran had never shared his shit on there but sometimes Tim would get very very drunk and say things like, I think about hurting myself more than you probably should, and someone would respond, yeah I think you're not meant to think about it at all, and then someone else would post a picture of a man with his cock out swimming in the Thames and say looks like he'll be telling the boys it was cold, at which point the whole whether or not you were meant to think about hurting yourself question would kind of fall by the wayside. Then Kieran would feel guilty and turn his phone on airplane mode and try not to think about it for the rest of the day.

Tim said I think it was at Katy's party I saw you last. Kieran had not been at Katy's party but he did not correct him. Tim said Kieran had been wearing a very extravagant hat and singing very questionable songs about dictators and their wives. Ellie made a dismissive motion with one hand and went to the sink to wash the vegetables. Tim looked at Kieran and made a gesture like he was doffing an invisible cap.

Nina said you must let me help and Ellie said no, really, it's fine. Nina moved towards the stove anyway and picked up a knife and just sort of held it as if that was doing something. They were finding their feet, Kieran thought, trying to keep in time to a rhythm that had once been familiar but was now just out of reach, muffled behind a pane of thick glass.

Ellie said that she had just got back from Scotland and that she'd found the best veggie haggis recipe on Earth. She said it was a miracle.

Nina said nothing miraculous had come out of Scotland since Russell Crowe.

They stood for a while in the kitchen drinking wine. Both Kieran and Nina had brought a bottle, but Nina's was the one open, and Kieran's had been placed tactically all the way at the back of the fridge. Nina tapped her glass with a nail and said I really needed this.

Kieran watched them. He could see the people they had been ten years ago: the way Nina insisted on helping even though she had no clue what she was doing; how Ellie fussed over everyone's glass and seat until it was just right; and Tim, stood at the end of the island, watching, with a face that could not be read.

Tim and Ellie were an unlikely couple. Tim was kind of serious in a strange way and Ellie was, at university, very 'fun', which meant she did a lot of drugs. Sometimes she would just say things, seemingly out of nowhere, like, I'm that bitch. She would finish a glass of wine and hold it up to the light and say, I'm just that bitch. Tim could be awkward and was notorious for turning up to house parties and making small talk with girls about the technicalities of the stock market and then going on to outstay his welcome, sitting alone on a sofa long after everyone else had gone to bed.

But they made some sort of sense now, Kieran thought, they had an ease with each other which only came with time, and when Tim asked Nina if she was still on the fags Ellie wafted her hand in his direction like he was a bad smell and everyone laughed.

They sat on tall black stools which Tim said they never really used, and Kieran studied the lighting fixture above his head, which seemed to be a deconstructed stage light suspended on thick metal cables. There was a large stainless-steel fridge that imposed itself on the space and had only one magnet that said GRAND CANYON NATIONAL PARK in a font you might see in the Old West. The canyon itself was red and looked like a scab. At the bottom it said in white Comic Sans: JUMBO SIZE FRIDGE MAGNET.

Kieran thought that you were maybe meant to tear that off, but said nothing.

Nina was stood by Ellie who was chopping a romanesco cauliflower. She put her hand on Ellie's shoulder and they laughed about a friend of theirs who'd had a baby. Ellie wiped her hands on her apron and took out her phone and the two of them made cooing noises and stroked the screen with their nails.

The men were in their own pocket of the room. A space grew between the two of them and hung there, unfilled.

Tim nodded at the fridge and said she's a beauty.

Kieran took a sip of wine. It was heavy and coated his tongue. He gestured to the fridge with his free hand and said keeps it cold, I assume?

Tim laughed and raised an eyebrow.

It was always like this with Tim, Kieran was starting to remember. These half-jokes, stating the obvious in a way that made it ridiculous. Sometimes you'd talk to him for ten minutes before you realised the whole thing was a construction, that he was in some way playing a character who was meant to bore you.

Kieran asked what Tim was up to and he said ah, still with the asset management stuff, you know how it is. All very boring, really. But it pays the bills.

As he spoke the tips of his fingers traced the grey veins on the surface of the island, lovingly, as if the marble could respond to his touch.

Ellie clapped her hands and told everyone to take their seats. There was a small performance over who should sit where, and the couple argued for a moment about what they had agreed earlier. They took their places, the men at the ends of the table, the women sandwiched between. Ellie took off her apron and brought over slices of vegetarian haggis on a bed of spiced quinoa, with turnips and swedes that were a crisp brown at the edges, and apologised for the cauliflower being late. She said they could have it as a palate cleanser.

Nina said the food looked amazing but quite medieval, not that that was a bad thing. Tim said Steve Bannon says we're all serfs anyway and Ellie said right but I'm not exactly eating oats and grain, ignoring the fact that she was, actually, eating oats and grain.

Right, Kieran said, and what did Steve mean by that?

Tim winked and said Steve Bannon in a New York accent. Nina laughed and said Bannon again, but slower, making the 'a' sound into a high whine.

Then Nina said that she found Steve Bannon quite sexy and Ellie said that was probably actually quite immoral. There was a silence and Ellie filled their glasses again. Kieran watched the dark liquid fill his cup, and started the process of subtracting each drop from the next day. That was his routine: each sip, each mouthful, was taken from what he was going to eat tomorrow, bit by bit, until he had hollowed out each of the next twenty-four hours in his head.

Kieran felt like he should join in, make some sort of comment. But it was difficult to engage like this, two steps removed. He ventured that he could imagine Steve Bannon was pretty good in bed, and that he probably had a 'swinger'. Ellie rolled her eyes.

Tim stood up to get a beer and threw some of the plastic from the table in the bin and Ellie said recycling! in a loud voice. There was a pause and then Tim said he wasn't too bothered about the whole recycling thing and Ellie gave a big sigh and said can we just not tonight.

Kieran and Nina shared a look and then Ellie said well Tim did go veggie a while ago. She said it like it was something to be proud of.

Tim shrugged and just said I like animals. As if that somehow resolved the conversation.

Nina updated everyone on her charity and Ellie said that it was 'really impressive' and gave a thumbs up that was so bizarre it made Kieran wince. He had called Ellie stupid once to Tim, and said she just wanted to be seen to care, and every time he thought of that moment his insides seemed to shrink and pull away from his skin. He wondered if Tim had ever told her.

Someone had asked him a question and he only realised when Nina tapped the table by his hand with her nail.

Tim looked at Kieran and said, you used to talk a lot.

Kieran said sure. Probably, yeah.

Ellie said hey Tim be nice and Tim said I'm not *not* being nice, I'm just saying. He's got quieter.

Nina said I think everyone gets quieter with age and Tim said not me and Nina said we can see that, yeah.

At university, Kieran had been loud and Tim had been quiet and that was how they had been together. Tim had a genuine strangeness and when Kieran was either anxious or in large groups he could make Tim seem stranger, turning him into a caricature, and he could have the whole room laughing, not just because it was funny but because they all wanted to communicate somehow their discomfort at the way this small man talked and held himself.

And Kieran had savoured that feeling. Making everyone laugh, having everyone on his side for a moment. He thought all that time Tim had been laughing too.

They all ate a few more bites instead of speaking. Kieran cut up several pieces of the haggis but just moved them about the plate. Ellie stood up and said she had to check on the cauliflower.

Tim said can you pass the butter and Nina said what else's changed, Tim?

Tim said the butter, please, and then Ellie shouted from the kitchen oh fuck, fuck, Christ. The fucking romanesco is burnt to a cinder.

She came over holding the glass tray containing the bits of charred vegetable in pink oven mitts and said why do bad things happen to good people, as if they were all in agreement that they were, in fact, good people.

Tim said they could always order food online and Ellie gave him a look, like, don't you dare. Kieran mentioned you could pay for that with bitcoin now and Nina said she had no idea how any of that actually worked.

Kieran said don't you farm bitcoin and Tim laughed and said no no you mine it, and Nina made a joke about a poor Chinese farmer with a straw hat waking up at dawn to pluck strings of binary code from the trees and Ellie said that was maybe a little offensive and Kieran said OK but you do kind of farm it.

The conversation slowed for a while, swollen with wine, and pulled itself gradually across the next ten minutes. Kieran thought he could see the way it avoided him, parted around the topic of Kieran like a river around a stone. They had all pushed their chairs back so there was more space between them and Kieran watched the wax from the candles gather in pale orbs and then trickle down the long white stems.

Ellie said she was going upstairs to show Nina her paintings whilst the ice cream softened on the table.

Tim said he wanted to show Kieran something. His man cave.

Kieran laughed. I'm sorry?

My man cave, Tim said.

Nina said that's kind of sad, Tim.

Ellie laughed. She brushed Tim's shoulder with the tips of her fingers and left them there. It's our joke, she said. Can you imagine Tim actually calling it a man cave?

Tim was beaming. That smile he always did when you couldn't tell if he was joking, if the Tim who had just said that was a character, some version of himself he was doing for his own amusement.

Ellie said she'd never been down there, that it was important they had their respective spaces. She had upstairs where she painted, her studio, with the north-facing windows and the hardwood floor, and Tim had downstairs. It's a trust thing, she said. It's like, I wouldn't want Tim watching me have a shit.

Tim raised his eyebrows. I've seen that a couple of times, he said. He rubbed his stomach and said Delhi belly.

Ellie said babe in a small, hard voice and then Tim was quiet.

The women went upstairs and then Tim and Kieran were alone. Kieran thought about saying excuse me, and leaving the table to make himself sick, but Tim stood up and cocked his head and Kieran followed. There was a sense of relief – the decision was made for him. The two of them made their way through the kitchen and Tim opened a white door that led down some battered stone steps into the cellar. They descended in silence, for so long that when Kieran turned back to look at the door he could not quite make it out in the darkness. He guessed they were maybe ten feet underground.

There was a small click and then Tim gave a push and a door opened. They stepped out.

The basement was all concrete. A single bulb hung from a thick black cable. It was cold and smelt of bleach, and, alone, tied to a square pillar that stood in the centre of the room, was a shaved horse.

As they approached Kieran could see that the horse's skin was the colour of the inside of a frankfurter sausage and when it heard footsteps it flattened its ears to its head and pulled away, as far as it could get. There was something dark on its ribs that might have been a shadow or might have been a bruise. The rope grew taut and strained.

What is that?

It's a shaved horse, Tim said.

Right, Kieran said, I can see that, yeah.

Kieran squinted. But what, he said, does it do?

Tim shrugged. Whatever horses do.

Whatever horses do?

Yeah.

Which is what?

You tell me.

Tim.

Kieran.

Are you deliberately avoiding my question?

What do you want me to say?

OK, Kieran said. OK.

Kieran ground his heel into the concrete and lifted his toes upwards. When he spoke again his voice was quiet. Considered.

But you shave it?

Every morning, crack of dawn. Tim said this with some pride, like it was an achievement.

Kieran stared at the horse, the vacant black globes of its eyes, the mottled curve of its hooves. It would occasionally shake its head and blow air through its nose. There was a white chalk circle drawn on the concrete around the horse, and, at the side furthest from Kieran, a faded brown stain.

What's the stain?

Ah, Tim said, *that*.

They stood for a while. Kieran chewed his lip.

So, Kieran said, what else do you do with it?

Ah, Tim said, you know.

No, I don't.

Well.

Tim inhaled as if he was about to speak but said nothing.

They fell into an uncomfortable silence.

Tim walked forward and took a stick of chalk from his pocket, using it to smooth out the white circle around the horse, filling in the gaps, creating one unbroken line. He slipped the chalk back into his trousers and wiped the dust on his thighs. Each time he approached the circle the horse would pull back with a swing of its long head and turn its body away from him. Then it would move so that one big eye was visible. Watching them.

The horse gazed back out at the two men, all smooth flesh and small eyes, their tight faces, and the way the shorter one moved made it shake. It could smell their sweat and the sharp thin scent of aerosol and the wine that made their breath heavy. It gave a little stamp. Flared its nostrils. Memories surfaced as a tremor in its flank. It only knew the dark and the room and the man. It urinated a little.

Kieran looked at Tim, the funny way he had cocked his head, the way he had his hands now clasped behind his back as if he was in a museum or an art gallery. He wasn't smiling – but he wasn't not smiling; he was holding his face in a strange sort of stasis, a halfway point between the two that was neither and both. There was no way of telling.

Does Ellie know? Kieran asked.

Tim turned to him and tapped his nose, before clapping twice. Well, he said, that's enough of that. He led Kieran from the room, fiddling with a set of keys in a way that made them faintly echo from the cellar walls. Before Kieran left he turned his head to look at the horse, smaller now, its two eyes fixed on the exit.

The men climbed the steps and just before they reached the top Tim turned around and said it was very important to me that you saw that. Then he pushed open the door and the sound of music and the smell of burnt romanesco and gravy filled the air and there was no question of talking about it further, because Tim had put his arms around Ellie and was kissing her face and saying did you show Nina your amazing paintings baby.

Nina said they were honestly just magic, pure magic, and blew a kiss at Ellie and did a little wiggle of her shoulders, leaning back so she could see Kieran and patting the seat next to her with a flat palm.

Kieran took the seat. For a while it was as if the floor was made of glass and he could almost see the horse, alone now in the dark, beneath their feet, but as the conversation grew between them and Nina poured him another glass of wine, the image clouded over. He watched Ellie's face for a glimmer of recognition. A look she might throw him that would mean I know and there is nothing that can be done. But there was none. She was drunk and her eyes were just starting to get that absent gloss and her teeth were stained a dark red.

Ellie filled Tim in on the joke they had been having upstairs, something about Jodorowksy directing *Toy Story*, and as Tim joined in, doing the voice of the caterpillar from *A Bug's Life*, Ellie made her way into the kitchen and returned with dessert. She served prim scoops of coffee ice cream topped with chopped nuts on little rectangular slates and said it was a bit naughty but why the hell not. Kieran looked at his and hoped that if he just watched it for long enough it would melt and it might look like he'd had a few bites. He moved some around with the curved side of his spoon and pinched his thigh under the table.

Ellie looked up and said but you are OK, aren't you, Kieran?

She said it as if they had all been talking about this prior, like this was the natural conclusion to a conversation that until now had gone unspoken. The room went quiet and Kieran could feel all the objects around him as things that were very hard and very real, and the way they occupied space made him feel like he had somehow shrunk into the hollow behind his eyes.

It had been his decision to come, really. Nina had said they should do something now he was out – and he had noticed the way she didn't say hospital, as if doing so would fill her mouth with the taste of bleach and antiseptic – and she had mentioned that she still did dinner with Tim and Ellie sometimes and Kieran had no choice but to say of course that'll be fine, and when she asked again he insisted that it was fine, really, and then there was nothing either of them could do. She couldn't push it further without forcing his hand, and he'd been so keen to seem normal he'd trapped himself.

You know, Ellie said, taking Tim's hand, we were all very worried about you. Kieran thought maybe Ellie was trying to embarrass him. Or trying to help. Or both, he supposed, at the same time.

Kieran could feel Nina look at him from the corner of her eye. He could also feel that he was actually quite drunk. Tim didn't smile at Kieran but looked instead at his plate and said nothing. Kieran wondered what they knew. He pressed his hands between his thighs.

Ellie gave Tim's hand a squeeze and Kieran could see the faint trace of chalk on Tim's fingertips, catching the light, leaving tiny white flecks on the dark wood of the table.

Kieran had only seen Tim break his act once. But they had not talked about it on the walk back from the hospital in the morning rain, stopping every five minutes so Tim could retch and spit on the side of the road, and they had not mentioned it when Ellie asked with a kind of limp curiosity where they had both been the night before, and Kieran was definitely not going to talk about it here, now it had calcified inside him, and become something he only returned to in the dark.

He had not said anything for a long while. The ice cream had started to melt and ran in a slow brown stream off the slate and onto the surface beneath.

Yeah, Kieran said. I was just very sick for a while.

A pause. Nina finished her wine and pretended to have another sip. Tim looked Kieran in the eye.

Kieran did not want to continue. He wanted to keep all that to himself, and the idea of it, under these lights, splayed on the table like a dissected frog, all tendons and dark dense organs, made his mouth dry. Then Tim made a joke about the fact that eating off stone was probably even more primitive than eating oats and grain, and everyone could tell Kieran didn't want to say anything else and so they jumped on the bit, and in that moment, as it was taken away, Kieran realised he wanted nothing more than to tell these people everything that had happened and when and why and what it had cost him.

But they were laughing again, and the moment was gone, and they were toying with the idea of Steve Bannon as a kind of feudal lord, picturing the bitcoin farmers with their tinfoil hats in hand, stood in front of his digital throne, and Nina gave him a smile that was familiar, that meant you can tell me anything, or almost anything, but then it was gone, he had missed it, and so he kept the feeling, hoping to revisit it, knowing that it would be gone in the morning.

Outside night had fallen and the glass now reflected a faint image of the four of them. Kieran thought of the sad long head of the horse and wished he had touched it.

Ellie asked what Nina was going to cook when she hosted next and Nina said she was trying to eat seasonally, and Ellie said that actually the concept of seasons was quite Western and oppressive and even, dare she say, a little cowardly. Tim did an impression of a cowardly season, shrinking into himself and muttering about how he was unable to face all the buds and new life, and Kieran laughed so hard he slapped the table and made his cutlery jump, and did his own impression of a season begging for mercy from the other, bigger seasons, and that opened it up to the room.

And the space then filled with their moody seasons: nervous winter and naughty summer on a date, confused and lecherous spring, autumn that spent its time smoking clove cigarettes and drinking expensive coffee, and the concept of all of these pressed together, smothered and spread thin over the surface of the globe, arguing and competing, freezing and thawing and freezing again, needing each other, only existing in relation to the next.

The Baron and
His Volcano

JAY GAO

Qiu, I escaped the company of the Baron and returned to Hong Kong. All those months stewing in the shadow of his volcano – was that a lifetime ago?

On the plane I picked apart the newspaper shoved down my seat's side. I recognised nothing. All the columns seemed to shift. The catastrophic blocks of black text and headlines rubbed onto my fingers – I recognised no language. Words kept breaking down before reassembling. Although the countries were picked at random, and their calamities recycled from some great heavenly wheel, every detail on those pages felt charged and subject to change.

I left the security of the Baron and returned to Hong Kong. All those years stewing in the shadow of his volcano – only now did it feel like I was about to wake from a short nap.

The empty plane was a ghost ship.

Around the invisible mark where we must have crossed silently from Europe to Asia, I had a premonition that our plane, besieged in the air by angelic creatures, would never land. The creatures had faces made from ash. In that vision, I was fumbling for a lifejacket underneath my seat; instead of finding plastic, my fingers pushed into a square of human flesh that parted at my touch like coral. The patterned blue veins on its yellow skin pulsed rhythmically, giving off a luminescence like a creature from the ocean floor.

Even in the dream I put the square of skin on over me. Even in the dream I did not want to die.

Even in the dream I put the square of skin
inside my mouth; even in the dream I did
not want to die.

Even in life I did not want to die. Qiu, I explained, that was why I had to leave the Baron.

I had expected a different weather of welcome after my plane landed at the newly relocated Hong Kong International Airport.

You should know, Qiu said, that events have shifted in your absence.

As she drove me out on the bridge from that reclaimed island – one that had been hooked and dragged from the bottom of the sea, against its will – I noticed a queue of tanks on the bypass, immobile, lined up like a row of dead black beetles.

You should know, Qiu said, that events have shifted in your absence.

She continued, Yesterday, I met a new patient who suffered from a rare condition called prosopagnosia. He developed it not long after his wife poisoned him with a faulty carbon monoxide heater.

It was as if Qiu was speaking through me towards someone else in the distance.

You should feel, Qiu whispered, that events have shifted in your absence.

She continued, Yesterday, I met an old patient who suffered from a rare condition called prosopagnosia. He developed it not long after his ex-wife poisoned him with a faulty carbon monoxide heater.

Have you heard of face blindness, she asked.

I shook my head.

Why do you ask, Qiu said, if events have shifted in your absence?

She puckered her face, Yesterday, I met an old patient who suffered from a common condition called prosopagnosia. He developed it not long after his ex-wife gifted him a faulty carbon monoxide heater. It was an accident.

An accident of love.

Have you heard of face blindness, she asked.

I shook my head even though I had.

A long time ago, Qiu continued, there was a German man who was shot in the head. After recovering quickly it became obvious that he had changed. He struggled to recognise, first, the doctors at the hospital; then he failed to recognise his friends, his family, his wife too, and, much later, the disease evolved to the point that he stopped recognising even his own face in his mirror.

Have you heard of face blindness, she asked?

I dared not move.

A long time ago, Qiu continued, there was a Chinese man who was shot in the head. After recovering slowly it became obvious that he had changed. He struggled to recognise, first, the doctors at the asylum; then he failed to recognise his enemies, his family, his first wife too, who had already died a few years earlier from heartbreak. The disease evolved to the point that, eventually, the man stopped recognising even his own face in the reflection of the water in the toilet in his cell.

Was it a woman who shot him?

Why do you think it was a woman?

Qiu paused. How, exactly, did you survive the volcano?

Was it a Chinese woman who shot him?

Why do you think it was a Chinese woman?

Qiu made sure nobody was eavesdropping before asking, How, exactly, did you survive the volcano?

After we finished lunch I asked her again about her patient. She added hot water to our pot of pale chrysanthemum tea; the grim flower buds bobbed like heads on the surface. I could not shake off the feeling that the Italian restaurant we dined at – that it used to be a bookshop; the more I looked around, imagining shelves instead of tables, and books instead of diners, and words instead of spaghetti, the less certain I was that I had, a long time ago, been in that very spot, reading a book about Italian cuisine.

Qiu, not noticing my confusion, stared out towards the harbour as if she was waiting for some shimmer to appear on its edge.

Was it a Chinese woman who loved him?

Why do you think the shooting was a result of love?

Qiu made sure nobody in the bookshop was watching us before writing a message on a bookmark. How, exactly, did you get away from the Baron?

Ignoring her question I stared out towards the harbour. For some days now, Qiu explained, the streets were filling up with yellow artificial flowers that fell, ceaselessly, from the rooftops of the highrises. Nobody knew which separatist group was releasing them. An ongoing strike of public services meant that the flowers accumulated like sloughed skin in the cracks on the pavement, bursting through the doorways of our apartments, invading the lobbies of empty hotels and abandoned offices.

I was waiting to see if I could see a shimmer, as fine as pollen, fall from the tips of those skyscrapers across the bay.

After lunch Qiu walked me back to my apartment block between the university and the pressing shadows of the Mid-Levels, occasionally picking off the yellow petals that caught in my black hair. As we hugged she whispered into my ear, You have come out of the well only to be dropped into the pond. Be on your guard. Trust nobody.

After lunch Qiu walked me back to my apartment block between the park that used to house the university and the pressing shadows of the Mid-Levels, occasionally picking off the yellow petals that caught in my black hair. After we kissed she whispered into my ear, You have come out of the pond only to be dropped into the well. Be on your guard. Trust nobody except for the Baron.

After lunch I walked back, alone, to my apartment block between the park that used to house the memorial for the university and the pressing shadows of the Mid-Levels, occasionally picking off the yellow petals that caught in my black hair.

Near my feet a large congealed mound of flowers refused to pass through the grating over a drain. I was repulsed by it.

Were the petals real or were they fabric? The more I rubbed the petals between my fingers, the more I struggled to tell the difference between those two textures.

If Qiu were here she would say something like, Does it matter if the petals are real or if they are just bits of torn fabric?

For a long time I had wanted to leave; I was already plotting a way to escape this city and return to the Baron.

All the people seemed to pass me on the street with an urgency. Was there a curfew Qiu had forgotten to tell me about? They walked through the walls like anxious ghosts. I could sense, still, the invisible fuzz from the neon signs, now unlit, lingering from the hot night before. My ears had yet to pop.

Were the petals real or were they fabric?

Why do you think the petals are a result of love?

All the people seemed to pass me on the street with an urgency. Qiu texted me about the curfew. They walked through the walls like anxious spies. I could sense, still, the invisible fuzz from the neon signs, now unlit, lingering from the cold night before. My ears had yet to pop. My body refused to correct itself.

If Qiu were here I would have said something like, I want to stay but I know that I will soon be pulled out, restless, too eager to escape, to put myself, once again, in the way of danger.

Car horns cursed up and down the roads. The bamboo construction poles wailed in the harbour breeze, and I could smell the sweet salty air of the ham and egg buns coming from a nearby bakery.

It was all here, more or less.

But there was this feeling I could not get away from, ever since I had stepped off the plane, that I was still sat there in my seat in the sky, dreaming, still so far away from arriving home at all.

Car horns cursed up and down the roads. A woman wailed. The crash of collapsing bamboo construction poles, and then the sirens started. I was too far away to see the accident, but I heard it all from the harbour breeze. More or less.

Was it all here? What was missing?

There was this feeling I could not get away from, that ever since I left the Baron, and stepped onto the plane, that as I sat there, in my seat in the sky, I was inching closer and closer towards a nightmarish version of a future where I never arrived at all.

I was flying overhead in circles, watching the distorted bubbling world through the oval passenger window beside me. I was sat next to the Baron. We were circling his volcano. Although I tried, for many hours, I was unable to loosen that seat belt which held me so absolutely in my place.

I was flying overhead in circles, watching the distorted bubbling world through the oval passenger window beside me. I was sat next to Qiu. We were circling the island upon which they had just relocated the Hong Kong International Airport. The plane refused to land, and nobody could tell us why. Although I tried, for many hours, I was unable to loosen that seat belt which held me so absolutely in my place.

You should know, Qiu said, how to do this by now.

I shifted uneasily in my seat and waited for her fingers to reach over and unbuckle my belt.

I shifted uneasily in my seat and waited for her fingers to reach over and unbuckle my belt. I waited for her fingers.

Earth-Grown Bodies

AOIFE INMAN

In the month before they begin burning animals on the Gower farm, there is a party in the village hall. It is organised by the Young Farmers' Club. There is a bar serving cans of Coke and 7UP and the committee repurpose the silver Christmas streamers they used during the infant nativity as decorations for the windows. By seven the hall is busy. The Gowers' eldest boy, Liam, hangs around the entranceway with James Trewin and Moira Lewis, slouching against the doorframe and blocking it just enough that people have to step over his feet. He kicks his younger brother, Dylan, in the shin as he passes and flicks a red plastic lighter with his thumb so that the flame dances on and off. Liam is taller than his peers, with pale, almost-white hair, shaved to the scalp. There is an inch-long scar on his ear lobe where Moira once pierced it with a safety pin and slipped. The three of them laugh disparagingly at the younger children darting back and forth from the dance floor, faces red with exertion, and at half past eleven they stalk off towards one of the old barns on the edge of the Gowers' land. They've bought pills from Dom Evans, hidden in a plastic tampon applicator in Moira's bag, though there is no one on the door of the village hall to search their things and the pretence feels childish now. They climb up onto the roof to take them. It's a full moon and the corrugated iron ripples like the surface of a lake. From a distance they can hear the music blaring from the hall. 'Cotton Eye Joe'. The sky is vast and black. Liam opens his mouth and imagines it pouring inside him like tar. A torch beam swings across the hill and at some point they climb down and head back to their respective houses, running blindly up the empty country roads, their pupils wide.

There is talk of what is coming long before it arrives and the village takes precautions. The Lewises leave buckets of bleach solution at the farm gate and the sound of hosepipes sluicing down cattle grids seems to last all day.

Gwennol Day comes and goes. The livestock shows are cancelled so the celebration feels smaller than usual without the Trewins' barns set out with rows of pens for all the rams and heifers. Still, the parade in the centre of the village goes ahead and the rain holds off.

A man from the council comes on a weekend and helps to close the footpaths that lead through the fields, until the valley is bisected in every direction by yellow tape.

This works for a while. Spring settles in as normal. Overnight, there are swallows nesting on the side of the schoolhouse and snowdrops appear on the verge by the newer housing estate at the base of the village. The ten o'clock news shows videos of fires on the Devon border. The cameras cut away to shots of empty yards and redundant milking equipment. Everybody in the village watches, switching channels when the news returns to the presenters in the studio, to catch the last few minutes of a programme about trains or weight loss on one of the satellite channels.

'It doesn't mean anything till it's here, just a lot of words to scare us,' Liam's mother, Roxanne, tells her sons, frying sausages on two flat griddle pans. Fat from the meat spits up onto her jumper, her forearms, her hair and she rubs it in with her damp fingers.

Liam shrugs his shoulders. 'You can't stir shit without a stick.'

'Language. Your brother's sat right there.' Roxanne looks over at her husband, Martin, slumped by the window overlooking the field. He massages the corner of his jaw with two fingers, frowning. He has been grinding his teeth in his sleep again. She calls his name and flicks her eyes towards their eldest son.

He sighs. 'Whatever you're doing, Liam, stop it.'

'Right, that'll be nothing, then. I'll stop doing nothing.'

Martin presses his wrists into the arms of his chair, exhales, and leaves the room. Roxanne hears the latch on the front door click to and she jostles the sausages in the pan so hard their skins split, juices hissing against the hot oil.

Roxanne Gower isn't a superstitious woman, but she isn't one to take chances either. There is a psychic from Trennelow Downs whose number Polly from the PTA meetings had slipped her last week.

'I can tell there's something on your mind,' Polly said across the table when they stopped for a smoke break. 'And she's not half-baked this one. It's the real deal. It was her that told me to get my thyroid checked last January, you remember?'

When the boys have left Roxanne rings her. The dialling tone goes on for a long time and the voice that answers the phone is low and hoarse. It has a smoker's crackle to it and Roxanne hangs up before she can ask her name.

In March a calf is born on the Gower farm. Liam is driving round the slope of the back field when he spots the heifer lying flat on the grass. The calf comes out legs first, body lodged between the safety of its mother and the spring air.

'I don't blame you, my love,' Liam says when he climbs down. 'It's a right mess out here. Best to hang tight.'

He holds the stiff, still legs of the calf and strokes the stomach of its mother, taut and dark. The field is quiet. Reaching up inside the animal, he twists the thick fleshy band that has caught around the calf's neck. He feels it is dead before it concertinas out, slick with life, stiff with the lack of it. Waiting in the cold air, he calls Kathy Morley, although he knows there is nothing to be done. The mother hangs her head back against the ground for a moment, eyes silted, before getting up, walking off the loss.

'That there's a sign,' Roxanne Gower says when she comes down from the house with Liam's brothers, and, sure enough, it is. When Kathy arrives, there are blisters on the feet of half the herd, small enough to miss the first time around, but clear enough to see now.

Roxanne doesn't know quite what to do with the news so she invites the young woman inside the house. She makes a pot of tea, sets her youngest boy down in front of a video. She wonders where Martin is. She hasn't seen him since the morning. He'd been down on the east fields tedding grass for silage. The hum of the tractor had woken her and she'd looked over at the empty space in the sheets beside her, running her fingers over the dip in the mattress, noticing the hairs caught on the pillowcase.

It doesn't take long for news of the infection to spread. Vans and army transport trucks arrive on the farm, loaded with paper masks and polythene sheeting. They replace the troughs of household bleach solution at the entrances to the barns and fields with buckets of lye and stiff brushes. The air smells so clean there can be no doubt the land is sick.

As soon as the quarantine is placed on the Gowers' farm, James Trewin is seen taking one of his calves, a steer, down the cliff path to the bay. He has remembered a story he'd been told once as a child, about a ritual amongst sailors. They would carry an ailing man down to meet the incoming tide and when the water retreated, so would his fever. James bargains something like that will work as good for cows as it does for men, as a pre-emptive measure at least. He leaves early, dressed in a rugby jersey, jogging bottoms and flip-flops. He leads the animal out of the farm's western gate and round the headland. There is a thin path, worn into the heather of the cliffside, that curls steeply down towards the sand and he takes this, holding on to the rope around the calf's neck with one fist, coaxing it slowly down the hill.

Ruth Kessell is standing on the flat serpentine rock beds at the far side of the bay. Her son Isaac is collecting hermit crabs in a bucket by the edge of the water. She spots James and watches for a while. She is waiting on the tide too. Right now the beach is half its full length, but when the waves have waned, exposing the pale body of sand, she will head out to the surf rocks where mussels grow in thick bunches. Nobody bothers to collect them here any more; most don't even know they grow on this coast.

When boy and calf arrive down on the sand, James slaps the skin behind the animal's shoulders, rubbing the clay-coloured hair into a cowlick, then brushing it flat with his fingers, the way his mum had done with him when he was small. They walk to the shoreline, sinking ankle-deep into the silt.

The tide is going out. Ruth zips up her parka, calls out for Isaac, and makes her way through the tide pools to where the water cracks into foam over the green rock heads.

James leads the calf into the water. He slips his palm under the rope on the calf's neck and feels the warm heat of its body against his skin. He closes his eyes and imagines the infection running out of every orifice, clotting in the water like oil. When he looks up, the calf bends its neck to the water and sinks its nose in, dark eyes damp with salt. He stares at it for a while. Well, that'll be something, he thinks to himself, nodding.

Dripping, they turn and head back up the way they came.

***

When the MAFF vans come to the Trewin farm the following day, James tells them they must have got something wrong.

'We've got no sick animals here. You want the Gowers over the way.'

The man on the doorstep nods sympathetically. 'Is your dad around?'

'The Gowers' land is on quarantine – they've got cases up there, it was on the news.' James nods his chin towards the van on the driveway. 'Have you dipped the wheels on that? You shouldn't even be coming up here if you haven't.'

The man clears his throat. 'Listen, we called ahead, spoke to your dad. It's a pre-emptive measure,' he says. 'We're taking all the animals in a three-kilometre radius of the test site.'

James grips the doorframe with his fists. 'That's fucking illegal, that is. You can't take shit without a warrant. Come back with a warrant, yeah?'

Harvey Trewin appears in the hallway behind James and places a hand on his shoulder, squeezing softly. 'It's all right now. Let him in.'

Harvey is a soft-spoken man, which has never mattered much to James until now. He shrugs off his dad's palm and curls his face into an expression of disgust, wiping the hair from his forehead with his fingers.

'You bastard,' he mutters, loud enough to hurt, and disappears out into the yard.

When it starts, Martin Gower insists on helping to bring the animals up the field, although Roxanne tries to persuade him otherwise.

'You'll only make a mess of yourself. No need to put yourself through all that. Let them do their job.'

'They're my animals,' he says. 'My responsibility what happens to them.'

'I'll help,' Liam says, leaning through the kitchen door on his way upstairs.

'You'll do no such bloody thing,' Roxanne hisses.

'He's man enough now,' Martin says calmly. 'If he wants to.'

'I'm his mother. I'll say when he's a man and it isn't now.'

'I'm not going to sit in the house while it's happening.'

'You'll do what you're told.' Roxanne spins round to face her son.

'Let him help. It's the best thing. Got to learn to deal with all things on a farm, death included. That's just the way of it.'

'This isn't death, Martin. It's the whole bleddy farm. You want him to watch that all be taken?' Roxanne cries then, ugly sobbing, wiping down her cheeks with the back of her hand. 'You selfish bastard.' The men in the room – because they are now, both of them, men – look away, fidget with their hands a little, picking the dirt under their nails. Martin Gower mutters his wife's name quietly under his breath, pleading something, although the request never quite falls out straight and they exchange a cold stare.

'Well, I want to help,' Liam says, unfolding his arms and helping himself to a slice of toast from the table.

Roxanne turns away towards the hob and takes a boiling pan off the heat, using a slotted spoon to remove the eggs, the steam condensing on their shells like a second skin. 'You don't know what you want,' she says softly, tipping the eggs into a bowl in the centre of the table, before leaving the room. It is important, she thinks, to have the last word, even if it means nothing at all.

***

The following day they begin burning livestock on the Gower farm. The parish newsletter announces the time and date of the fires on its back page beneath the obituaries, although it's clear from the sound what is happening. They build the pyres on the top field, the bodies of the animals partially obscured by an outbuilding. Six hundred Holstein Friesians. On the road that leads up towards the farm, the gate is drawn across and men in white coveralls are seen on the bridleway, moving the last of the cattle from the Lewis and Trewin farms up the track and spraying down their vehicle tyres with bleach.

The smoke begins in the evening. Isaac Kessell leaves his bedroom blind open and presses his forehead against the windowpane.

'Jonah's dad is taking him up to watch from the field,' he tells his mum, eyes fixed on the road outside. 'Everybody'll be there.'

'It's a school night,' Ruth says, rubbing her thumb over a grease stain on her son's blue football shirt. 'Why d'you want to go watch that anyway?'

Isaac wriggles his shoulders out from her grasp. 'Jonah said, last year, Martin Gower put a fridge in the bonfire on the hill and when it caught light it exploded. That's why he's got that funny scar on his eyebrow. It got all singed off with the sparks.'

Ruth presses her lips together, trying not to smile.

'Well, it's cows they've got on those fires, not fridges.'

'I know that.' Isaac rolls his eyes.

There's a small moon-shaped night light in the corner of the room, which Ruth switches on. It casts a faint yellow glow across the carpet. Isaac can't sleep without it, even though he's nine. Ruth has tried removing it and stowing it in a drawer in the kitchen, but he finds and puts it back every time. She frowns as she watches him climb into the bed, his feet, pale as minnows, slipping out from beneath the covers.

'Do you think he's too sensitive, the way he is?' she'd asked her mum the previous day as they took Isaac for a walk down through the woods where the crocus bulbs were coming through. Isaac had been showing them how to spot vole holes in the dry-stone walling that ran along the edge of the path, running his fingers through the tussock grass and revealing opening after opening, each one dark brown, damp, and as delicate as an egg.

'He'll toughen up,' her mum had replied. 'And then you'll wish he hadn't – I remember when your brother asked for a Swiss Army knife for Christmas, I near on cried.'

Isaac's small body softens as he drifts to sleep, knees tucked to his chest, and Ruth sighs. She walks downstairs, runs the water hot to soak the chicken pan and opens the back door. The daylight has stretched a half-hour thinner than the previous evening and the air is murky and rust-coloured, illuminating the quiet farm and smog gathering on the hill.

Later, Liam drives around the fields with his father. They don't talk. They have never been good at that sort of thing. Martin Gower lets his son take the wheel as they loop to the south fields, their backs to the pyres at the top of the hill. Once, when Liam was small, he took his son around this very route. 'One day, this'll be yours, eh now? What about that?' he'd said aloud, one broad palm clasping Liam's tiny chest to his own.

Now, he leaves Liam to drive the rest of the route alone, checking for any calves that are left, that have managed to squeeze past the old fence posts and down to the river. Martin stands and watches his son, one hand on the wheel, the other hanging languidly at his hip, as the tractor bounces up the curl of the hill and out of sight.

The weather over the weekend is damp and changeable, and the fires have to be reset several times as new banks of cloud roll over the hills. It's the fine sort of rain, the kind that hangs threadlike, suspended rather than settling, and it can't clear the smoke from the air. The smell of the burning animals lingers, a noose around the B-road that leads down into the village.

In the evening, on the television, they show footage of the fires and Ruth lets Isaac stay up to watch. He's wearing Batman pyjamas and the elastic around the cuffs is thin and loose from where his limbs have grown too quickly. When the camera pans out to show the pyres at the top of the hill behind their house, Isaac leans forward on his knees and points out the navy hoodies and trainers of his school friends at the edge of the frame.

'If you'd let me go, I'd have been on telly too,' he says. 'Then Auntie Sue could have watched.'

Ruth mutes the broadcaster, who is repeating the same well-worn statistics about infection rates that they've been hearing for weeks. She accepts an orange segment from her son and they watch the screen as a blue lorry with an open storage bed empties carcasses onto the grass, their thick bodies crumpling into one another like paint squeezed from a tube. Martin Gower is standing in the foreground, behind the correspondent with his clean wax jacket. His face is gaunt, the burst capillaries on his cheekbones bright under the camera lights. Isaac drops the orange peel onto the coffee table and climbs onto the sofa, sliding his head under the crook of Ruth's arm.

'Will they get more animals now, new ones?' he asks.

'I expect so, yeah. They'll have to, else it won't be a farm, not really.'

Isaac screws his face into a knot. 'How do they kill them?' he asks.

'The vet shoots them in the head – that's what's kindest.'

He hugs her then and Ruth wonders if this is too much detail for a nine-year-old.

Ten days after the ashes are buried, the quarantines on the farms are lifted and one by one the MAFF vans leave the village, but the acrid smell of the fires lingers. Liam, James and Moira are seen at the White Lion. The barman, George, knows their parents, their farms. He serves them halves of pale ale, which they take to the corner and drink quickly, in silence. A small group sets up the pool table in the back of the pub and the gentle click of cues echoes across the bar.

Moira unrolls a packet of gum on the table.

'Dad heard from Harry Pope that they think it was some cows up at Holsworthy Market that brought it down this way.' She flicks her gaze between the boys' faces, then shrugs and slips a piece of gum between her teeth. 'I don't know, you know, but that's what people are saying.'

James picks the edges of a beer mat. 'Your dad buys from Holsworthy, doesn't he, Liam?'

Liam spits into his empty glass. 'Whole bloody county goes there, dickhead.'

'I'm just saying . . .' James shrugs.

It's Liam who swings first. Something smashes, cracks, and people turn expecting broken glass and the sticky residue of spirits. The boys are not really fighters but they make a good go of it. They throw their bodies at one another and push their fists and teeth into the skin of shoulders and cheeks. Moira flattens her back against the panelled wall of the alcove and the boys slam one another onto the dirty carpet in front of the bar. The pool cues at the back of the pub are leant against the table, and George drags the boys out into the street, one under each arm.

'That'll do,' he says, wiping his palms against his thighs and picking up the bottles that have been left on the doorstep by the early-evening drinkers. 'I think we've seen enough of all that. Piss off before I ring your dad, Liam.'

The boys spit on the tarmac and walk off. Whatever has been said in those punches feels beyond repair.

That summer is cooler than the previous year but people still come down for the holidays. Ruth Kessell drives over to the rental cottages by the bay in early July and goes around opening the upstairs windows. She bleaches the sinks and the showers and lays out fresh towels in the bedrooms. The bookings on the website are full until September. People seem to have forgotten about the images of vets in paper coveralls patrolling the countryside. Good, Ruth thinks, the sooner the better.

A family from York arrive midweek and park up on the verge. Ruth recognises them. They come most years at the same time, like clockwork. A mother, a father, two young children, a boy and a girl.

'Your husband took them to feed the calves up at the farm last time we were here. They loved that,' the mother tells Ruth animatedly when she drops round the following week to replace a bulb in the kitchen. 'Is he around?' she asks.

'Nah, not any more.'

'Sometimes they're more trouble than they're worth.' The woman laughs lightly and touches her hand to her mouth. Behind her, the man is teaching his daughter how to shuffle a pack of cards. Ruth smiles and asks if they have enough loo roll in the bathrooms.

'We saw the news, you know . . .' The man is standing now, one hand around his wife's shoulders, thumb to her collarbone. 'About the farms,' he continues, 'but we didn't know if it was here . . . whether they would have had to . . .'

Ruth nods and the woman frowns, chewing her lip. 'Oh that's awful, just horrible to think about.'

'Yeah.' There is a small silence. Ruth wipes her hands on her jeans. 'That's all done for you now so I'll be off.'

'Oh right, thanks, that's great.' The woman slips a hand into her pocket and pulls out a fiver.

'You're all right.' Ruth shakes her head. 'It's just a bulb.'

'No please, you went to all that trouble.'

Ruth's cheeks feel hot but she pockets the note and slips out onto the road. She spots Liam Gower in the village-hall car park at the base of the hill. His bike is leant against the low wall and he is rolling a cigarette with his back to the sea.

'You all right?' she calls.

He nods.

'Need a lift home? You can chuck the bike in the back if you want.'

'Nah, I'm grand.' He gives her a half smile and cups his hand around the lighter, chewing smoke into the air. Moira Lewis comes out from behind the hall itself and shifts her eyes about from Liam to Ruth.

'All right, Mrs Kessell,' she says, biting her nail. 'How's Isaac?'

'He's good, thanks for asking. You lot off for summer now?'

'Something like that, yeah.'

'How's your folks holding up?'

Ruth has seen Martin Gower round and about. He looks

old now, and worried. She knows money is tight. Compensation is meant to be coming but there are still infected sites up around the Welsh border, Yorkshire, Dartmoor. Everything has ground to a standstill.

The two of them shrug. 'You know,' they say. 'It's all . . .' and they tail off.

'Yeah,' Ruth says, nodding. 'Been a bit like that.'

On the farm, Roxanne Gower wakes up next to her husband for the first time in years. The air is hot in the small room and she moves the covers from her legs, aware of the damp warmth that has greased itself around her ankles and toes. She lies there as the sun creeps across the duvet, scattering fragments of warm summer light along the opposite wall.

Martin is awake too. Roxanne can feel the slackness of his breathing against her arm, his spine turned towards her. She pretends to fall asleep again, and when she opens her eyes he is gone. The back door scuffs. She hears his footsteps on the gravel drive and she exhales. Her children are waking up. The toaster pops. The smell of lemon shower gel and steam from the bathroom seeps across the landing; the window has been left shut again even though she tells them every day it will rot the woodwork. Her younger boys are arguing over the television remote. She closes her eyes and tries to remember what it was like before she was married but it is so long ago now that the memories are dull, their surface scummed over by age and tax bills.

The day of the rescheduled school exams is warm, too warm, and the teaching assistant, Cathi, opens the row of windows in the eaves of the school hall to let in a small breeze. Only Moira and James turn up. Moira lingers in the entranceway, wrapping a hair elastic around her wrist and snapping it against her skin, but eventually she slides into her seat. Cathi keeps the door open a few minutes longer than she should. She is hoping Liam will saunter in, trainer laces trailing along the corridor, but he doesn't.

'Miss, it's nine, can we turn these over now?' James chews the end of his pen and tries to read the questions through the back of the paper. Someone has written the sine formula in blue biro on the desk he is sitting at and he holds his finger over it, feeling the little ridges in the wood.

Cathi exhales, frowns, shuts the door. 'Let's go, then. Forty minutes, you know the drill.' She walks back towards the stage, pausing to pick up the spare answer paper from the desk near the front.

A group of walkers come to stay at the holiday lets over the bank holiday weekend. The footpaths around the village have been reopened but they are quieter than usual, even on the popular routes. James Trewin finds two of them out by the lower fields, climbing over a stile that used to lead around the peninsula to the smaller cove, a half-mile along the cliffs.

'Have you dipped those?' He nods to their boots, caked in river mud and gravel dust.

They smile and rub the insect bites on their lower arms. 'Sorry, mate. We didn't know.'

There is a bucket of bleach and water, along with a brush, stacked against the metal livestock gate. James sucks in his cheeks and a muscle in his jaw flexes.

'There's a sign up,' he says. 'Might be right of way, but don't be a prick about it.'

The taller of the two men holds his hands up. 'Honest mistake,' he calls. 'You have a good day.' He turns back towards the stile and James shakes his head. 'Wanker,' he mutters and clicks his tongue.

The summer turns over and the schools go back. The roads are quieter. There are crab apples on the ground by the wall of the church, their skins wrinkled and reddy-brown.

Liam Gower is seen up at the old bird-watching hut with Moira Lewis. Nobody says anything to their parents. Some things are best kept quiet – this is the general consensus.

The post office closes down. A fundraiser is held to keep a volunteer there one day a week – cake sales, a tombola, guess the name of the bear – but it turns up short and they have to shut anyway.

Ruth drives down to the holiday lets and strips the beds, airing the mattresses and wiping down the skirting boards. There are two bookings for October, one for New Year's – plenty of time to prepare.

Just before the first cold spell begins, Martin Gower's body is found slung up in the copse of trees near the church. Roxanne senses something is wrong from the hum of the village when she wakes. The earth outside is quiet. Downstairs the boiler moans and she hears the taps going in the kitchen. The bedroom window is open a crack and the siren whistles up the lane, quietens, parks, pauses. She rolls over and slides her feet out to fill the space on the far side of the bed, waiting for the knock at the door.

TODAY, AT THE DUMP, THE WORLD IS IN THE BIN

ANDREA MASON

TODAY, AT THE DUMP, the world is in the bin: a classroom globe, tossed into TV & MONITORS, sits on its head, a round peg in a square crate wanting the hard angles of a TV or a monitor. She has tasked herself with visiting her local waste facility once a week for a year. She wants to know about waste. She needs to know the nature of it, and the volume of it, like a storm chaser terrified of storms. She will examine the discarded goods with a dispassionate eye, in the way that a hospital consultant matter-of-factly dispenses with the person in front of them, writing a follow up letter which cites that 'this pleasant woman' has a bone density, for instance, that implies a fragility that the woman does not recognise.

Yesterday she watched a YouTube clip of Slovenian philosopher Slavoj Žižek. A dramatic soundtrack accompanied the camera as it panned down from a shot of industrial fluorescent strips to a heap of mixed waste: plastic bags and clothing. *This where we should start feeling at home. We are used to our waste disappearing, like shit*, he said. *In fact, waste is our nature and we should love it. Love is not idealisation. True ecologist loves all this.* He gestured to a heap of plastic bottles as the camera panned around to reveal that he too was standing in a London waste facility.

George, a site worker, waves cheerily at her as she notates the TVs and monitors: BUSH, DELL, DAEWOO, SHARP, GOODMANS, JVC, SAMSUNG. An Apple iMac has dints on its back, either side of where the stand is attached.

In *Viet-Flakes*, artist Carolee Schneemann's film-montage, composed of Vietnam atrocity images, plays across fourteen old-school, boxy TVs, which hang from the gallery ceiling; cables drape down like tendrils and spool on the floor around fourteen DVD players.

The world in TVs.

TODAY, AT THE DUMP, a forest: pine prunings cover the concrete floor. The green against the grey reminds her of a sweatshirt she bought at H&M, attracted by a green forest transfer which contrasted pleasingly with the grey of the sweatshirt. Back home, she found the sweatshirt too thick. She felt heavy. She improvised by rolling up the sleeves each time she wore it. Then, she chopped off the waistband and cuffs and slashed the neck, *Fame*-style. It was ruined: unreturnable, unfit for the charity shop, nonrecyclable. She stuffed it into a binbag alongside other similarly neutered items and sent it off to landfill.

In *Make a Salad*, artist Alison Knowles stands at a table, knife in hand, on the bridge of the Turbine Hall at Tate Modern, and chops cucumbers, radishes and tomatoes to the accompaniment of a live orchestra. On a count, she throws the salad onto a giant green tarpaulin which covers the concrete floor, chucks over the dressing and descends into the hall where she forks it into colanders from which the salad is served. *Every time you eat a salad*, Knowles says, you are *performing the piece*.

TODAY, AT THE DUMP, a headless horse: a hand-carved decorative rocking horse. As she walks along to get a better view she sees that the head has been sawn off. *Spooky*, Denise says when she tells her later. *Last week we had a dead cat and a dead dog.* Denise is her portal into the dump. She writes her name into Denise's open book, and Denise gifts her a hi-vis vest and a red hard hat. Entry is via an open hangar. She's always careful to look left for exiting traffic (she has watched the Health and Safety video and signed off her compliance), and takes the pathway alongside a low aluminium barrier, which leads to a small flight of metal steps. Up here, a ribcage-height concrete wall is all there is between her and PLASTERBOARD, METALS, HARDCORE

& RUBBLE, GARDEN WASTE, WOOD & TIMBER, HOUSEHOLD WASTE, CARDBOARD. She looks over this wall as one might look over a cliff edge, to see what's been dashed against the rocks. PLASTERBOARD and METALS sit side by side in large containers. The other categories are partitioned by concrete walls, which taper down to the ground floor, down there, to the land of JCB crushers and diggers, and men with long-handled brooms.

Two diggers, travelling in opposite directions, draw alongside each other. The nearest driver shouts across to the other driver, who wears ear protectors. George, wearing scarf and woollen hat – *to keep the flies off he says* – shouts to this driver.

She walks back along to METALS. George follows her, wheeling a red trolley full of bikes and scooters. The JCB driver is using the digger arm to bash down the metals, making room for these new bikes and scooters. A trolley catches in the teeth of the digger. The digger arm bashes repeatedly against the side of the container in an effort to dislodge the trolley, like a horse kicking its belly to dislodge a fly. George flings his arms up and down. The driver presses the trolley against the inside edge of the container, and jerks the digger arm upwards. The trolley falls off, and George raises his arms in celebration.

TODAY, AT THE DUMP, in FREESTANDING APPLI-ANCES, a Hoover Link washing machine stands alongside a Flymo EasiMow stands alongside an electronic clothes dryer stands alongside an oven stands alongside a Zanussi Electrolux. The appliances stand on the ground floor, where she can walk around them.

She has tried running, to tamp the bones, but then her right knee throbs.

In *In the Kitchen (Fridge)*, artist Helen Chadwick stands coffined inside a tall fridge freezer, its interior upholstered with white PVC. Chadwick's body is just visible through a layer of PVC, the dark upside-down triangle of her pubic mound, the shape of her pink body. Her head, uncovered, pokes above the top shelf.

The lightbulb is on.

In SMALL APPLIANCES: a black boombox, a cassette deck, a kettle, a transistor radio, a Portable Powerfoot, two coffee-makers, a fan heater, a toaster, a car tyre, seven bicycle tyres.

The tyres are interlopers.

Alongside SMALL APPLIANCES, a large red wire crate contains CAR BATTERIES, inside which a brown dog finger-puppet is categorically misplaced.

In *Orange Lion,* by Paul McCarthy, a dirty toy lion sits sad-eyed, legs out in front, its tail poking out – 'penis-like', Max Glauner tells us in *Frieze* magazine – between its legs, its left paw 'about to grab hold'.

She has tried hopping, less impactful on her knees: fifty hops on each leg, ten on the spot, ten forwards, ten backwards, ten sideways, outwards and in. One day, she entered the park and started hopping, thinking she was alone. Ten hops in she heard a shout. Oi. Oi. A man sat on the low stone bench secluded by a yew hedge. She stared at him as she walked on. *You look like someone from a mental hospital though don't you, don't you.* He gestured at her with a can of lager.

In *Babel*, artist Cildo Meireles has stacked radios in a spheri-cal tower, progressing through radios of the ages: the oldest styles – big, wooden, boxy, form three base layers. Smaller boxy shapes in metal and black plastic and even smaller silver-coloured plastic boxes with rounded edges form a series of concentric rings, some of which sit proud, giving the look of a thing with moving parts, like a camera lens. Tuned in to different frequencies, the radios emit a cacophony of sound, asking her to listen.

TODAY, AT THE DUMP, in HARDCORE & RUBBLE, a handheld showerhead covered in dust pokes out from a broken-up concrete floor heaped against the retaining wall. Breezeblocks sit heavily on top of the rubble. It is just six weeks since the recent earthquake in Turkey and Syria. For some twelve days she has woken daily to images of rubble and dust-strewn people and things, this being the timespan during which one might expect to recover people alive from the rubble. After this, the story disappeared from the news.

In *Regular/Fragile* by artist Liu Jianhua a repetitious facsimile of everyday objects: shoes, toys, hot water bottles, hammers, bags, mobile phones, cast in shiny white porcelain, cascade down the gallery walls; made in response, the gallery info says, to a series of aviation disasters that happened in China when the artist was going through a hard time.

In Turkey and Syria, during recovery efforts, a hand was found in the rubble.

In *Cold Dark Matter: An Exploded View*, artist Cornelia Parker has exploded and reconstituted a garden shed: shards of wood, wheelbarrow wheels, tattered wellington boots, and bent bicycle frames are suspended by wires from the gallery ceiling, lit by a single bulb which creates shadow play.

In Turkey and Syria, during recovery efforts, a foot was found in the rubble.

LATER, AT HOME, in a dream, a woman is on a hospital trolley. She has three toad-like eyes. Her skin is warty. The woman stares at her. Beseeches. She is beseeching. She is something. The nurse talks as she inserts her hand into the woman's left eye socket and rummages in the woman's face, in the way that we see vets' forearms shoving into cow's uteruses. Poor cow. Like in *Cow* by Andrea Arnold. Poor bloody cow.

TODAY, AT THE DUMP, in HOUSEHOLD WASTE, a copy of *The Tipping Point* by Malcolm Gladwell. The paperback book has a pale yellow band, top and bottom on its front cover; pale and pissy, not unlike the colour of the stained patches of the mattress it sits atop. She presses her ribs against the cold dusty wall as she leans in to read the subtitle: *How Little Things Can Make a Big Difference*, just as a man gently floats pieces of bubble wrap and polystyrene packaging over the cubicle wall, which obscure the book's title. To her left, at WOOD & TIMBER, a woman throws in pieces of a cupboard with abandon. With release. A satisfactory thwuck, thwack, crack, as each item meets the criss-cross pile of Victorian pine doors, wooden pallets and broken-up particleboard kitchen cabinets.

In *Der Lauf der Dinge* artists Fischli and Weiss harness the energy of never-ending collapse: tyres and wood and tables and bags of rubbish spin and turn and flip and fall, substances ignite and explode, and drip and drop, chemical reactions cause explosions and foamings and eruptions, expansions and contractions; dust flies, fluids flow, chairs tip, tyres roll, carpets unfurl, planks topple, wheeled contraptions power along tracks, barrels barrel, sparks fly, oil burns. At midpoint, a weighted object on a string ignites and flies around a central pole like a comet circling a Swingball; clogs trundle, air gusts, a cardboard box floats. And, fin, a volcano of white steam explodes out of a bucket.

LATER, AT HOME, she opens up her laptop. The screen

moves, rebooting the episode of BBC's *Sort Your Life Out*, a reality TV programme where families clear out their houses of all their possessions in order to radically declutter, which she was watching before she fell asleep. It's the part where the family come to see their stuff laid out on the floor of a mega warehouse, organised by category and colour, like a Tony Cragg sculpture. This family watch now in wonder as the shutter goes up to reveal 111 bottles of nail varnish, 80 packets of out-of-date medicine, 203 hair accessories and 1,000 books. She imagines every person, everywhere, emptying out everything from their homes, turning the streets and roads the world over into one gigantic categorised and colour-coded artwork. In the programme the families displace the problem of what to do with usable but unwanted items by taking them to charity shops, creating an endless feedback loop of donate, rebuy, lay out, donate, rebuy, lay out, donate, rebuy, lay out: a merry-go-round of buying and giving and buying and giving and buying and giving of goods, that we must love.

Tapestry

AISHA PHOENIX

Loom woke on the morning of her fourteenth birthday feeling exactly the same as she had the day before. She had convinced herself that The Change would come. Like so many girls before her, she would be stuffed full of tiny sweet cakes and juicy sugar fruit, and given glasses of wild-grass juice to drink. She would be carried down to the Tapestry on the donkey that belonged to Mother Yemi, the leader of the village women, and her destiny would be decided. She was born to be a storyteller. Soon everyone would know that was what she was.

She rose early and went outside the small, tin-roof wooden cabin she shared with her mother to watch the firebirds drink nectar from the crimson flowers of the flame tree.

'Hear me and I shall tell it,' Loom said, and she began rehearsing her story of how the firebirds came to the island. She waved her arms, whispered and shouted to give life to her words. When she became a storyteller, she would be paid handsomely to tell such stories. There would be invitations to mark special occasions, and sponsorship from the wealthiest families on the island.

By the time she set off down Nest Hill, she was already running late for school. Her path was flanked by nest trees with thick, interweaving roots until she arrived at the wooden cabins where her friends, Tress and Taya, lived with their mothers. Loom abandoned the path and half ran, half slid down the side of the hill through lizard ferns that reached up to her waist. She rejoined the path where the ground levelled out, catching up with Tress and Taya.

To her right was Little Boat Harbour and the sea that stretched to the horizon. Braid, her mother, would be out catching ocean seed. As she and her friends made their way up the hill to their dusty white school with its rusty tin roof, she told them the story of the firebirds, which made their eyes widen with wonder.

While Mister Thomas wrote equations on the board, she scrawled stories in her exercise book, only turning to maths when he began prowling between the rows of desks.

When Loom returned home, Braid showed her the silverfin she'd saved for her from the day's catch. That was the only thing that made the day different from any other. After supper they sat together on the step under a lantern and her mother helped her with her maths. Loom hated equations, but they delighted her mother more than words.

Three weeks later The Change came – sticky brown, then red. It was her fallow day, the day she tended the earth seed, the hairy brown-skinned milk fruit and the small knobbly moon potatoes they cultivated on the patch of land behind their home. Usually, when she finished, she would go down to Black Sand to tell Tress and Taya stories and play in the waves. Today she ran barefoot down to Little Boat and stood in the shadow of the gnarled knowledge tree, waiting for Braid to return with the catch. She helped the women haul in the shimmering ocean seed, and watched as her mother calculated in her head how many fish to give to each of the women, dividing the catch according to the size of their family and the number of days they had each worked. The rest would be sold in the market and the profits shared according to Braid's formula.

When her mother had finished, Loom leaned in close and said, 'The Change has come.'

Her mother pocketed the knife she was holding, wiped her hands on her overalls, and gave Loom a hug. Then she took off her headscarf, releasing her colourful yarn-woven plaits, and tied the heavy cloth over her daughter's afro. 'It's come,' she said to the other women, with a slight nod of her head.

The women clacked their wellies together in a show of respect, and as Loom passed by, they touched her headscarf and offered blessings. Braid held her hand, which she hadn't done for years, and led her back up the hill to their home. For once, Loom sat while Braid fetched buckets of water to fill the bath, and it was Braid who soaped and washed her, her rough hands gentle against Loom's skin. Then Loom knelt over the bath as Braid poured buckets of water over her head, then massaged her scalp and kept massaging it, as though to wake some sleeping thing inside her head.

'Ma,' Loom said.

Braid fetched lengths of cloth to wrap Loom's hair and body. The fabric was orange and green and made of the heavy material she only brought out on special occasions. She wrapped Loom into it so tightly she could barely breathe.

'Pick the flame tree flowers,' Braid said.

Loom picked the crimson bells she was normally forbidden to touch and laid them on the white cloth her mother had placed on the rock outside the cabin.

They sat on the step until they heard the procession and spotted Mother Yemi, resplendent in gold, in the cart pulled by her donkey, followed by women in bright headscarves and girls with neat afros carrying treats.

'For we wel-come a daughter,' Mother Yemi sang.

'For we wel-come a daughter,' the mothers and girls sang back.

'Her new life is before her,' Mother Yemi sang.

'Her new life is before her,' they chorused.

Loom and Braid stood up.

'Give a flower to each of the mothers,' Braid said. 'If there's any left over, give them to the girls.'

Loom picked up a flower.

'Mother Yemi first,' Braid said.

There were two flowers left when the mothers all had theirs. Loom gave one to Tress and the other to Taya.

As they drank wild-grass juice and shared Loom's sweet cakes and sugar fruit, Tress whispered, 'You feel different?' She looked longingly at Loom's headscarf.

Loom touched her tummy, but shook her head.

'You'll tell us what happens . . . in the Tapestry?' Taya spoke so quietly Loom had to lean in to hear her.

'You know I would if I could,' Loom said.

Revealing what happened in the Tapestry was said to ruin a woman's destiny. Loom wasn't about to risk that, not even for her best friends.

Mother Yemi approached and placed a hand on Loom's shoulder. 'It's time.'

Loom walked towards the donkey – the same one her mother had ridden eighteen years ago – and wondered how its tired legs would carry both her and Mother Yemi.

Many arms lifted her onto the animal, seating her sideways. Braid told her where to put her feet so they didn't get caught in the wooden shaft at the donkey's side. She kissed Loom's hands, turned, and started walking back to the hut.

Loom's eyes filled with tears.

The bony creature picked its way down the steep hill, followed by the procession of women. They turned right along the path that led to Little Boat. Instead of going towards the harbour, they took the incline that led to the Tapestry, the tallest building on the island, painted yellow like the sun. The women got Loom down and helped Mother Yemi out of the cart, then

Loom followed Mother Yemi to the ornate door beyond which her destiny would be decided.

'For we wel-come a daughter,' Mother Yemi sang.

The Tapestry door opened and two barefoot women stood in the doorway. 'For we wel-come a daughter,' they sang back.

'Her new life is before her,' Mother Yemi sang.

'Her new life is before her,' they echoed.

'Faith, Earnest.' Mother Yemi nodded at the two women.

They bowed, put their arms around Loom and led her into the building.

She followed them through a long water trough into a room like nothing she had seen before. The walls, ceiling and floor were covered in bright, intricate tapestries that seemed to be giving off light. Around the room, there were men working at looms. In the centre was a chair that looked like a low-backed throne and a carving that resembled a small tree.

'Sit,' said Faith, the smaller woman, pushing Loom into the chair.

'For we wel-come a daughter . . .' the women sang.

A door at the back of the Tapestry opened and a short man with grey hair and a round stomach walked in. This had to be Pregnant Man. Loom and the other girls had heard about him. 'Her new life is before her,' he said in a flat voice.

Loom sat in the chair. The man cast his eyes over the tapestries. He raised a hand abruptly and Faith handed him a stick with a metal hook. He jabbed it into the bright weaving in front of him. Faith rushed forward, took the stick and with some twisting and sharp yanks she pulled out strands of enchanted yarn from the wall. She untangled them from the stick then handed it to Earnest.

Pregnant Man looked down and grunted. Faith rushed to him with the stick. He thrust it into part of the tapestry on the floor and left her to pull the yarn out. He continued to do this for what felt like hours, with Faith retrieving the yarn, then handing it to Earnest, who hung it on different branches of the sculpted tree.

Then, without a word, the man walked towards the wall, reached into the tapestry, opened a door, and disappeared. The men who had been silently working at the looms got up and followed him through the door.

'We'll make it special for you,' Earnest said, unwrapping Loom's hair. She put her fingers into Loom's curls and pulled so hard that Loom's eyes started to water.

Loom watched the women pick up strands of yarn, whisper to each other and return them to the tree. Whatever was in the yarn, she knew, would indicate her destiny. The Pregnant Man had decided it. Faith turned Loom's head abruptly and the hair on her temples tightened painfully as the two women plaited scratchy lengths of yarn into it.

'She'll marry a weaver,' Earnest whispered.

'Mmm . . . They'll have two children . . . No, three,' Faith said.

'She a fisherwoman?' Earnest asked.

For a moment they let go of her head and rustled about behind her.

'No. She not like she mother.'

'She's a farmer,' Faith said.

Loom closed her eyes. A farmer – with three children, married to a weaver, who would spend his weeks in the Tapestry, which she would never be allowed to set foot in again. A weaver like her father, whom she had hardly seen before he passed. She wanted to rip the plaits from her head and run.

Tears welled in her eyes.

***

Faith and Earnest worked on her head through the night. At dawn, they lit yellow candles, using the melted wax to seal the bottom of Loom's plaits.

'We've wel-comed—' Faith and Earnest began, but before they could say 'a daughter', Pregnant Man appeared, carrying an engraved silver bottle.

'Be blessed,' he said, pouring oil from the bottle into his palm and sprinkling it on Loom's head.

He retreated. Faith and Earnest wrapped Loom's hair in her headscarf and tied it tightly to hold the weight of the plaits on her aching head. Then they kissed her on the cheeks and led her back to the entrance.

The light outside surged at her. She closed her eyes and took a step back, but Faith pushed her forward and a hand took hers. She knew it was her mother's. They walked together in silence along the dusty path that led to Nest Hill. Loom kept her eyes on the earth, a tightness like tangled roots in the pit of her stomach. How was she going to tell Braid that Pregnant Man had decided she was no more than a farmer?

They took the hill slowly. It seemed steeper somehow. She felt the ground undulating beneath her feet, and Braid squeezed her hand, as if to say, 'It's OK.'

When they got to their hut, Loom sat on the step while Braid unwrapped the fabric that held in her hair.

'Ah!' Braid said, holding up some plaits. 'No boats?'

Loom shook her head.

'Probably for the best. The salt air ages the skin.' Braid ran a hand across her face. 'And you're going to marry a weaver, like your mother and grandmother before you.'

Her mother walked into the hut and didn't come out for a while. Loom wound a couple of plaits around each index finger until Braid emerged, red-eyed.

'At least if destiny puts you with a so-and-so, you won't have to spend much time together,' Braid said.

She examined Loom's plaits again. Eventually she said, 'So what are you?'

'A farmer,' Loom said quietly.

'A farmer?' Braid shouted. 'You, a farmer? What farmer do you know who lives and breathes stories?'

Loom watched her mother's chest rise and fall and knew to remain silent.

'Did they mention a hidden destiny?' Braid said softly.

'What's that?' Loom said.

'Every couple of generations a woman is given a vocation, with a hidden destiny. You might be a farmer for a while, but then discover that you are meant to tell stories.'

Loom shook her head. 'They didn't mention that.'

Braid sat down on the step and covered her face with her hands. Loom put her arms around her mother. 'It's OK. I'll tell tales to the milk fruit to help them grow.'

The next day, after Braid had gone down to Little Boat, Loom made her way to school.

'Your presence is no longer required,' Mister Thomas said.

'But I still want to learn.'

'You'll learn plenty with the women in the fields.'

Loom stood there looking at him.

'Go on before Mrs Cane canes you.' He chuckled to himself and dismissed her with a wave of his arm.

Her legs were heavy as she climbed further up the hill to the fields.

Her task was to pull out the chokeweed strangling the crops.

It was exhausting, but as she got into the rhythm, bending, twisting and pulling, she told stories about the farmers of old to help pass the time. The women listened and laughed and in return they helped her pull up chokeweed when Mrs Cane wasn't looking. At dusk, Loom made her way home to her cabin where her mother waited.

Braid took her in her arms and massaged her shoulders. 'You get on good?'

Loom raised her shoulders, then let them drop.

'I grilled silver,' Braid said.

Loom smiled and sat on the step to eat her favourite fish with boiled dumplings, milk fruit and moon potatoes.

'I wish Pregnant Man had woven a different future for you.'

Loom nodded and closed her eyes. Braid put down her plate and wiped Loom's wet cheeks with her hands.

This new rhythm in her life meant getting up early, going to tend the fields, coming home to eat with her mother, and going to bed. She missed Tress and Taya and thought about what they were learning at school while she worked the land. Her favourite time of the week was first light on Sunday before her mother got up. She would leave the cabin quietly, her hair unwrapped, and meet Tress and Taya. Then they would run down to Black Sand where Loom told them tales about sea creatures, then watched them play in the waves.

'Why don't you swim any more?' Taya asked.

Loom pointed to her bright plaits with their yellow-wax tips.

'Well I hope The Change never comes,' Taya said.

'Hush, Taya,' Tress said. 'Do you want to remain a girl for ever?'

***

243

The rhythm of Loom's life stayed the same until a month after she turned fifteen. She got back from the fields and found Braid leaning against the cabin, almost doubled over, coughing. She rushed to her mother and massaged her back, then fetched the jug and poured her a cup of water.

Braid coughed some more and then took a sip.

'Has it passed?' Loom said.

Braid nodded and Loom tucked her into the bed they shared.

The next day, when she came home her mother was already in bed.

The blood came a few weeks later. Braid tried not to let Loom see the red on the cloth she put to her mouth when she coughed.

Loom began getting up earlier to help her mother get ready for work and insisted on walking her down to the harbour.

A few weeks later she came home from the fields and Braid wasn't there. Loom went to the yard out back and called for her, but there was no answer. She raced to Little Boat.

A crowd of women huddled near the moored boats. Loom pushed her way through and saw Braid propped up on a colourful tapestry.

'It is as it was woven,' Mother Yemi said. 'No more fishing for her. She can't take the sea air. Help her up to her hut. Let her rest there.'

The women shooed Loom out of the way.

She rushed up the hill ahead of them to light the lantern and pull down the sheets for her mother.

'No need to fuss, I fine,' Braid said, when she was back in their cabin.

***

For a few weeks, the women passed by in the evening with food, then one by one they stopped coming. When Loom ran into them in the market they wouldn't meet her eyes.

Loom started working seven days in the fields instead of five, but it still wasn't enough to provide for the two of them. Every now and then Tress would come by with a little parcel of food, but Loom knew her family couldn't spare it, so she would send it away. She kept asking herself why she had to be a farmer when her talent was for cultivating words. And why was her mother a fisherwoman when she knew numbers better than anyone?

If she were a storyteller, she could earn enough for them both. Just a couple of engagements a month would pay far more than she could ever earn toiling every day in the fields.

One evening, on her way back home, she bumped into Taya who was sweeping the ground outside her cabin. Taya put her arms around her and then gently felt her ribs. She shook her head. 'The Tapestry changed you.' She placed a hand on Loom's headscarf and felt the plaits beneath it. 'Shame you can't just take them out.'

If women undid the life stories woven into their hair, they died. Everyone knew about Spool, the woman from the other side of the island who undid her plaits and dropped down dead that very night.

But what would happen if Loom undid just *one*?

The next day after working the fields, she went to find Mother Yemi, who lived in the grand brick house at the top of Sunset Hill. Loom brought a flower from the flame tree by her cabin to bless the old woman. Mother Yemi sat alone on the porch, drinking from a tall glass of wild-grass juice and eating rarenuts.

Loom had never been this close to a brick house before, let alone a double-fronted one with two floors. There was a stone path in front that cut through an immaculate lawn, surrounded by sky bushes laden with velvet petals. It was all contained by a white picket fence with a large gate.

Loom called from the street.

When Mother Yemi beckoned, she opened the gate, closing it carefully behind her, then made her way up to the porch, where she bowed and handed Mother Yemi the flower. 'Can you help me?'

'That depends.' Mother Yemi sniffed the red petals. 'What kind of help are you seeking?'

'I need to know which bit of the weaving in my hair means I'm a farmer,' Loom said.

'Why do you come to me with such questions?'

Loom massaged Mother Yemi's shoulders as she'd seen her mother do.

'Not just anyone has that kind of learning,' Loom said. 'Few can read the weaving just so.' She craned her neck to see whether her words were having an effect on Mother Yemi. 'Am I correct in thinking you're the only woman on the island who knows how to read *all* the weaving?'

Mother Yemi straightened in her chair.

'I heard that you read weaving better than most men.' Loom saw the beginnings of a smile on Mother Yemi's round face. 'They say that you are an expert reader—'

'Flattery holds no sway with me,' Mother Yemi said.

Loom looked down at the floor, her hands resting on Mother Yemi's shoulders.

'Don't stop,' the old woman said.

She wasn't sure whether Mother Yemi meant don't stop the massage or the flattery, so she continued with both. 'I bet I'm correct in thinking you are the most expert reader on this island.'

'Fetch the looking glass from beside my bed,' Mother

Yemi said.

Loom dusted off her feet and hesitated at the door.

'There's no snake in there to bite you,' Mother Yemi said. 'Go.'

Loom ran in, the tiles cold beneath her feet. Ahead of her was a wide staircase with a gleaming wooden banister. Loom wasn't sure where Mother Yemi's bedroom was, so she opened one of the two doors on her left. It was a bright room four times the size of her cabin, with cream sofas and armchairs, and portraits of families dressed in finery on the walls. The second room was a study with a large desk and hundreds of books. On the other side of the hallway, there was a dining room with a long polished table. The fourth room turned out to be a kitchen with marble countertops. A thin woman in an apron was washing dishes under running water.

'Mother Yemi's room?' Loom said quickly.

The woman looked her up and down. 'Upstairs. First door on the right.'

She ran up the stairs and found the vast bedroom with a long balcony overlooking the sea. Behind the bed was a tapestry of the island with every cabin and house. Loom grabbed the mirror.

'Did you get lost?' Mother Yemi said, frowning. 'Sit and hold up the glass.'

She pulled Loom down in front of her and unwrapped her headscarf. 'You see these strands here?' She held up a plait that looked like a yellow flower emerging from a plant rooted in the mud. 'They mean you are a farmer. Look how the green weaves into the yellow, surrounded by brown in that pattern there.' Mother Yemi ran her hand down the length of the plait. 'You're not like your mother. You'll farm until the end of your days.'

Loom nodded slowly.

'It's a shame though,' Mother Yemi said. 'I heard about the stories you tell . . . But the weaving's the weaving and it says you're a farmer.'

'Perhaps I have a hidden destiny?' Loom said, barely audibly.

Mother Yemi searched through Loom's plaits, lifting and dropping a few at a time. After a while she said, 'No.'

'How come Pregnant Man gets to decide?' Loom asked.

'His name is Mister Yarn.' Mother Yemi looked at her for a moment with narrowed eyes. 'He has the sacred authority. It was passed down to him.'

'But why does he make it so Nest Hill women are only farmers or fisherwomen? Why can't we be storytellers or—'

'Because that's not what he sees in the tapestry.' Mother Yemi frowned. 'You're a farmer. The weaving says so.'

'What if I took that plait out? What if I changed it?' Loom said, glancing up at Mother Yemi.

'Then you would drop down dead. You understand? You would surely die. You've got no business messing with the weaving. No business at all.' Mother Yemi's voice had a sharpness to it that Loom had never heard before.

'But why do girls in some families get to become doctors and storytellers, while the rest of us—'

Mother Yemi struggled to her feet and waved towards Nest Hill. 'Go home. Your mother needs you.'

Loom bowed, turned on her heels and ran home.

Loom returned from the fields one evening with a bag of overripe milk fruit that had been given to her by Mrs Cane, who'd prodded her ribs and said she was scrawny. She cooked just enough for her mother. She had to make them last. She missed the days when she would come home to freshly grilled fish. Braid had worked harder than most other islanders and all she got in return was a little earth seed.

What if she just undid the *end* of the braid that made her a farmer? That wouldn't kill her, would it?

On a day when the dirt track scorched her feet, she arrived at the fields to find Mrs Cane standing under a tree fanning herself. As Mrs Cane mopped her brow, she started yelling, though not at anyone in particular. Then she saw Loom.

'I give her plenty milk fruit, but she's still skin and bone. How am I supposed to grow fine earth seed with this skeleton?'

She made Loom work harder than the others and when the women took their break under the shade of a tree, Mrs Cane found her more chokeweed to pull.

That night, while her mother slept, Loom went outside, lit the lantern and sat on the step. She took up her mirror and found the green plait, woven into yellow, surrounded by brown. Holding it in one hand, she fetched a knife and cut off the bottom of the plait, where it was fused together with candle wax. She checked herself. She did not feel any different. With tentative fingers she began to undo it. Once she'd loosened an inch or so, she checked her pulse – racing but fine; breathing, fast, but fine. She extinguished the lantern and went back to bed, but wouldn't let herself sleep in case she didn't wake again.

She rose late in the morning. She felt the same as she had the previous day. That night she went outside and sat on the step. She said a prayer, then began to undo more of the plait, her scalp aching as she pulled at the yarn. She kept undoing it until only soft black curls remained. She rubbed the freed hair between her fingers as she tried to slow her breathing.

When she went to bed, island stories about Spool dying after taking out her plaits circled in her mind. She tossed and turned, sweat dampening her nightgown until finally she succumbed to sleep. Late morning, she opened her eyes and started to giggle. If the enchanted yarn had made her a farmer, she was a farmer no more.

'Mother Yemi,' she called, as she entered the old woman's front garden, her hastily wrapped hair leaning to one side. 'Mother Yemi, am I a ghost?'

'I doubt it,' Mother Yemi said from her seat on the porch. 'I never did meet one so noisy.'

Loom went up to the old woman and whispered in her ear. 'I undid the weaving that says I am a farmer.'

'You did what! You're too young to die. Too young . . .'

'I'm not dead, Mother Yemi. I'm as alive as you.' She reached for Mother Yemi's hand and held it in her own.

'You're breathing now, but it's sure to kill you in the night.' Mother Yemi rocked in her chair and moaned.

'But I undid the weaving yesterday.'

Mother Yemi turned and frowned at Loom. 'Yesterday?'

Loom nodded.

Mother Yemi made her sit and examined her hair. Then she pinched Loom's nose closed, forcing her to breathe through her mouth.

'I want to be a storyteller,' Loom said.

'I saw Spool's body – stiff and cold,' Mother Yemi muttered to herself, as though she hadn't heard. 'They said she died because she tried to change her destiny. I thought it was the enchanted yarn.' She shook her head.

Finally, she stood up. 'Come back tomorrow afternoon,' she said.

When Loom reached the porch the next day, Mother Yemi handed her a plate of meaty crescent fish and a cup of wild-grass juice. 'Do you know who my husband is?' she said, without meeting Loom's eyes.

Loom shook her head.

'Mister Yarn.'

Loom's eyes widened.

'Eat,' Mother Yemi said.

Loom broke open a crescent fish, sucked it and pulled out the flesh with her teeth. It was delicious. Why had she never tried it before?

'I know how to get the enchanted yarn,' Mother Yemi said.

Loom stared at her.

'And I know how to weave hair.'

'You worked in the Tapestry?'

'Exactly so,' Mother Yemi said. 'How do you think I met my husband?'

Mother Yemi shuffled into her house and emerged with a box. She lifted the lid and revealed brightly coloured yarn on a bed of white satin. 'If you don't want to be a farmer, I can make it so. Sit!'

Mother Yemi began humming. Loom recognised the tune of 'We wel-come a daughter', only it sounded mournful. Gently, Mother Yemi began to plait the yarn into Loom's hair.

When she was finished, Mother Yemi rubbed her hands on Loom's skirts and said, 'I have given you a hidden destiny. You must never try to change your hair again.' She looked Loom straight in the eyes. 'Your life depends on it.'

'What have you made me?' Loom said.

'See this plait that is blue, woven into green and aqua?' Mother Yemi gave the plait to Loom so that she could examine it. 'It means your hidden destiny is to weave hair.'

Loom stared at Mother Yemi, then her eyes dropped down to the earth, cracked and dry beneath her bare feet.

An Account of the [War Heroines] of the First Independence War by [An Unnamed Soldier]

ISHA KARKI

An unnamed soldier's diary was recovered for the Great Independence Exhibition, which took place three decades after the First Independence War. Archive restoration and translations were sanctioned by the current Leader of Nayadesh, who famously pledged allegiance to Truth when first sworn in. These extracts were showcased at the Exhibition, where a monument to the War Heroines was also unveiled. Unfortunately, the monument, which paid tribute to the design of the original, has since been defaced and stolen. The Exhibition was generously funded by our international benefactors, still affectionately known as Friends. For details on renewed public interest in the War Heroines, see previous entry on the #justiceforourmothers movement.

In armoured jeeps, they were taken to the camps and [safe-kept]. It wasn't a hostage situation. We knew from the beginning – even if we didn't want to admit it – that this was [something else].

The first night, it was my squad posted at the No-Man Zone. We saw the women come out one by one. A couple of boys shouted [in surprise]. The rest of us, trained under the iron rule of the Commander, knew better. Fingers stiff on our rifles, we tried to keep count. Each time we thought our census complete, another shadowy form emerged, as if the women had been stacked in like sticks of wax on a shelf, slowly melding into each other's shapes.

The moon was high and bright, an uninterrupted circle. We sensed something amiss. Was it that the women's saris were askew, the ties of their bhotos unloosed? Or that they wore no jewellery, and so carried no markers of age, religion, marital status, community? We only knew them as ours because their footsteps rang with the same pauju our mothers and sisters wore at home.

Why had those pauju remained around their ankles when everything else was stripped?

Later, when we compared counts, the numbers varied wildly: anything from three to thirty women per vehicle. The Commander knocked our heads with his pistol. We must have seen ghosts, he said, because how could that many people fit inside a vehicle that size?

As the moon dissolved and became sickle-edged, there were more jeeps, at least two if not more than twelve at once.

Even from our campsite, a mile from the No-Man Zone, we heard the women [talking]. The soldiers were [relieved]. Some thought they recognised a neighbour, an old schoolteacher, their bank cashier. A week later, after lines of bodies had been swallowed by the enemy camps, we thought we recognised our friends' wives, our distant cousins. Another week and we thought we heard our sisters and mothers.

What was more [remarkable] was the times of silence. We heard nothing, as if the camps were really peopled by ghosts.

Suman was so [moved] by the sound of [talking] that one night he crept across the No-Man Zone. He'd been posted there every day since the first jeeps. He kept mumbling that he'd seen his baby sister. A red blotch marred her right cheek, he said, he could spot her from miles away. He had to go. Don't be [hasty], we said. Breaching the Zone meant death on sight. We thought we managed to talk him out of it, but he slunk off when no one was expecting.

He came back two days later. We'd lied to the Commander for him and were furious, but seeing him made the [sympathy] inside us grow. We gave him hot water, a ball of stale rice, wrapped his shaking body in our own blankets. I still see that ashen face. Those [soft] sounds he made.

This is what Suman saw:

[*illegible script*]

He became agitated. Some muttered he was possessed. Most found his account [humorous] and [pleasing]. They told him to [get some rest] and tried to [take him to his bed]. We protected him [from further agitations]. After lights out, some of us went to speak to our squad captain in private. I was unable to go because I was on reprimand for [antinationalistic behaviours]. I kept thinking about what Suman said of the [enemy soldiers], how dirty and bleak their camps, how [barbaric] and [cruel] their faces.

When the squad captain heard Suman's account, he didn't say anything for a long while, just stood with his head cocked. Finally, he said he would speak to the Commander and the strategy committee. We looked at each other with [relief]. No one wanted to approach the Commander, but we believed he was a man of principles. The strategy committee, however, had only one of our own within its ranks. The other five members were [Friends], the same advisors who once [guided] us on [morality] and [supervised] our governance, culture, civility and religion. We [were indebted to] them. They had [magnanimously agreed] to [grant] power to our new Leader and were invested in [seeing us emerge victors], in possession of the new nation we dreamed of since they [helped us dream of it].

Our people usually [welcomed] the [expertise] of the [Friends]. We knew what the [Friends'] strategies led to in the past, so we weren't surprised when the [Friends] decreed [yes]. It took twenty-nine days for this decision to arrive. The nights we waited, the chham chham of pauju [serenaded] us. Even the soldiers who ignored the sound were affected: we saw how their fingers trembled as they polished their boots. I kept dreaming of a girl I used to know, startling awake every morning, face wet.

The committee said [nothing was more important] than our civilian women. Since [safe-keeping wasn't] happening to war regulations, [a rescue mission] was planned. Most of our squad was of the same mind. At this crucial point, when so many soldiers had been lost, they said, the women [were] important.

We decided to [volunteer].

But by then, the day now marked as Independence was upon us. That was perhaps the last time the women in the enemy camps had names like Rani and Komal and Chameli and Aneeka, because after that they were only known as War Heroines.

[*missing pages*]

Some [fell in love] and when those enemy soldiers vacated our borders, the women [chose to leave with them]. We watched them go with bellies swollen, hair adorned with gajra, saris draped in the old way. The women didn't glance at us, which was a blessing, for who could bear the weight of their gaze?

During the exodus, the Leader pronounced that these War Heroines were paving the way for future peace. We will gift these women to the other side. Do not think of them as 'our' daughters. Down the line, when their descendants meet our descendants, they will look at each other and say, Brother.

When the Leader visited the first [Rehabilitation Home], I was assigned a spot in his security. I found myself shaking as we neared that [pleasant] building. All those nights I had listened to the women [talk] and now I would come face to face with them. The rifle almost slipped from my sweat-slicked hands. The squad commander looked at me sharply. I kept my eyes on the Leader's head, a perfect circle of skin that shone like the moon that first night. I didn't let my eyes waver.

The Leader walked up to the women lined up in the courtyard. He clasped the hands of the first one and said, You are a Mother of this Nation.

I knew from her tender wrists she must be young. I saw the protrusion of her belly and her shorn head. Her scalp was clotted with scabs, like she'd wrapped her hair around her fists and pulled with all her might.

I couldn't look at her face.

We will take care of you, Mother, the Leader said, placing palms on her stomach. We will take care of this.

The Leader presented them all with saris, blood red, the colour for new brides. As we were leaving, I heard murmured voices.

She will burn that sari.

Why?

Because of what happened at the camps. The enemy took their saris so the women wouldn't knot them up and [shame] themselves.

At those words, my very bones trembled. The [War Heroines] must have been kept [in different clothes]. Had I known this? Had Suman in fact told me a long time ago, and I scrubbed the knowledge from my mind?

It was that same day the Leader ordered the mandatory [care] of all pregnant War Heroines. Only when they are looked after can we look towards the future, he said.

[Unfortunately] within two weeks, the unborn babies had all [perished].

The new government poured in funding to train the [War Heroines] so they could re-join the labour force, provided [financial incentives] to any man who married them. We want them to re-enter society, the Leader said, and the [War Heroines] cried [over his goodness] and [thanked] him whenever he visited.

The Leader also ordered the women's families to come and claim them. I found out later that many retracted their family names from the [War Heroines] and [gave them freedom to carve out new life paths]. They didn't want [to diminish the War Heroines' fame].

During this time, as I trailed after the Leader on his visits to the [Rehabilitation Homes], I kept a lookout for the girl I dreamt of. Some fog had seized my mind, and I could no longer remember her name. But I knew her face, the dimples and pointed chin that accompanied me through gruelling tuition classes and wooden rulers on palms, that appeared to sneak me guavas through the fence. I looked in every centre, and later, when we were discharged, every town I passed.

What did I hope to see when I found her? A sign, a medal,

or a wound visible to the eye? I realised I was no different to those droves who gathered outside the [Rehabilitation Homes], peering through windows as if it were a zoo, whispering:

They don't *look* any different.

No, see there, that one's face, and that one's neck is covered in [gold].

How can we tell when they're out among us on the streets though? It's not right, I want to know who was in those camps, who was [talking].

I kept dreaming of that beloved face in those cells Suman described. Where had my friend disappeared? Where had they all disappeared? That first time we'd thought of them as ghosts, it was like we'd predicted the future, seen their true forms.

[*Missing pages*]

The statue in the middle of the square had a green tinge. Pigeons roosted on it, and it was always hot to the touch. This was the highest honour bestowed on the [War Heroines]. There was something [distinct] about the monument: the woman's face was [shielded] by her own hands like she couldn't bear the [bright of day].

It was here that I met [the War Heroine]. Every day, I saw her sleeping by the statue, wrapped in rags, dull coins scattered about her. When she was awake, I offered her some sips of water. She didn't thank me but accepted. Another time, I brought her a thick woollen blanket. Another time, I took over hot paratha and we sat, breaking off pieces, chewing in silence.

Finally, one day, I asked for her story. She turned her head, looked at me without blinking: a clear gaze, bright as the moon.

She said yes when I asked her if she'd been at the war camps. I wanted to know what her life was like after, if she married, if she worked. She nodded, but there was a gaping in her eyes, a slackness to her mouth, the kind I was used to seeing on the faces of fellow soldiers. I asked her where her husband was and why she was at the feet of this statue.

This is what she said:

[*illegible script*]

No Phones at the Dinner Table

JACK HOUSTON

it's a hippo and I've got the ears just about right I think and the roundness of its nose and the eyes and that's about it for a hippo because all I have to do now is draw the water around it and I hear step into the light shine so bright sometimes which is my WhatsApp alert and Dad says no phones at the dinner table and I didn't even remember he was on the sofa that sort of separates the TV from the dining table because I was concentrating on my hippo's left ear which just about matches the right ear now and I say but we're not even eating yet

Dad gets up and walks over to the kitchen the entire kitchen dining table TV area of our front room an L-shape and says it doesn't matter a rule's a rule and then says is that your WhatsApp? you should mute the notifications like I told you to but I won't because I need to know when my friends are saying the things they're saying and I sigh loud enough so Dad can hear me but not enough to get in any more trouble not that I am in trouble and I put the phone on the shelves squashed behind the dinner table and Dad stands in the kitchen and I can tell he's thinking something and maybe wants to say something but maybe doesn't know what because normally he wouldn't be that bothered by me using my phone at the dinner table even if and when we are actually eating dinner

Lorna! Dad calls into the rest of the flat which is only three more rooms and that's including the bathroom Lorna! Dad calls again and we wait in silence for Lorna to come Lorna! and Lorna shouts from our bedroom that she's coming Lorna always puts off coming to the table every dinner time and breakfast and lunch at the weekend not that Dad's even started cooking dinner and she's supposed to have a snack in between each meal even in school because the hospital said she has to but Lorna still somehow manages to hide food in her baggy jumper or I don't even know where and Dad doesn't like us saying the word anorexic because I think he thinks us not saying it will somehow make it not true and Dad smiles at me weakly in that way he used to when I was little and calls Lorna! again and it's not like I can blame her because everyone wants to be thin or at least thinner all my friends at school do and I suppose it's something I think about too and even Dad's a bit the same but Lorna's so thin the consultant at the hospital said it will start to affect her fertility and all sorts of other health things perhaps

my eldest sister Evie isn't here yet because she's at university up in Birmingham which is far away and is a good university I know this because Dad said it is though Dad was quite upset when she went there last year because Dad thought Evie could have got into Cambridge or Oxford had she not messed around with Dan who got her pregnant and messed with her A levels not that Dad told me any of this I overheard him talking on the phone to Auntie Barbara his sister and I'm not supposed to know this because Dad didn't want me to find out because I'm only nearly thirteen but Auntie Barbara said something on the other end of the phone and I don't think Dad realised I was at the table drawing a picture of a horse quite a good horse I got the head and the way its back swept all the way down to its tail just right and its legs but I still wasn't happy with the hooves hippos are much easier because of all the water after I heard Dad on the phone to Auntie Barbara I asked Evie and she told me but also told me not to tell Dad that I knew and Harry Styles sings from my phone again on the shelf behind me but Dad looks at me with one of those don't even think about picking it up to check it looks as he calls out Lorna! again and Lorna comes in flustered pulling her jumper sleeves over her hands as if that will hide how skinny her hands are and she sits down and Dad sits down

and now both of them are sat here watching me draw a hippo

today Dad says we're going to be having clam pasta Dad's favourite like the one he and Mum had on holiday back when she was still here and he starts telling me and Lorna the story he's told us like a thousand times but we don't stop him of how the man in the swimming trunks came up the beach when they were staying near Rome and they were on the beach and the man who was selling the clams tried to proposition Mum and he was holding his bucket of clams and trying to proposition Mum whilst also trying to sell his bucket of clams and Dad always tells us she didn't know where to put her eyes because the man's trunks were so small and so tight and he tells us of how she told him later she was worried he'd be upset because the man with the tiny trunks was so obviously trying it on with her but she didn't know where to put her eyes and Dad laughs again as he says he wasn't fussed because he knew Mum loved him and after they'd left the beach without the man in the tiny trunks or his clams they ordered the clam pasta at the restaurant they went to and it was the best thing they'd ever tasted and he's never quite been able to do the recipe as good

I can tell Lorna's been crying and it's probably Mark but she can't say anything about it to Dad because Dad doesn't know about Mark and she can't say anything to me because Dad's here in the room with us because Mark's old

267

really old too old to be going out with someone who's only fifteen like Lorna is and it is a bit weird because I've seen him and he's got like a proper beard like how Dad did around the time of the clam incident in the photos we've got up on the shelves behind where my phone sings again but this time Dad doesn't give me the look because he's concentrating on Lorna and asking her if she's all right and Lorna just gets up and runs from the room and Dad goes after her and I am starting to get a bit hungry but I suppose I can wait a bit longer and will have to I suppose because Evie's not even here yet so I pick up my phone and check my messages and there's three from Sam asking what we think of Jamie and what she should do and then WHERE ARE YOU GUYS???!!!

none of us are supposed to be on Tinder because we're too young but it isn't difficult to enter your date of birth in so you're over eighteen that's what we do that's what Josie and Jessica and Sam did and that's what I did and most of the boys at Drayton and so is how to tell if a boy in your class or your year or maybe in one of the other years fancies you or not before you go and make a big fool of yourself by letting him know you fancy him and Sam wants to know if she should swipe right on Jamie and I'm a bit shocked and don't know what I should say because she knows I fancy Jamie and have done since we were in primary school and to say she fancies him now is to totally ignore the fact that she's heard me saying so many times about how much I fancy him and my feelings and to go and ask me if it's OK if she swipes right on him is not right I don't think

Lorna started not eating properly when she started at Drayton which was when she was my age which was nearly three years ago but we didn't notice at first and only found out how long it had been going on when Lorna told us at one of the family therapy sessions the eating disorder clinic made an appointment for because Dad didn't know what to do not that I know what to do because I'm the youngest one in the family and I can hear Lorna and Dad talking in our room and I wonder how much longer they're going to be in there because it's not like she's going to tell him why she's so upset he could be in there forever and it could be forever until Dad starts cooking and I've finished the head and the eyes of my hippo and have even drawn one of those little birds that live on their backs I think there are little birds that live on the backs of hippos I'll have to check and I really am actually starting to feel quite hungry

step into the light shine so bright sometimes sings my phone again and I pick it up and turn the ringer off and I don't want to look at it or try making Sam feel any better over what is in fact a massive betrayal but I can't help but try and peer at the screen to see if it is her who's messaged the group again or one of the others and it is her and I bet she's already sent Jamie a picture of her boobs like Jess who said about sending a picture like that to Dean and then was worried Dean would show it to his friends but I don't think Dean did or would because Dean's actually quite nice but then I suppose people always seem nice until they aren't though it's not as if any of us have even got much in the way of boobs though I suppose Jess does a bit more than me and Sam or Josie and in the light of the phone's screen I can see Dad's face in one of the photos that's been lit up by my phone screen just his face not anything else the photos lined up along the shelf in a sort of shrine I say sort of but it really is a shrine

269

what we try to do is reframe what has happened to us it's a sort of instinct the family therapist said even if that thing is terrible we will reframe it in an attempt to find some kind of peace but sometimes if the bad thing that happened is bad enough that's just not possible and all we can hope to do then is realise that it's OK for it to be bad the family therapist said and if we can do this then Lorna will be able to eat properly again not that the family therapist said that last bit about Lorna but I know that's what we were all thinking as Dad nodded and said mm-hmm

Mum died when I was three Lorna doesn't really remember all that much about her either because she was only six or something and it's not like I'm sad about it all that much because like I say I didn't really know her but I suppose she knew me and loved me and that's what Dad says he says she loved me loved us all very much but she had to go but the family therapist says that it's OK for me to be as upset as I like about it because if something is hard to process it's hard to process but I'm not sure I've processed anything

it's all I know

when Mum died Dad quit his job but we don't talk much about what happened then but we did have to sell the big house on Chisholm Drive only two roads away from here but we often walk past it on our way to and from school which Evie told me she remembers I'm not sure Lorna does but the flat we live in now is smaller and high on the fifth nearly the top floor of the block and has a really big

window in the front room which is also the kitchen which catches the sun which makes the flat really warm even in winter and
sometimes too hot in summer and Dad and Lorna come back in
and Dad smiles at me sort of weakly and Lorna doesn't look at me

and now Dad's phone rings
and he gets up and answers it which isn't fair if you ask me because
how is he allowed to answer a phone if I'm not? and we hear him
say hey and oh and no don't worry about it it's OK and I look at
Lorna and she lifts her eyes to mine for just a second and then
looks away and Dad says it really would be nice if you could try
and make it and then he says oh no it's OK I quite understand and
then he hangs up the phone and goes back over to the hob and
looks at the kitchen as if that is going to tell him what to do and
he doesn't say anything was that Melissa? I ask and he doesn't say
anything so I say Dad?

it's a bit
weird anyway Dad inviting his new girlfriend over on the night
we're having our special clam pasta because we only have our
special clam pasta on their anniversary his and Mum's anniversary
which is why Evie is coming all the way from Birmingham and
why Dad probably shouldn't have invited Melissa no matter how
much he likes her and don't get me wrong I like her too she is
actually quite nice and likes Dad even though he's quite old and
going a bit bald and has a bit of a belly so could definitely do
worse Melissa is obviously not Mum and never will be but even
thinking this makes a funny kind of hollow feeling in my tummy
because I don't even know if she is like Mum at all she looks a bit
like her I can tell that from the photos but is her laugh the same?
or her voice or the way Mum would have listened to me as if I was

the only person in the world can she do that? and it's Dad and Mum's anniversary anyway and Evie's not here either

Lorna shifts in her seat and I think she's actually going to say something

but she doesn't

Dad's still standing in front of the hob like he's waiting for permission to start cooking and I hope he does soon because I am getting quite hungry and he sees me staring at him but instead of starting to make the food he gives me that weak smile of his that hasn't made me feel any better about anything since I was at least eight and turns and looks back at the hob so I look at Lorna who's just staring down and picking at one of her nails so I just start drawing another hippo in the pool a smaller one next to the bigger one and think that in the wild I guess a hippo would have a baby hippo with it are hippos mammals? we learnt about what makes a mammal that it's the milk they make and some other things but how does a baby hippo suckle with those big wide mouths and in all that water?

and Dad's phone rings again and he picks it up and says hi yes and I can tell he's smiling even though he's got his back to us and he says that's great OK then we'll see you soon and he hangs up and says to me and Lorna that was Evie she's at the station already she's getting in a cab I guess I should get the dinner on and Dad turns on the radio and takes the chopping board down from where it hangs on the back of the kitchen door and starts slicing into an onion

Dad always listens

to classical music while he's cooking he says it relaxes him and it is sort of OK but not as good as the songs me and my friends sing in school in the playground or the songs we play at my after-school street-dance lessons and Dad starts to hum along to the music and there's a sizzling noise as he puts the chopped onion into the oil and the kitchen is filled with the smell and I look at Lorna but she's just staring at the tabletop probably planning how to get through dinner so I go back to my hippo and her baby and start drawing a few trees behind her but then I remember hippos live in the jungle and that they've got to be jungle trees and I wonder how a jungle tree might look different to the trees we have in the parks and along the streets around here

my phone vibrates and I know I could take it to Lorna's and my room or just the sofa but then I decide I don't want to get into discussion with Josie and Jessica and Sam about Jamie because I don't like talking about what he might look like naked and I think jungle trees have big leaves like the cheese plant we have in our front room and isn't that a funny name a cheese plant? makes me wonder what kind of things we could have named plants after like bread plant or sausage plant or clam pasta plant

Lorna fidgets in her chair and I bet she wants to get up and walk out again but Dad's probably already spoken to her about spending more time in here with the two of us even though I'm still drawing my hippo and her baby's jungle and Dad's now chopping the garlic so none of us are actually saying anything to each other not that I would know what to say to Lorna any more not since she came into our room after a shower and I saw the marks on the tops of her legs near her hips deep red scratches but I knew they weren't just scratches from itching herself because she was bitten by a mosquito or something but that she'd been at herself with some scissors or something because we talked about it in our PSHE lesson with Ms Clarke who said she used to do it when she was younger and later Sam said her mum has scars on her arms and Dad says right and gets a tin of tomatoes from where we keep them on top of the fridge and pulls the ring pull open and pours it on top of the onions and garlic and says right again and then comes and sits down at the table and says ooh what are you drawing but then says the clams and gets back up again

and Dad tastes the sauce with the spoon he's using then stirs some more which is a bit gross because of germs and then grinds something salt or pepper into it tastes it again and says I'm putting the clams in now as if we need to know that and I look at Lorna and try to catch her eye as Dad takes the kettle that's just boiled and there's a whoosh as he pours the boiled water into the already heated pasta pan and says I'm putting the pasta on too

the buzzer goes on the intercom and Dad turns off the radio and walks into the flat hallway and picks up the phone receiver thing that you talk through to speak to the person who called up to the flat from the street and I hear him say honey and you're here and where's your key fob? and says anyway you can tell us about it when you're up here and presses the buzzer and then turns to us and smiles but not one of his weak ones a proper one and then he walks towards the front door but stops and turns around and comes and sits back at the table with the two of us and I put the green-colour pencil I was doing the

leaves of the jungle with down and Dad smiles at me again and I
smile back and look at Lorna who also smiles

and in the quiet of the flat
we can hear the lift murmuring up the lift shaft and then the click
click click of the key-code door to the hallway outside and it
creaking open and then our front door opening and there's Evie in
her big coat and her hair piled on top of her head and saying hey
how is everyone? and she puts down her bag and sighs and she
looks funny different but I don't care and I get up from the table
and leap the two to three steps across our small kitchen and wrap
my arms around her and I've started crying and can feel Lorna
hugging as well and she's started crying too and now Dad wraps
all three of us in his big arms and Evie says hey it's OK it's OK

someone clears their throat
from the doorway to the kitchen and we all look up from our
group hug and Evie says oh yes this is Michael and there's Michael
who's actually quite hot-looking in a normal sort of way and Dad
wipes the tears from his eyes with one hand and offers the other
for Michael to shake as Evie says we're not to worry as Michael's
parents live not far from here well not too far and that they are
going to stay with them while they're here and Dad asks if she's
sure which is silly because we've only got the bigger bedroom
between all three of us and Lorna and I have long piled Evie's bed
with a load of our dirty washing and schoolwork and other bits
and bobs and god knows what else and Dad smiles at Michael and
says but you are eating with us right?

La Calima

SIRI KATINKA VALDEZ

'La Calima is a vast cloud of fine sand
kicked up by storms in the nearby Sahara
Desert, sometimes carrying locusts with it,
and does nobody any good.'
Araguyan Island travel guide [1]

There were German hippies scattered everywhere. Naked, half-naked, wet, sunburned – passed out. After three days and three nights of full-moon partying, only one of them seemed to be awake. A twiggy woman with short auburn hair, a washed-out tank top and a knitted shawl wrapped around her hips. She paced barefoot up and down the black, sandy beach. Mumbling, then shouting, then laughing. Calling out to anyone and no one:

I have a clownfish in my belly

>*Big clownfish in my belly*
>>*Ich habe einen großen*

Clownfisch in meinem Bauch

The soft waves tuned in to her little chant – creating a cacophony *mashuhshhhhh*. Mediating the language of the Thieides, who once walked this land. MAYUC–MOTHER/ N-ÏNET–BONE/O-CHE–BUTTER/XERA–SKY. *Skybutter, motherbone. Motherbutter, skybone. Mashuhshhhhh.*

The Thieide people had settled here aeons ago – unknown exactly how they got here. Perhaps wandering Imazighen from the Sahara, they were tall, had fair eyes and blond hair. They herded sheep, drank the juice of the prickly pear cactus and made gofi flour from crushed xaxti roots. They named these things after the letter

---

1 We gratefully acknowledge the source: *La Gomera: A Guide to the Unspoiled Canary Island*, by Tim Hart (Colley Books, 2004)

A: *Amän, ayuh, awan, anaïs* . . . water, skull, milk, honey. They hunted giant rats and ran from mad dogs, the Presa Canarios. They leaped up and down the ravines with long wooden poles, criss-crossing through generations. They used the wind to communicate, with a bird-like whistle. *Phhhhhiiiuuuuu.* Messages whooshing over the island – as if the wind was their shared lung.

SONG OF THE THIEIDES

Phhhiiiiuuu. We call upon *Ara'che* for nourishing rain. We call upon *Chiraxi* for blessed abundance. We fear *Gyoto* – the black dog *cancha* nestling in the volcano, violent and vindictive. If he crawls into our minds, we pierce a hole in our skull to let his spirit out. When our bodies are old and the red owl calls, we are carried to the mountain cliff to die in peace, with a bowl of fresh goat milk.

CORRECTIONS

Or maybe this was not true. Maybe after the Spanish invaded and the indigenous culture perished, they recorded it wrong, they got the names all mixed, and the archipelago's place-specific cultures confused. And the name for *butter* was actually *bone*. And the God of the Sky was the Goddess of the Sun, and the Dog Devil nestled in the details.

—Did you ingest something? a man yawned to the clownfish woman as she passed him.

—No, I only had three beers.

She sat down beside him. Fiddled with her jade ankle bracelet as he rolled her a Manitou. She began telling him about ze *cool* clairvoyant dream she had had, six years ago. About three purple and orange planets that formed a triangle in the Milky Way. She showed him the tattoo on the inside of her thigh, as proof.

—See? Ze triangle?

The guy nodded, searching his leather pouch for a lighter.

—So you see, ze energy of this triangle will protect us, when ze shit hits ze fan.

—Well, take it easy, OK? the guy said, handing her the cigarette. The woman got up and continued on with her soliloquy.

. . . *Clownfisch . . . meinem Bauch! Haha!*

The moon faded as the sun made its way up from behind the jagged mountains, bathing the ridge in a warm, yellow glow: slabs, rocks, lizard, lichen – a neon-blue string tangled in the shrub. A vintage can of Coca-Cola. An island outside of Africa. Its tip soaring up from the middle of the Atlantic Ocean, the rest of the land submerged in saltwater. Civilisations long lost at the bottom of the sea. If there ever was an Atlantis, it was here.

From bird's eye, the eroded, volcanic landmass looked like the lower jaw of a fossilised giant. Skull above water, torso wrapped in a velvety blue cape. Crooked, canine teeth piercing the landscape. And in the middle of her jaw; a moist, spongy tongue. A turtle-bellied organism – green moss, laurel trees, black ants, fungi, lost species and cultic shrines. Such as the mighty molar Cerro Grande – a mountaintop so flat it served as an altar for the gods.

***

The fresh-seafood truck that had come from San Andrés navigated around the mesas between the villages of Hierro and Arure – final stop Valle Dorado. The two brothers liked to get an early start, so they could stop at their childhood village, Truches, and stretch their legs at the foot end of Cerro Grande. Twice passing the cementerio where their parents and younger brother were buried. Twice crossing themselves to the Wunder-Baum-scented Virgin of Candelaria, dangling in the windshield before continuing on with their route.

Pescadito fresco! Fresh fish! The distorted sound from the loudspeakers reverberated through the narrow walls of the gorge. Like a revolution was happening: *Viva la swordfish!* Truck scurrying down the terraced ravine, a flock of fleeing birds, a *beep-el-li-beep* in every sharp turn to notify oncoming traffic. Descending alongside the cluster of houses on the hillside of La Calera. Straight through the rotonda – first stop La Playa, in the valley of gold. A gameshow-esque *ta-da-ding-ding-dei* announced the brothers' arrival. A quick exchange of money for goods, a few familiar *¿Cómo estás?* and off they went. Passing the clownfish lady and the full-moon people, *ta-da-ding-ding-dei*. Stopping by old Señor Rasca y gana on his bench, with a stack of scratching cards and an aluminium-coated dream.

—Any luck this morning, Señor?

—Ojalá . . .

Here's hoping.

A naked, herculean man climbed down the boulders to the small, secluded beach nestled between Puerto Alto and the so-called *babybeach*. He began washing his body, dipping his tangled hair in the glistening saltwater. He seemed to have appeared from nowhere, as if he stepped out from a history book, a Greek glitch, only to disappear again into the rockpile, into a fracture of time.

A man who needs no one, craves nothing, sustained only by sunlight and fresh coconuts – with the aid of a Swiss Army knife.

A while later, he was driving around in a shiny Jeep Wrangler, the canvas sun-roof flamboyantly flapping. Nodding to the old man who ran the supermercado by the wharf. The old man nodded back, searching his pocket for cigarettes before he remembered that his daughters had made him quit.

The supermercado had beach balls and nets, snorkelling gear and flip flops. It had instant coffee, stale white bread, evaporated milk, multicoloured markers and expired sunscreen. The sunglasses-and-postcards-from-the-eighties thingy, that rotated halfway before it got jammed. Ice cream, crisps, slimming teas, sodas, tampons, toilet paper, neon-coloured dishwasher soap. Clusters of short, brown-spotted bananas, straw hats and Spanish romance novels.

Puerto Alto was its own little ecosystem, a fermented brew of symbiotic commerce. There was the tiny pizza-place, that made *damn good pizza* that you ate on the kerb. The Lebanese restaurant that had the greasy baba ghanoush. The costly hiker's store, with the vegan jerky and weightless hammocks. The dusty fish restaurant that had been there since the seventies, and the back alley of the restaurant where a colony of cats would linger after closing hours, devouring fish heads and shrimp shells. *A sublime carcass feast.*

Today the waves were calm. The fishermen had already taken out the boats, those still anchored seemed to serve only a decorative purpose. Other days, the harbour was like a sea monster regurgitating objects it had devoured years back.

Last spring, an unidentified body had been found floating in the water – face down. Juan Carlos had come, the Chief of Police, together with a forensic pathologist from San Miguel

– and that was that. The black body-bag was hauled up on the truck, three scoops of ice cream for lunch, and the tourist season was officially open. But now it was February and the season was almost over, and La Calima was coming – and then the air traffic would halt, and the tourists would disappear, at least those that had read about the island before they came, and knew this was not the right time to stay. At this time of year few people came, and most people left. The same way the tide retracted, the tourists flew home, flew north, to their *lebkuchen* and grading of grammar papers, to their staff meetings and laundry days.

But the locals were still here, and the mute, ethereal Fincaresidents were still here. Those that pilgrimed into Puerto Alto once a week, supplying their sprouted-chickpea diets with ethically scrutinised items from the supermercado. And those that had left society for an indefinite amount of time were still here – those that lived in caves, on the beach—for nothing, of nothing. Los Salvajes, the feral ones.

SONG OF LOS SALVAJES

They call us the feral ones. Los salvajes. We drum to the beat of barking black dogs. We dive into dumpsters for cruelty-free treats. We are nihilistic nomads, foraging for kicks. We'll drink your wine and smoke your weed. We do not want to fight with the local police. We want to sit in peace and stare at the moon. The moon is full of feelings. It collects all our dreams. It wells up inside like a warm, salty teardrop – it moves the ocean. It transforms the world.

***

Near Nouadhibou airport, Mauritania. Fine grains of sand swirled up from the rocks and sandbanks, creating a cakey substance of debris and particles. The thick, heavy smog hovered above the ground before continuing north, riding the southeastern winds. Vacuuming up whatever came in its way; iridescent beetles, bar-tailed larks, oil refinery residue, plastic pebbles, lost thoughts. A tangled nest for the world's loose ends, huffed and puffed on by the storms of Sahara. A maroon, sultry cloud – La Calima, little sister of Sirocco.

The iron-red, ectoplasmic substance oozed in over the archipelago, over the Araguyan island, drifting on top of Cerro Grande. The cloud began to descend the hill, towards the bottom of the valley. Behind it, more clouds came. Clinging together to form a massive fleet of red, heavy dust – moving down the mountainside, onto the valley of gold. La Calima meandered like a fat red snake, through the little streets and narrow pathways. Slow-moving and determined, swallowing whatever was in her way. In every crevice, on every windowsill, on every eyelid, a thick red film of dust gathered. No visibility, no clarity, no horizon, no future, no past, no language.

Just a low buzzing, cacophony – a distorted hymn.

SONG OF LA CALIMA
ICH EK I CALIMA   ich EK i calima

        ek WIND spirit

ek carry oil refinery dust   and   fluttering   LOCUST
wings
        and iridescent   plastic STUFF

EK huff   EK puff   EK BLOW your casa POOF!

ek cloud exchange for HONEY LAND

                              ek carcass on cementerio head
beep-el-li-beep   and there goes the body bag
beep-el-li-beep   three ice cream
SCOOPS

               oops buried flapper wrangler jeep danger!
               orange skies danger! blood rain
     airborne   *dust, dust, dust*

ha! choking seizure   regurgitates ectoplasmic
                                  BABY milk

                    Here! Sun holder of the Maker World
Ek thank you great DESERT
Ek thank you RED owl
                    for this here multicolour MOON
                                        for this here
telenovela
     And for this here
THIEIDE lung. *Mashuhshhhhh*

                    Listen

     Ding-ding-ding
it won't help closing the curtains

286

filling the cracks under the door with toilet
paper   *ding-ding-ding*   closing   the
eyes   closing   the
mouth

ding-ding-ding
   and the night comes too slow and the mouth drinks too fast
   and the fan stops working and the toilets are overflowing

   head under pillow eyes under pillow   suffocated   thoughts
under pillow
   the wind is stuffed with broken words
                  tattle tales in every crack
              Mashuhshhhhh

   what comes after you
ATLANTIS
   what comes after you LANGUAGE after plastic tangled
DOLPHIN
                  after CLOUD circuit
   breakdown
                  after   news   FEED
breakdown
         after feral cat
                        eats
   RAINBOW?

The Bhootham in the Mango Tree

Mango Tree

RAJASREE VARIYAR

'There's a bhootham in that mango tree,' my father says.

My eyes follow his outstretched finger to where it levels accusingly at a grand, leafy specimen of the bearer of my favourite fruit. The tree stands proud in a field of long grass that holds the ominous potential of lurking cobras.

'Is it there now?' I ask.

Acha beckons me closer.

'She's there,' he says, pointing again, and I squint. Just beyond the shade of the balcony, the heat of the midday sun creates a distinct shimmer above the Keralan soil.

The mango tree is immune from the sweat I can feel trickling between my breasts. It protrudes from the edge of the tangled jungle that borders the field, currently empty of grazing cows. Its only inhabitant – that I can spot with my two mortal eyes – is a coal-black bird, glossy in the light, grooming its feathers. I watch its wicked beak bobbing up and down beneath its left wing.

'Do you mean the crow, Acha?'

Other than the odd word that works best in Malayalam – the *Achas* and *bhoothams* of our conversation – we're speaking in English. I'm not complaining. I love my mother tongue, the soft syllables of the word for 'father' sounding like a caress. But my Malayalam's terrible. I can understand it, but I have the vocabulary of a seven-year-old. To comprehend my mother tongue but speak it like a child – it's a cruel oxymoron.

He looks at me as though I'm crazy. I know the look – people throw it at Acha all the time, although thankfully he never catches it.

'Don't be silly,' he says. 'There, sitting in the tree. All dressed in white.' The frown creasing his brow eases, receding like the tide from the shore, and his eyes drift away. They widen, with a child's wonder. He's remembering, although these days his memories are a swirl of fact and fiction, mingled and kaleidoscopic, like a rainbow Madeira cake.

'That's where I saw her first,' he says. His gaze wanders back to the tree. 'She had hair like yours, thick and long. But she wasn't sitting in the tree. She was walking under it, towards me. Singing.'

I watch him carefully. He seems calm. I imagine his mind as a placid valley in summer. The days when the calm rolls away before a raging storm of delusion and paranoia never seem far off. I hope this peace will last, just for one more week, until we're safely back in London.

'Do you know what a bhootham is?' Acha says. He always starts a story with a question. He's holding my hand. His long, elegant fingers would have been amazing over the keys of a piano. Until the first storm, they'd been tapping at computer keys, speaking languages like Ruby and Python. Sometimes Acha's stories are about computer code, about it spiralling around him or telling him secrets, and I'm lucky if I understand one word in three.

But he's not talking about that now. Bhootham. I used to hate it when he tested my knowledge like this, back before he began to change. Now I'm glad. I wrinkle my nose and try to think through what I learnt from the comics he used to buy me at the railway station when we travelled by Indian sleeper train. 'Some sort of demon or banshee?'

'Ghost,' he says, 'They're chained to this world by tragedy. That's what a bhootham is, a disturbed, searching soul, unable to escape its desire to remain here.'

Creepy. The words seem at odds with the sunshine outside, the lapis lazuli sky, the moist smell of soil and vegetation. I look at Acha, his face so like my own other than a slightly squarer jaw. His cheeks seem thinner than ever, making his dark eyes, framed with lashes almost as thick and long as mine, look huge. The question slips from my mouth almost reluctantly. 'Where did your bhootham come from?'

'Right here,' he says. 'A long time ago. She speaks to me sometimes. Sometimes she sings.'

I stay silent, waiting, but it seems he's run out of words for now. Instead, he shivers, from a chill that can only be imagined in this heat. I lean forward in my plastic chair, sticky with the sweat seeping through my salwar trousers.

'Are you OK, Acha?' I ask.

He blinks and his head jerks, as though he's forgotten I'm there. Maybe he has. He moves in and out of worlds in fits and starts, as though he's living many lives in one. But then his gaze meets mine and he smiles.

'Do you smell that? It's lunchtime.'

We've been in Thrissur almost a week now. At first, it was good to be away from uni – Warwick is miserably grim at this time of year – and the looming threat of graduate programme applications. Thrissur is apparently some beautiful ancient Keralan city, complete with Bronze Age stone temples and medieval palaces. My experience of it is patchy wifi and having to visit swarms of relatives. Most pay as little attention to Acha and me as possible, as though we're carrying an embarrassing contagious disease. My patience for the whole thing is fraying. I'm thinking enviously of my mother, who refused to come.

Acha is right. It is lunchtime. The dining room is cool and dim, just like most of the chambers and crevices and niches in this centuries-old house. It used to lodge several generations of the family, all living together in a mad, chaotic, loving tangle. Now, my grandfather lives here alone except for a few loyal house staff and a steady stream of relatives paying respectful social calls. The thick stone walls and small windows keep the heat at bay. The rooms smell of incense, old wood and must.

My grandfather sits at the head of the table, my aunt, uncle and cousin, down from their home in Bangalore, arrayed around him like retainers. He's a doctor, respected and revered in the town for years, and each year has added another layer of lacquer to his character. I call him Achacha – another beautiful word, a susurration, a soft caress. Acha's Acha. He's not a soft caress. He views his patients as puzzles. He views his younger son as an incomprehensible mistake.

Acha and I are seated at the end, the hangers-on, listening to a seamless mix of English and Malayalam conversation. My cousin Sanjana is on my left. She leans towards me.

'How's your acha going?' she whispers. They all refer to him like that, 'your acha', as though he's not their uncle, or their younger brother, or their son. They don't want to be reminded they're that close to him.

'He's great,' I say through a mouthful of fried fish and warm chapatti.

Sanjana hesitates. She wears full make-up and her hair's streaked with red-brown highlights. I remember the days when we used to play tag in the long grass of the fields, heedless of death by snakebite, and eat chocolate Nesquik powder out of the tin in the pantry, and paint each other's nails.

'You spend a lot of time with him,' she says. 'What do you talk about?'

'Of course I do,' I say. 'He's my father, not a stranger with a coke habit. We've got plenty to talk about.' I smile to take the sting out of my words, although I only half mean it. She can't be expected to understand, I tell myself.

The tops of her coffee-coloured cheekbones have turned a deep mahogany. She turns back to the main conversation.

Acha says to me, as though we had never paused to come inside, 'This bhootham used to be a young woman. A house maid.'

I nod in encouragement.

'She had a lovely voice. She'd sing as she swept the floors with the coconut-palm broom. At night, she sang to the children of the house and her voice was like silk.'

'Don't forget to eat, Acha,' I say.

At the other end of the table, my aunt calls Narendra Modi a hard-line Hindu and a dictator-in-training. I resist the urge to applaud. A hush falls over us. All eyes are on my grandfather. He waits, although he already has our attention. 'Any man,' he says, 'who upholds and fights for Hindu values must be respected.' My aunt looks like a chastened but defiant schoolkid. 'For centuries the Hindus have been downtrodden and now it's our time to be—'

'She's hiding,' Acha says suddenly. He's louder than he has been for a while. His voice cuts through my grandfather's voice, startling him into silence. Everyone turns to stare at him. He doesn't seem to notice. Instead, he's looking past us towards the kitchen, as though he can see something we can't. 'Just like she used to hide in there. She doesn't want to face us all.'

I put my hand over his. His fingers fold into a fist beneath my palm, and he leans forward as though he's about to stand.

'It's OK, Acha,' I say. 'There's nobody there. I'm here.' Stay calm when he's not, I've learned. Calm's contagious.

The family are lowering their gazes from us, then turning away. Murmurs are starting up, soft as the hum of bees. My grandfather is still silent. He's staring at Acha, his upper lip curled.

'We should find her,' Acha says, still too loudly. 'She's

hungry, and alone. Out by the mango tree.' He's still fixated on something visible only to him, his eyes bulging, but he's settling back into his chair.

My uncle looks concerned. His mouth opens, but before he can say anything my grandfather speaks. 'It's rude to interrupt, Arun,' he says, his voice quiet. 'You never could understand that, could you? Even before you lost your mind and spoke nonsense.'

'He can't help it, Achacha,' I say. 'And it's not nonsense. He just sees the world differently.' I want to scream at him, Screw you, you're a doctor, shouldn't you know?

My uncle jumps into the gap. 'Hey, Arun, guess what's showing at the Ganam Theatre? They've remastered *Manichitrathazhu*. Arun? Do you remember watching that, years ago?'

Acha's gaze moves back to us, seems to focus finally on his brother. I feel his fingers relaxing.

'We can go tonight,' my uncle says. 'Who's in?'

Sanjana's all enthusiastic agreement, and grudging gratitude sweeps through me. I muster a smile for her as the conversation steamrollers on.

I've lost my appetite. So, it seems, has my grandfather. He sits back in his chair, his eyes flicking over each of us so deliberately it's clearly no accident he never once looks at Acha.

In the end, we all go to the cinema, everyone but my grandfather. I haven't seen a Malayalam movie in years. They ooze with drama so thick and sticky you feel as though there's a spiderweb wrapping around you, trapping you in your seat. But Acha's more animated than I've seen him in a while.

The movie's about a young couple who buy an ancestral house that looks like the one we're currently staying in. The house is haunted, by a nineteenth-century dancer forced to become a concubine and then murdered in a jealous rage. We watch the young wife become possessed by the dancer's vengeful spirit – her bhootham. Despite the music, complete with piercing soprano voices and pulsing colours, I can hear my uncle snoring beside me.

The movie stops halfway through. The lights beam on, blinding me, and I'm confused until I remember the unique phenomenon of the Indian movie interval. Sanjana turns to me, grinning.

'How great is— Her eyes move past me, past my sleep-dazed uncle. 'Where's your acha?'

The seat between my uncle and the aisle is empty.

He's left his glasses behind.

Thrissur at night is more chaotic than it is by day. The tumult has become a thousand moving points of light breaking the darkness. Glaring headlights, flickering lamps, multi-tiered, hanging outside temples, harsh fluorescence spilling from the always open streetside shops. My chest is tight with lack of air as I sit in the back of my uncle's Toyota. The window's open, the air as heavy as a moist towel. The cloying pungency of vegetables on the verge of rot settles in the back of my throat. It mixes with the smell from the roadside restaurants, curries and dosas and frying samosas. The traffic's forcing us to move so slowly I'm struggling not to cry. Surely a car should be travelling faster than a meandering man on foot. Instead, we're waiting as a cow takes its easy, oblivious time crossing the road.

We've assumed that he's walked down the main road alongside the cinema. The alternative's horrifying – that he's wandered blindly into a tangle of streets and alleyways, to get hopelessly lost, to run into people who might beat him for his wallet or his strangeness. The others have taken a cab home, in case he heads that way.

The cow moves off and so, finally, do we. I scan the faces flashing past us, watching for Acha's hunch-shouldered walk, my eyes searching for his thin arms and the pastel green of his shirt.

We drive ten minutes down the road, further than he could walk in an hour.

Nothing.

Turning back, we hurtle as fast as we dare to the cinema complex. The car weaves through the maze of streets around it, dodging stray dogs and street vendors packing away for the night. We get stuck behind a random procession of priests and devotees hefting a golden deity above their shoulders. As they sing, the smell of jasmine and marigold seeps through the air-conditioning vents.

No sign.

My uncle suggests we head back to the house. His voice is tight. Eventually, he says, when whatever spell's beckoned him out of the cinema fades, Acha will head home.

I nod, wanting desperately to believe it.

I run up the front steps into the house. 'Did you find him?' Sanjana and I ask at the same time, answering each other's question.

'I'll go out again now,' my uncle says.

My grandfather sighs and raises a hand to his head. '*Kashtakaalam*,' he says. Hard times. 'He'll wander back eventually.' And he mutters, in what his old ears hear as an undertone, 'No bad thing if he doesn't.'

I can't be here any more.

'Maya,' someone calls as I run out of the room and keep running, down the steps and across the drive.

At the back of the house is an artificial lake, an ancient

man-made pool. Time-worn stone steps lead down into the cool depths. This is where my father bathed at five in the morning and six in the evening, every day, for the first seventeen years of his life.

A stone bench stands in front of the pool. I sit down, the granite still warm from the day's sun, and look out over the water.

Long minutes pass before my breathing slows and I can think again. I don't want to think again. I want to lie down and sleep and wake up to find my father standing over me, smiling, like he used to do when I fell asleep stargazing on the trampoline at home.

I can't just sit here. I'll walk around, willing him back. I'll be a beacon, guiding him.

The night's a sheet of darkness rippled with moonlight. It's starting to rain, thick, solid drops that splatter like water balloons in the dirt. Mosquitoes keep me company as I carry on beyond the back of the house.

I turn the corner.

There's a figure under the mango tree.

For a moment, I think someone's abandoned a statue there, kneeling, hunched. But then it moves, straightens, its head turning up towards the branches, and the faint light turns the pastel green of its shirt even paler.

I'm running.

My sandals slap the ground, drowning out the cicadas, but he doesn't seem to notice. I stop inches from him, breathless with relief. 'Acha? Acha, where have you been? What are you doing here?'

He continues to stare into the tree, milky light leaking through the leaves and dappling his face. 'She keeps calling me,' he says. I wonder if he knows I'm here, but then he looks at me.

Rain is dripping from his hair and down his face. He seems as tired as an ill child, the bags under his eyes ugly as bruises, and even though he's gazing at me, I'm not sure if he's seeing me.

I feel terribly, angrily alone.

'Acha, we've been searching for you. I've been so worried. How did you get back?'

His eyes roll to the left, as though he's searching for the memory.

'I took an auto rickshaw,' he says, as if it's the most obvious thing in the world.

What idiots we've been, assuming he'd hightailed it away on foot. He's schizophrenic, not stupid.

'Why did you leave?' I say.

He's confused.

'I had to ... had to ...' He holds up his hands. I take them. They're covered in dirt, mud embedded under his chipped fingernails.

When I stare at him, his eyes drop to the ground beneath my feet. I follow them. There's a single patch where the mud's even blacker than the surrounding moist, fertile soil.

He's been playing in the dirt.

I lead him back into the house in silence. My salwar is almost soaked through and my braid swings like wet rope against my back. Acha obeys mutely when I order him to wash the dirt from his hands. Voices sound from the drawing room and I follow them to find the family sitting stiffly together, living versions of the stern photos of our relatives on the walls behind them.

'He's here,' I say.

My aunt leaps up. 'Where?' she says. I point back towards the bathroom and she hurries past me to meet him as he emerges.

My grandfather sits expressionless.

Acha enters with my aunt as thunder crashes through the night air. He's dry and clean, and has found a burnt-yellow shirt that he wears over his lungi.

'I've told Deepak,' my aunt says. 'He's on his way home now.'

We settle Acha in a chair. I bring fresh water from the kitchen, and the lukewarm, cardamom-flavoured drink that soothes my father but I find disgusting. We sip without speaking, the TV providing ambient noise, until my uncle appears. His face lights up when he sees his brother. He crosses the room, claps him on the back, smiles at his wife.

'I'm glad you called when you did,' he says. 'I was at the police station.'

My grandfather stirs. 'The police station? You told them about this?'

'Yes, Acha,' my uncle says. 'We had to tell them he was missing, especially because he's . . . vulnerable.'

I feel Sanjana looking at me, but I'm staring at my grandfather. His face has hardened.

'So now everybody knows,' he says. For the first time this week, he looks directly at Acha. 'What were you doing, you idiot? You mad fool?'

There's an intake of breath as my grandfather stands and steps towards him, a hand raised. I move in front of him without thinking.

'Acha!' my uncle barks.

We all freeze into awkward, ominous silence. My skin is burning. I feel the blood rushing to my cheeks, hot as lava. My grandfather's eyes move down to mine and his face twists.

'Let's all sit down and have some chai,' my uncle says.

I want to laugh, a raging laugh. He sounds like a souvenir

in some tacky shop in Soho, *Keep Calm and Drink Tea*. From the corner of my eye I see my aunt start, turn and disappear into the kitchen.

My grandfather's hand lowers. Light glints in his eye, tracks down to tremble at his lower eyelid. 'I'm going to bed,' he says. He exits with a speed that belies his eighty-five years, shoulders only slightly hunched, head high, unassailable.

The door closes behind him and I turn to Acha. He looks back at me, uncomprehending, like a wounded child.

My aunt returns with the tea. Steam spirals into the humid air above the steel tumblers. She urges us to sit down.

The words pushing impatiently behind the barrier of my teeth are going to cause pain to the wrong people, but I can't hold them back.

'I don't think we should stay here any more.'

I'm looking at Acha, but I'm speaking to everyone else. When my gaze flicks to them, I see their shame and shock – and relief.

My aunt approaches me, her arms reaching out to wrap around my shoulders. A second later, I'm crying, and Sanjana is there, too, stroking my back. My uncle tries to dissuade me, but I can see his heart isn't in it. He can't change his father. Finally, he calls a hotel he knows, some four-star luxury. He'll drive us there in the morning, he says. And he insists that he'll pay.

'We'll visit you every day,' he says. 'Next time, come to Bangalore. Stay with us.'

He looks at Acha when he speaks. I see the awkwardness and guilt on his face, that he can no longer understand the younger brother he grew up with, that he can't help him.

I feel as though my father's been banned from his ancestral home, from his family's history.

I put him to bed. He looks exhausted following his exertions, but he doesn't sleep, staring at a ceiling that, in the darkness, looks distant as a starless sky. I stand for a while, looking down at him. I can't leave. Sitting down on the floor, my back to the bed, the sharp wooden edge of the frame digging into my spine, I pull out my phone. The world beyond, flickering through the hazy wifi, pulls me away from my thoughts.

'Maya?' His hand is on my hair.

I turn and wriggle around until I'm on my knees by the bed, as though in prayer. The whites of Acha's eyes gleam at me in the scant moonlight that filters through the window.

'I haven't finished my story, little one.'

I want to tell him to sleep, but I want to hear his voice more.

'The singing maid. The whole household loved her. The other servants. The children, who no longer had their mother to hug. Their father, too. He loved her even more after his wife had drifted off on the smoke of a funeral pyre.

'Then, something changed. She wasn't happy any more. Her singing no longer echoed from the walls. Now it was her soft sobbing that floated through the trees. The children gave her helpless kisses, but she had stopped smiling. The servants brought her sweets, and she must have eaten them, because her stomach grew rounder every week. The children's father spoke to her too, even getting angry with her. But still she became quieter, shrinking into sadness even as her stomach got bigger, and the father avoided her, as though she had a disease. Then one day, she was gone altogether.'

He's returned to staring at the ceiling and I'm as transfixed by his storytelling as I was as a five-year-old.

'She'd gone to get married, they said. But the younger boy didn't believe she could leave him. He went looking for her that night and he found her. Dressed in her white cotton sari, in the mango tree. Hanging. The rope creaking in the wind.'

He falls silent. I feel sick. 'Acha?' I ask, an odd tightness in my throat. 'What did . . . what did the boy do?'

Acha looks at me. 'He ran back to tell his father,' he says. 'The father told him to go to bed, but he didn't. He followed him in sneaking secret to the mango tree, and watched him dig. Watched her disappear into the ground. He never told anyone, not even his older brother, what he had seen.'

His face crumples. 'He told me it was a dream,' he says. 'Just a dream.'

I place a hand on his cheek, feeling the rough stubble under my palm. He lifts his hand to cover mine. We stay like that until exhaustion drags his lids down and his arm falls limp to the mattress.

I leave him snoring, and I hope he's dreamless. The house is heavy with empty darkness. I walk through it, bare feet soundless. At the door to my bedroom, I stop, and my swirling thoughts fall into a mad decision.

The huge archaic bolt on the front door scrapes free.

The rain's passed. It's pleasantly cool now. As I stray from the path, mud embraces my toes over my sandals, and the grass paints water drops onto my salwar trousers. I step slowly, trying not to think about cobras and cockroaches.

Head down, head down, until the mango tree looms above me. I look up into its branches, feeling an electric thrill of fear. The crow's gone, and there's no sign of a young woman with long black hair. Just leaves, trembling with rainwater, and the graceful, curving outlines of ripe fruit.

Acha's scrabbling at the earth had been less like digging and more of a transfer of the rain-softened dirt from one place to another. I've brought with me a trowel, a small, mud-encrusted thing I found lying by the side of the front porch. It sinks into the ground with ease, as though it wants to search.

The trowel digs and finds dirt, and more dirt. I dig, ignoring the sting of salty moisture in my eyes, until the trowel hits something less easy to loosen and coax to the surface.

I take a breath and let my hands do the searching. I tug and tug until something breaks free and I can lift it to the light of the rising sun.

Stained white cotton drapes over my fingers.

Contributors

Tom Benn is an award-winning author, screenwriter, and Associate Professor in Crime Writing at UEA. His first novel, *The Doll Princess* (Cape), was shortlisted for the Dylan Thomas Prize and the Portico Prize, and longlisted for the CWA's John Creasey Dagger. His essays and fiction have appeared in *Granta*, the *Paris Review*, *The Book of Manchester* (Comma Press) and *Bog People: A Working-Class Anthology of Folk Horror* (Chatto). His first film, *Real Gods Require Blood*, premiered in competition at the Cannes Film Festival, and was nominated for Best Short Film at the BFI London Film Festival. *Oxblood* (Bloomsbury), his fourth novel, was longlisted for the Gordon Burn Prize, the CWA's Gold Dagger, and won the *Sunday Times* Young Writer of the Year Award.

N.G.F. Clark is an award-winning author from Leeds. In 2020 he won the Alpine Fellowship Writing Prize and in 2023 was runner-up in the Desperate Literature Short Fiction Prize. His stories have appeared in publications from *Tethered by Letters*, *Fresher Press*, *Eyelands*, and elsewhere.

Kate Ellis is a writer based in London. Her short fiction has been published in the *Open Pen Anthology*, *The Mechanics' Institute Review*, *100 Voices*, and *The London Short Story Prize Anthology* among others. She runs the Brick Lane Bookshop Short Story Prize, hosts the *BLB Podcast*, works for Inpress Books, and one day might finish writing her short story collection.

Wendy Erskine is the prize-winning author of two short story collections, *Sweet Home* and *Dance Move*. She edited the art anthology *well I just kind of like it*. She is a frequent broadcaster and interviewer, and works as a secondary school teacher in Belfast. Her debut novel, *The Benefactors*, is published in 2025.

Jay Gao is a poet from Edinburgh, Scotland, living in New York City. His most recent books include: *Bark, Archive, Splinter* (Out-Spoken Press, 2024) and *Imperium* (Carcanet Press, 2022). *Imperium* was a winner of the 2023 Michael Murphy Memorial Prize, an Eric Gregory Award and a Somerset Maugham Award. Currently, he is a PhD student in English at Columbia University.

Danielle Giles was born in Germany, and now lives in South West England. Her short fiction has been published in *Extra Teeth* and *Dear Damsels*, shortlisted for the Bristol Short Story Prize and the Brick Lane Bookshop Short Story Prize, and longlisted for the Galley Beggar Press Short Story Prize. Her novel, *Mere*, is published by Pan Macmillan. In her spare time, she enjoys marshes and misidentifying birds.

Katie Hale is a novelist and poet, based in Cumbria. Her most recent novel, *The Edge of Solitude*, won a Northern Fiction Award, and was a *New Scientist* Book of the Month. She won a Northern Debut Award for her poetry collection, *White Ghosts*, and is a former MacDowell Fellow, and winner of the Palette Poetry Prize, Munster Chapbook Prize, and Aesthetica Creative Writing Prize. She has held Writer in Residence positions in numerous countries, including Australia, the US and Norway, and is a member of the Polar Artists' Network. Katie also mentors young writers as a core team member of the Writing Squad.

Alice Haworth-Booth is a writer of short stories and non-fiction. She is the co-author, with her sister Emily, of the children's book *Protest!*, an illustrated history of social movements. She has a background in activism and campaigning, and works as a freelance graphic designer for community and grassroots groups.

She is currently writing a collection of short stories which explore political and personal agency.

Jack Houston is a parent, writer and part-time public librarian whose short fiction is published in *The Cardiff Review*, *Far Off Places*, *The Interpreter's House* and *Litro*, and, together with being shortlisted for the Brick Lane Bookshop Short Story Prize, has also been shortlisted for the BBC National Short Story Award.

Aoife Inman is a writer from West Penwith, Cornwall. Her short fiction has been published in *The London Magazine*, shortlisted for the V.S. Pritchett Award and won the Brick Lane Bookshop Short Story Prize 2021. She has an MA in History from the University of Manchester, where her research focused on the relationship between memory and landscape in post-conflict communities. By day she works as an assistant editor at 4th Estate Books. Previously, she was a development executive at Bosena, an independent Cornish film production company, and a junior agent at Felicity Bryan Associates, where she worked with award-winning authors including Damon Galgut, Reni Eddo-Lodge and the Estate of Derek Jarman. In 2021 she co-founded FBA New Voices, a talent development programme for emerging underrepresented writers in the UK.

Gio Iozzi a writer and teacher, recently completed a PhD in Creative Writing from Goldsmiths University. A winner of the Pat Kavanagh Prize, her stories have been published and listed in various places including the Brick Lane Bookshop Short Story Prize, the Bridport Prize, the Bristol Short Story Prize, *Ambit Magazine*, the Nature Chronicles Prize, *New Writer Magazine*, the Brighton Prize, Fish Short Memoir Prize, Exeter Writers and athousandwordphotos.com. Writing and art: joiozzi.com. X: bristlingnarratives@gioiozzi. She also campaigns to protect trees and set up Haringey Tree Protectors @justplanenews.

Isha Karki is a writer based in London. Her short fiction has won the Dinesh Allirajah Prize, Galley Beggar Press Short Story Prize, and Mslexia Short Story Competition.

Suey Kweon was born in Incheon, South Korea and grew up in the UK, where she lives today. Her short story 'Mapping Chillies' was shortlisted for the Desperate Literature Short Fiction Prize.

K. Lockwood Jefford is from Cardiff and is a former NHS psychiatrist and psychotherapist. She completed an MA in creative writing with distinction at Birkbeck. Awards for short fiction include first prizes in the Brick Lane Bookshop Short Story Prize (2023), Bath Short Story Award (2021) and the V.S. Pritchett Short Story Prize (2020). She was shortlisted for Hay Festival Writers at Work in 2024. Her work appears in *Prospect Magazine, Aesthetica, 100 Voices* (Unbound, 2022) and many short story prize anthologies, including those for the Brick Lane Bookshop, the Bristol Short Story Prize, Fish Publishing and the Rhys Davis Competition. She completed a collection of short stories, *In Bed With My Sister*, and is currently working on a novel inspired by South Wales and Federico García Lorca's play, *The House of Bernarda Alba*.

Robert Loyko-Greer is a writer based in London, where he works for the publisher Profile Books. He co-founded the Desperate Literature Short Fiction Prize in 2017.

Max Lury is a British writer based in London. He received the 2022 Curtis Brown Prize whilst at UEA, and won the 23/24 Galley Beggar Short Story Prize, alongside being shortlisted for the 2022 Brick Lane Bookshop Short Story Prize. His work has been previously published in *The End*, the *Lighthouse Journal*, and *Tar Press*. His debut novel, *No Ghosts*, is forthcoming in 2026.

Andrea Mason is a London-based writer and artist. Her fiction pamphlet *Waste Extractions* was published in 2022 with Broken Sleep Books. She was runner-up in the Desperate Literature Short Fiction Prize 2023, won the Aleph Writing Prize 2020, was shortlisted for the Manchester Fiction Prize 2020, and was shortlisted for the inaugural Fitzcarraldo Editions Novel Prize, in 2018. Journal and anthology publications include *Cybernetics, or Ghosts? Stories from Myth to A.I.*, edited by Michael Salu, *Eleven Stories*, *UEA New Writing*, *3:AM Magazine*, *Failed States*, *Tar Press*, *Seen from Here: Writing in the Lockdown*, *The Happy Hypocrite* and *Frozen Tears*.

Leeor Ohayon is a writer from London, based in Norwich where he is working on his PhD in Creative and Critical Writing at the University of East Anglia. His work has featured in the *London Magazine*, the *White Review*, *Apartamento*, *Brick Lane Bookshop New Short Stories 2021 and 2023*, *Paper Brigade*, *RSL Review* and *Prospect Magazine*.

Aisha Phoenix is an African Caribbean British writer based in London. Her story '(Un)welcoming' won the Spread the Word City of Stories Home prize for Haringey and her speculative short story collection, *Bat Monkey and Other Stories*, was shortlisted for the 2020 SI Leeds Literary Prize. Her stories have appeared in anthologies, including: Peepal Tree Press's *Glimpse: An Anthology of Black British Speculative Fiction*; the *Leicester Writes Short Story Prize Anthology Vol. 5* and *Vol. 7*; the *Brick Lane Bookshop New Short Stories* (2022), Inkandescent's' *Mainstream*; National Flash Fiction Day's *Root, Branch, Tree* and *Bath Flash Fiction Volume Two: The Lobsters Run Free*. It has also featured online, including in: *Strange Horizons, Litro* and the *Mechanics' Institute Review*. Her poetry has been published in Peepal Tree Press's *Filigree: Contemporary Black British Poetry* and the *Oxonian Review*.

Melody Razak is a British Iranian writer who lives in Brighton. Melody has had short stories published in the *Mechanics' Institute Review*, the *Bath Short Story Anthology* and *Brick Lane Bookshop Short Story Prize Longlist 2019*. She has also written for the *Observer Food Monthly* and *The Sunday Times*. In 2021 Melody was selected as one of the *Observer's* 'Ten Debut Novelists' for her novel, *Moth*. *Moth* went on the be shortlisted for the Authors' Club Best First Novel Award, longlisted for the Desmond Elliot Prize, and was selected as the readers jury for the Festival du Premier Roman. Melody is currently writer in residence at Birkbeck University.

Francesca Reece is a writer from North Wales. Her debut novel *Voyeur* was published by Tinder Press in 2021, followed by *Glass Houses* in 2024. She was the 2019 recipient of the Desperate Literature Short Fiction Prize and has had work featured in *The London Magazine, Banshee, Literary Review, Elle UK* and on *BBC's Short Works*. After several years living in Paris, she is now based in London.

Shola von Reinhold is a writer and artist. Her novel *LOTE* (Jacaranda Books, 2020) won the Republic of Consciousness

Prize and the James Tait Black Memorial Prize.

Mariana Roa Oliva co-authored the book *Seedlings_: Walk in Time* (Counterpath, 2023) alongside media artist and programmer Qianxun Chen.

Siri Katinka Valdez is a bi-lingual writer from Norway/USA, living in Oslo. She is the co-founder of the small press and feminist writing collective Blomster & Bureau. Siri has published the short story collection named *Det ble Bud* (Gyldendal, 2012), as well as *Snille Djevel befri meg* (Blomster & Bureau, 2019), a translation of, and a homage to, the forgotten writer Mary MacLane. Siri also co-created the audiowalk *Sans for Finans/Money & Magic* (Echoes app, 2022), about money systems, debt creation and magical thinking. She is currently learning Esperanto.

Rajasree Variyar grew up in Australia and now lives in London, where she juggles writing alongside a career in insurance product development. She received her MA in Creative Writing from the University of East Anglia. Her manuscript of *The Daughters of Madurai* (then called *The Wanted Girl*) was shortlisted for the 2019 Mo Siewcharran Hachette Prize. Her short stories have won second prize in the *Shooter Literary Magazine* short story competition and been longlisted for the Brick Lane Bookshop Short Story Prize. *The Daughters of Madurai* is her debut novel and was published by Orion in the UK in April 2023 and in the US by Union Square in February 2023. It was a Barnes and Noble Book Club pick, a Lilly's Library book club choice, and won the *Times of India* AutHer Award for best debut novel in 2024. She is currently working on her second novel.

Joanna Walsh is a multidisciplinary writer for print, digital narrative, installation and performance. The author of twelve books, including several written with AI she hand-coded, her publishers include Semiotext(e), Bloomsbury and Verso. She is a UK Arts Foundation fellow, a Markievicz Award and DAAD awardee. She has also worked as an editor, illustrator, academic researcher and arts activist. She founded and ran #readwomen (2014–18), described by the *New York Times* as 'a rallying cry for equal treatment for women writers', and @noentry_arts (2019–2024), changing the conversation around age and arts opportunities. She writes a monthly fashion and theory column, 'Theory of Style', at *Spike Art Magazine*.

Acknowledgements

Thank you to the twenty-two brilliant writers whose work this collection champions. Thank you to Wendy Erskine and Joanna Walsh for their excellent Introduction and Foreword essays.

Thanks to Martha Sprackland for commissioning the project and copyediting the final text, and thanks to all at CHEERIO Publishing – Darren Biabowe Barnes, Clare Conville, Harriet Vyner, Maude Elms and Labeja Kodua, Edward Wall – for making the book happen.

Thank you to everyone at Desperate Literature and Brick Lane Bookshop who has supported the creation of this book, particularly to Terry Craven, whose role as a creative consultant on the project has been highly valuable throughout.

Desperate Literature

The Desperate Literature Short Fiction Prize was launched in autumn 2017 by Terry Craven, Charlotte Delattre, Robert Loyko-Greer, and Emily Westmoreland. Since then, the prize has published seven collections of eleven pieces each, published in limited edition titles under the name *Eleven Stories*.

Thank you to every writer who has ever submitted to the prize (including those re-published here, of course), to anyone who has ever sought out or stumbled upon our books, and to anyone who has ever attended our events in Madrid, London, Paris and Edinburgh.

Thank you to the de Groot Foundation for their generous support of the prize since its inception, to the Civitella Ranieri residency for hosting so many of our winning writers, and to the Literary Consultancy and Spread the Word for partnering with us on the prize.

Thank you to our partner journals, who since 2018 have published pieces from the prize: *Prototype, Open Pen, The London*

Magazine, Hotel / Tenement, The Second Shelf, Gorse Journal, 3:AM, A Women's Thing, Structo, Kill Your Darlings, Minor Literature[s], Helter Skelter. You are the backbone of the literary world.

Thank you to our guest authors who have judged the final shortlist each year (roughly in order since 2018): Euan Monaghan, Hestia Peppe, Eley Williams, Claire-Louise Bennett, Sam Riviere, Rachel Cusk, Niven Govinden, Ottessa Moshfegh, Derek Owusu, Isabel Waidner, Natasha Brown, Anton Hur, Joanna Walsh, Mariana Enríquez, Tiffany Tsao, Megan McDowell, Samanta Schweblin, Alejandro Zambra, Henry Hoke.

Thank you to the bookshops who have hosted our events outside of Madrid – Burley Fisher Books in London, Shakespeare & Company in Paris, Typewronger Books in Edinburgh.

Thank you to the people and organisations who have helped and encouraged us along the way: Adriann Ranta Zurhellen, Jude Cowan Montague at Resonance FM, Charlotte Seymour, the British Council, the *Bookseller*, *Hate Zine*, BookBrunch, Porter Anderson at Publishing Perspectives, Martha Sprackland, Ines Gonçalves, Dostoyevsky Wannabe, and Deborah Triesman at the *New Yorker*.

Thank you to the Brick Lane Bookshop team for the spirit of collaboration in which they have worked with us on this wonderfully international project. In particular, thank you to the brilliant Kate Ellis for her fantastic ideas, energy and patience.

And finally, thank you to the wider Desperate Literature Prize team, which in the last eight years has included Terry Craven, Charlotte Delattre, Robert Loyko-Greer, Emily Westmoreland, Kate McCully, Layla Benitez-James, Moira McCavana, Paloma Reaño Hurtado, Joan Fleming, Dom Czapla, Vesna Maric, Kwaku Osei-Afrifa, Lara Alonso Corona, Bárbara Bianchi

Ceballos, Silver Sharma, Fatema Abdoolcarim, Dominique Chapla, Finola Griffin, Daniel Leal, Emma Kahn, Jacob Cantor, Carrie Amicucci, Claudia Fell, Danny Fier, Kate Golding, Jenny Mueller, Michelle Waslick.

Brick Lane Bookshop

The Brick Lane Bookshop Short Story Prize started life as a conversation behind the shop counter between former bookseller Kate Ellis and shop owner Denise Jones. They wanted to create a platform to find and promote unpublished writers and to celebrate and publish their work. So far, Brick Lane Bookshop have published seventy new writers in six anthologies. Many alumni have gone on to publish in their own right, receive critical acclaim and win other prizes. Thousands of the Brick Lane anthologies have sold in the shop, and elsewhere.

Thank you to the entire Desperate Literature team for being independent international bookselling and publishing legends. Special thanks to Robert Loyko-Greer for his vision, momentum and insight. This project wouldn't have happened without him.

Thank you to everyone who's been involved in the Brick Lane Bookshop Short Story Prize since it launched in 2019:

Every writer who has ever submitted a story to the competition.

All the writers we've published since 2019, including those in this collection.

Our insightful first- and second- and third-round readers, who number in the dozens, many of whom have been reading and sharing prompt, wise feedback for the competition since 2019.

Our prize judges, in chronological order: Emma Paterson, Zoe Gilbert, Kit Caless, Harriet Moore, Chris Power, Sharmaine Lovegrove, Kishani Widyaratna, Wendy Erskine, Elise

Dillsworth, Anne Meadows, Huma Qureshi, Chris Wellbelove, Melissa Cox, Gurnaik Johal, Kira Evans, Dan Bird, Lucy Luck, Vanessa Onwuemezi, Tom Clayton, Angelique Tran Van Sang and Saba Sams.

Polly Jones, Olly Crabb and Johanna Russell for being the best Short Story Prize team and keeping the competition running smoothly.

Bret Johnson for his work on social media.

Denise Jones for her forewords, initial belief in the project and continued support. The Short Story Prize has always been entirely funded by the shop.

Kalina Dimitrova, the bookshop manager who ensures the shop is a tightly run bookselling machine.

Sue Tyley, our copyeditor and proofreader from the beginning until 2024. Her meticulous work and extraordinary patience taught me so much.

All our indie bookshop stockists.

Everyone who has ever bought, gifted and read our anthologies.

Our partners Spread the Word, Scratch Books, Prototype Publishing and *the London Magazine*. Special thanks to Bobby Nayyar, Tom Conaghan, Jess Chandler and Katie Tobin.

Clays printers.

Turnaround book distribution, who make the Brick Lane anthologies available across the UK and beyond, especially Benjamin, Eleanor, Claire, and Jack for the intro.

Brick Lane Bookshop customers for choosing to shop in an independent.

Last but definitely not least, massive thanks to all the Brick Lane Bookshop booksellers during the Short Story Prize years: Denise Jones, Polly Jones, Kalina Dimitrova, Glenn Collins,

Andrew Everitt, Rachel Brook, Ríbh Brownlee, Bret Johnson, Johanna Russell, Georgia Sherlock Taylor, Jay Jones, Trish Mendiratta and Olly Crabb for their hard work keeping the shop so busy and brilliant.

NOTES
p. 26 - Photo: Rijksmuseum / Wikimedia Commons